Heirs of Sarah: The Hajj

This is a work of fiction. Names, characters, places, and incidents either are the product of the author's imagination or are used fictitiously. Any resemblance to actual persons, living or dead, events, or locales is entirely coincidental.

Copyright © 2022 by Jessica L. Jackson

All rights reserved. No part of this book may be reproduced or used in any manner without written permission of the copyright owner except for the use of quotations in a book review. For more information, address: jessljacksonllc@gmail.com

First paperback edition September 2022

Dedicated to my mother, father... and ancestors.

Preface

The concept of the Heirs of Sarah was birthed from a complicated and unconditional love for Black culture around the world. Growing up, I struggled with my image dictating which societal standard I had to fit into in order for people to digest my existence. Being Black meant adhering to capped ceiling constructs which nurtured the idea of an inferiority that enforced "getting by" as a dream or goal to strive toward. I saw the struggle around me and believed that as long as I could maintain that struggle I was doing everything I was supposed to do in this world.... but that never quite sat right with me. I was both mentally and physically famished with the nothingness of it all. In addition to being Black, I'm a woman. As women we're taught quietness, an acceptance of objectification, and a disciplined servitude to men. If ignorance was bliss, then I'd be alright with serving two cursed life sentences. To sprinkle on insult, 'the powers that be', have the audacity to add on time because I possess a sought after body shape, intelligence and beauty.... as if to tell God He made a mistake by loving me.

In 2019, I took a job as a project manager at a bank. My seat wasn't yet solidified so I sat in a random area at a dim lit work station. While there were plenty people assigned to seats around me, often times I was by myself. I had just got off the phone with a friend who loved commenting on my body shape and pointing out the similarities to a famous entertainer. I didn't care for the comparison because I was sick of Black women being sexually exploited in the music industry, it made me cringe. At the same time, Beyonce's Lion King soundtrack was just released and since I was alone, I decided to put in my earphones and listen. Pride filled tears snuck out my eyes and I felt seen, not merely with the naked eye, but with divine sight. My mind began to race with the struggles of Black women to be seen and appreciated as more than sex toys and the story that popped into my heart was that of Sarah Baartman's, so I began to write.

Historically speaking, our stories were robbed, hijacked and erased. So I thought to myself, what if Sarah could tell her own story her own way. What if her name was used to inspire and relate to in terms of rising from injustices? I used the exploitation of Sarah's body against the very evils of the world that used her life to cause Black women harm all round the world, past and current. "They know not what they do", jumped out at me and the story took life of its own. I began to toy with the idea of Sarah being a goddess sent to protect this world, only to find that hate's will would try to repurpose her life and legacy.

Later on, Beyonce would go on to release the visual album... that woman inspired millions of people. A few days late, a sexually charged over exploited beautiful Black woman's hyper sexual song was released and I thought to myself, "I guess they had to remind us of who they wrote us to be, huh? Can't be too proud of what we were really created to be, right?" My writing became more and more fueled. Not only did I see an opportunity to breathe hope into desolate stories, but I also saw an opportunity to relate and unite an entire people, encouraging us to break generational cursed chains and free us from a mindset of the lesser mentality of what we're told we have to be.

Yet, while writing I came to yet another issue. The issue being the heart of the exploited women around the world. The exploitation being learned and engrained so much that fake love was comforting.... I had to be gentle with this story because what and who they are is a part of history as well and it has its place no matter how they're viewed. They too deserve genuine and unconditional love. From that knowledge, my story grew and I found so many perplexing historical parallels to societal dilemmas we still face in modern times. So as the story grew, so did my knowledge. And as the knowledge grew so did my heart. As my heart grew, I couldn't help but pour out in hopes that you'll see it too.

Table of Contents

1. The (Un)Beautiful End
2. Trail of Tears
3. Seek and Find
4. The Great Unlearning
5. The Sentinelese Treasury
6. Plots for Ascension
7. Amanirenian Sanctuary
8. Kandake-Mino
9. Iji mesit' eti
10. Power in a Name
11. The Fallen and the Façade
12. A King that Findeth
13. Anointing Tresses
14. Mansa-ibn
15. Growing Pains
16. Tested Love
17. Fear Love, Not Evil
18. One Hurts, All Hurt
19. Kurati Homecoming
20. Orisha Gatekeepers
21. A Prodigal King's Worth
22. Higher
23. Beside the Still Waters
24. Rise of the King
25. Higher Still
26. Fallen Love

The Heirs of Sarah: The Heiress' Hajj

Jess L. Jackson

Chapter 1: The (Un)Beautiful End

Rest for the weary. Just one day to resonate with His glory. A simple moment to appreciate His many creations and observe His perfection in each intricately simplistic detail.

On a hidden beach along the Gamtoos River, the brightest pink orchids bloomed undisturbed. The blazing sun was at its highest, warming the gentle water for comfortable touch. A soothing breeze tickled the leaves and danced through furs and hair. From a safe distance, creatures watched over.... first with curiosity then in recognition as water, air, earth and fire harmonized in psalm. Bushes as high as small trees provided paradise for a family enjoying sanctuary among themselves in a peaceful place created by Him, with them in mind.

The goddess Queen was upright in the water offside her family. She forced herself to be strong while she led the most enigmatic orchestra she'd ever conjured, guiding the elements in a ballad unknown to herself.... and for once, she feared her song. Her silken hands gently swayed high as she could reach but shook violently at the same time. She prayed a prayer she'd hoped God heard and didn't hear, but she needed him to know that she knew what He already knows. She made every attempt to steady her heart and mind while ushering in caressing winds filled with delicate petals of exotic breeds of flowers, but it was mournful and the uneasiness wouldn't retire. Each second that passed was heavier than the second before but she dare not undo her part. She was key to that part of the prophecy.... That part of their stories. Her strength was a requirement for her purpose. She was in love with love but the moment drew nigh and tempted her to beg for a new course.... chart different waters.... rewrite what she felt belonged, but the sacrifice wasn't hers and yet, it was. However, to save herself would mean to undo the world, she couldn't bring herself to escape fate. For the sake of it all, she surrendered to trust.... and faith.... and love, she accepted that ultimately the last say so was what counted. So she bit down on her lip to hush her whimpers and took deep breaths to quiet her heart's storm. Nature listened intently, shedding tears of grateful empathy at the operatic beauty and wonder.

The high bushes blocked her King's view, but he knew. He knew what was to come but neither knew how it was to happen. Their resolve: give God room and remember His glory and mercy at the same time. He and the Queen carried the burden of knowing the day would come since their triplets were born. How was a King to protect his family from pained greatness and allow courage to be itself? So the King commanded one day for them to be no more than loving. And while his wife took a moment to herself, he played every single game he could. Explained every single thing that crossed his mind to those girls and hoped not to alarm them to reason. He sang every song they ask for at the top of his lungs, so sweet and tender. Provided every junky treat and spoiled his darling triplet girls with the milli seconds of time, the gift he knew was never his to control. The King thought if only he could fit centuries into a blink, he would so they'd forever know his heart for them. When the weight started to mount, he muscled more strength and grew silent and simply listened to the wind while his daughters rested in the safety of his name. They laid on a royal blanket looking out beyond the clouds wrapped in their father's wings while he hid his aching heart from their gifts.

Two minutes of somber morning proved too long for hate's sake and a mischievous gust interrupted the Queen's attempt at tranquility. She felt the wrinkle which alerted earth's energy, rippled the water and drew her attention. Her gentle reaction didn't disturb her family's day off. She refused to be startled in the face of the enemy. Remaining calm, she kept in mind the high bush obstructed the King's view as she slowly crept out of the water where she was bathing, each stride revealed her feminine essence.

The Queen caught a whiff of a stench louder than royal horns announcing evil's intent before she could bother to lay eyes. She stretched her neck in the opposite direction then rolled her eyes with repulse and started to pray again but her Highness knew the answer and mustered courage from knowing.

At first sight of them out the corner of her eyes, Queen Hadiat did not cry; she offered not one scream nor worry. She knew who she was. Her amber-melanated skin gave life to desert sands, piercing almond-shaped eyes had elegantly mounted phoenix wings, and the fullest lips had liberated waves of nations. She held allegiance with every tribe and moved boldly for her throne preceded her. Unashamed of her renowned figure she stood firm with long dark hair braided in the story of her tribe. However, *they* couldn't recognize which tribe it was.

They being the Dutchmen brothers, who went by the names of Hendrick and Peter Cesar found her alone, or so they thought. Dressed in their hunter's uniforms, they tried to sneak up on her. Although her face and hair aroused their curiosity, her naked supple skinned curves exposed their cowardly thoughts. They believed she was unaware as she didn't let on that they were in her peripheral until she was sure her King and their girls will not be bothered.

Careful to not disturb the nature's tranquil flow, she steadily turned staring them eye to eye while grabbing her clothes to dress. It sickened her that they had no idea they were in the presence of gods, instead they demoralized themselves at her humanity. The Queen focused her eyes at the brothers who resembled hyenas circling their prey while rubbing their crotches. She barely got her gown on when they began their drooling approach.

Hadiat planted her left foot then elegantly lifted her right heel and slid her toes inward. Shoulders high, body calmly aligned, she fought them off with ease never changing her peaceful breaths. She punched Peter so hard he fell unconscious but before he hit the ground, she moved a gust of wind to lay him gently, careful to remain silent and protect her family's rest.

The other brother Hendrick was overcome with frustration as he tried again and again to take her down while she side stepped him with poise, watching him stumble every time. He didn't want to kill her, but if only he could taste of her flesh. He drew his knife from his waist as to threaten. He tossed the knife back and forth from one hand to the other, trying to figure out how best to attack, searching for signs of her being intimidated.

Hadiat, fearful her husband will be disturbed by the sound, became impatient with Hendrick's impudent regard and decided not to waste time any further and chose to reveal herself as The Gift. She closed her eyes and began to commune with the elements. With a graceful lift of her finger, Hendrick was suspended in the air, screaming in pain as she poked at several pressure points with a mere thought. She walked closer and dropped her hand to her side slamming him into the ground.

A wrestling noise began to come from the bushes. Her husband heard the fighting and ran out spreading his majestic and mighty wings and with every muscle and bulging vain of his body he yelled "Sarai!" A now frantic Hendrick rushed to pull his gun and shot the winged man in the chest.

Hadiat froze in terror. She watched as her husband's steps slowed heavily until his body collapsed onto the ground. Her eyes jumped into a spasmatic quiver and her body jolted in place repeatedly. No prophetical writing could have ever prepared her for the pain; a million excruciating deaths before dying. Her husband lie on the ground dead. Before the first tear could roll off her chin, his body levitated as his Indigo wings wrapped around his lifeless body then dissipated into sand and departed in the wind that carried its King away. Hadiat barely exhaled and he was gone.

Scared and shaken, Hendrick pointed the gun at Hadiat and commanded her to be still.

It wasn't a normal gun. It definitely wasn't a weapon she could control. A gun fashioned from the confused thoughts of demons, the only kind that could drain or take her and her daughters' lives.... akrhh matter. The scant touch of any akrhh matter weapon could curse her and their souls or kill them instantly. The sight of it temporarily paralyzed her mind. She wanted to give in but didn't know what conceding looked like, in all her existence there had never been a need, but His will was to be done. Trying to come around to the reality of the moment, telepathically, Hadiat commanded her triplets, Aida, Liya, and Zoya, to remain hidden behind the tree. Even though she struggled to see a next step without her King, Hadiat knew what the purpose of her daughters' lives were, that they were greater than her own. And so she refused any further risk. She succumbed to the colonizers and they carried her away leaving her Heiresses there alone.

Chapter 2: Trail of Tears

The akrhh shackles placed on her wrists by the brothers disabled her powers and thus, her hopes. Every time she tried to even think of how to break free her mind snapped her into her predicament. Hadiat's tears left trails no one should ever have to follow. No bread crumbs to sweeter tomorrows, just fully numb to the circumstance. For the entire eight-hour incomprehensible drive, she wept. It was happening and the loneliness penetrated every crevice of her entire being.

The Dutch brothers, arrived in Cape Town, still unbeknownst to them, they'd captured the Queen. Once they were on the British military base they took her to see a military doctor named William Dunlap and explained all they'd experienced while never removing the gun from her head. Even in chains, they feared her power. However, their explanation was unnecessary. Dr. Dunlap knew exactly who Hadiat was, the goddess Queen to the Throne of God. He sent the Cesar brothers outside to await his orders while he circled his prey.

From the soulless burning markings on the doctor's hand, Hadiat knew he was no mere human but a pawn to a powerful demon named Tiago. He noticed she spotted his brandings and slowly rolled up his sleeves so that she can see the full picture. Dr. Dunlap had sold, murdered, and plotted against Believers and pledged himself to Tiago by shedding the blood of innocents in hopes to become a demonic vessel someday.

Hadiat's eyes continued to review his markings and her heart palpitated when a crazed grin crept across his face, casting shadows over her spirit. She understood his beliefs were firmly rooted in evil winning the war against God's children. Deep breaths escaped her chest and she could no longer hide her fears. She begged God yet again for mercy. She just lost her King and her babies, was that not enough? Now this? Now a pawn of Tiago? Her tears could fill the Sahara and spill over to quench the world's remaining deserts. The Queen knew Tiago commanded entire nations. Although she'd never seen Tiago's face, he knew of hers. She figured it must have been Tiago who put the bounty on her head sending the doctor and some demonic troops to find her and the King.

Dr. Dunlap immediately adorned her neck and shoulders balefully with additional chains made of akrhh matter. He leaned in close to her and whispered into her ear, "It's over now you little bitch!" His breath hissed her into repulse.

Too long a glance at her rare and exotic glory and the scoundrel hurriedly commenced to stripping her of her essence as he too had become hatefully enamored with such beauty, power and grace, the likes of which he'd never witnessed before.

The Cesar brothers heard her wrestle and cry from outside and fought themselves with what they were to truly understand. Once the noise died down, they reentered the doctor's home in enough time to catch him zip up his pants.

He noticed the attention on him after raping her so Dr. Dunlap asked her her name in mockery as though he didn't already know, a scandal she wouldn't entertain; she sharply turned away. His eyes widened with endless lust as she continued to sob. Dr. Dunlap knew he was supposed to turn her over to his boss, Tiago, but he couldn't bear the thought of losing his treasure even though he didn't truly understand her worth. Instead, he decided to keep her for himself.

Hendrick looked over all the broken plates and cups on the ground. There were books and papers scattered across the home from Hadiat fighting back. He stood numb while Dr. Dunlop sent Peter Cesar for the presiding military officer, Captain Alexander. A darkening feeling grew over Hendrick. He began to feel the pain he'd caused Hadiat as he watched her lay there stripped and shaken. Her shackles rattled against the hard floor and swirled through small puddles of her own blood and tears. His face turned up and just as he was about to vomit from it all being too much, he tried to offer his version of humanity. "The man we killed called her Sarai!" Little did Hendrick know, it was a term of endearment her husband used to show his love for his wife, the mother of their miracle children and Heiresses to the throne.

"Well then we'll call her Sarah." Dr. Dunlap paid the brothers thirty pieces of silver each for their troubles. "Now, when the captain arrives, let me do all the speaking." Dr. Dunlap's salacious mind pondered a story that wouldn't reveal her true identity. To increase his chance of keeping her secret, he had to seem unconcerned and aloof, appear normal. His thoughts ran wildly into ideas of disgusting and lewd worlds he would escape to with her whenever he pleased. "By chance, did she have a little girl with her?" The doctor knew of her Heir, but had no idea there were three. The smile on Dunlap's face emptied any remaining decency in his wicked body.

Hendrick, sickened by perversion, shook his head no and walked into the front room leaving the money behind.

When Captain Alexander arrived, Dr. Dunlap showed him Sarah and asked permission to take her to England to work as his house maid. Captain Alexander looked her over and nearly drooled at the thought of ravaging her. He felt alike in thought with Dr. Dunlap, therefore he did not deny him his pleasure.

Dr. Dunlap wasted no second. As soon as he'd been granted permission, he packed what he could carry and left.

Before she boarded the ship to Europe, Queen Hadiat's akrhh matter chains were replaced with gold akrhh matter jewelry. This was done by Dr. Dunlap to disguise her enslavement, however the curse of the akrhh matter began to sink into her pores.

Hadiat took deep breaths and whispered enchantments trying to ward off the darkness but the curse was too heavy. Passengers stared in confusion at Hadiat's bedazzled neck, wrists and ears wondering how a lesser being could afford such refinement. In Hadiat's misery, the passengers jealousy encroached her spirit and at times, she'd give in to the pettiness and turned her nose up or twisted her lips, forgetting the task at hand was freedom, not indulgence. After the boat docked, she was placed into a carriage by the doctor and his butler. She remained silent for the rest of the trip to his home in England. In a moment when no one was watching, Hadiat looked down at her hands and twisted her wrists back and forth. Slowly, she rubbed her fingers across the bracelets, then guided her hands to her neck. Her fingers shook harder and harder each time she tapped the necklace. Her hands worked their way to the earrings then quickly to her mouth as she covered her lips when a yelp tried to escape. Remembering her pain, she lamented over the unknown status of her children. She couldn't commune with them, couldn't hear them, couldn't feel them and longed to see them. She needed to be their protector in the most eager of ways but she was enslaved. She prayed God would grant them the mercy He seemingly denied her and protect her children to keep them aligned with His will. She also wept softly over the loss of her King, who did not have a proper burial. The lack of honor tormented her soul and she felt to blame. Thinking, "if only..." would last her an eternity. The ominous damp air of the Brit's land mimicked her heart's sentiments.

Dr. Dunlop perfected his lie by the time they made it to the polluted land and told stories over and over again about his now house servant and how he "discovered" her never revealing he'd found the Queen. His great idea was to hide her in plain sight. Although he didn't want to share his new prize, he knew the world had never seen such complete and rare beauty, they'd only heard of Africa and read about it in their history books. To keep her humble, he perpetuated the lies and decided to make her an attraction for his own profit. "You can no longer dance in the ways of your people's majesty; you will dance as I tell you." He trained her to hide pain, turn the other cheek, and paraded her around various amusement sites and museums while charging people to see the Afrikaan woman.

Men's minds regularly unraveled at the thought of fully unrobing her to have their way while women grew bitter and envious of the attention she held but never desired. Adults and children alike would poke sticks at Hadiat and screamed racial slurs.

Meanwhile, Dr. Dunlap reminded her, "You will take it and you will smile or I'll go find your heir," threatening her time and time again to displace her further and further from her reign.

It worked. Dunlap's warnings rang too loud and his desecrating scent wreaked over her thoughts. He smirked when she'd rock herself to and from to ease at least a minute portion of her worries and pains. He laughed when she refused to sleep knowing she feared her nightmares. He felt accomplished when she showed signs of losing sense of herself by the minute. The time passed by and before he knew it, he'd held her captive for five years. Dr. Dunlap kept her chained in the demonic weaponry fashioned as gold jewelry and groomed her to accept despair and her slave name Sarah Baartman. To his patrons, she had become known as "Hottentot Venus" a racist name she inherited while on stage dancing for the pleasure of men.

Hadiat, was already beaten down and worn. After a show in Paris, she sat in a wooden chair next to the back door of the venue. She exhaled thinking the worse had come and gone. After quieting her worries, she heard voices coming from the back office. To her demise, she overheard that she'd been sold by Dr. Dunlap to a delusional piece of a man named S. Reaux who was also very enamored by her. She thought she had no more tears to give until they quietly rolled down her face. After wiping the tears from her eyes she looked up and Reaux was standing right in front of her. Hadiat's heart jumped when the lunatic whispered that "he could feel that she's very different and wanted to dig deeper to find out."

Reaux grabbed Hadiat by the wrist and yanked her out the seat then drug her to his carriage and threw her inside. The voices in his head screamed out to him louder than ever before begging for him to perform his deranged experiments of persecution. When he got her home, not only did he rape poor Sarah, he plagued her with constant tests to try to prove why her skin is so different and inferior. He'd come up with theories regarding the reproductive system of Black women and decided to put his theories to trials by prostituting her out.

How much more was she to bare. Hadiat was beyond tired. Her head swirled back and forth through the putrid guises of her being less than. The Queen's mind was poisoned by the akrhh matter and she'd lost hope. The misery consumed her and she died daily, forgetting her crown.

The Venus Hottentot gained notoriety from sea to shining sea, but not everyone was sold on the idea of her freely making the decision to be used. One day a woman who posed as an abolitionist found Sarah Baartman. "Queen Hadiat, is that you?" The woman stretched her hand out to reveal its glow, showing Hadiat the light within, letting her know she was good.

Faintly remembering her own name, Hadiat looked up to see the woman and recognized her as a child of a Fallen Angel, known as a T'Malak. "Where are my daughters?" Tears spilled out seamlessly as he heart began to lift at another chance to live yet again.

"In hiding, great Queen. We separated the triplets to keep them safe. Come, let's get you out of here!"

"Separated them! They're strongest together! Do you even know which one you sent where? They are different! You know the prophesies. One to free, one to heal and one to lead. They can only do this together!" The unsettled panic made her look unappreciative which was not her intention. She calmed her words to bring down the heightened mood. She choked back her sniffles and searched the T'Malak's eyes once more for a bit more comfort. "I cannot break free. They have me in chained akrhh matter. See, this gold jewelry? Help me get it off?"

"Forgive me your Highness, me and the others cannot tell them apart. Only you and the King could do that." The woman pulled out small vile containing liquid that glowed iridescent purple and started to pour it over the bracelets.

"Is that?" Hadiat's muscles jumped at the sight of the vile, so ready to seize freedom.

"Yes, David's tears. Directly from the Judean oasis where he mourned". The T'Malak's voice raised in excitement. To play such an important role meant everything to her redeemed heart.

King David, humbly the beloved man after God's own heart. His favor with the Creator resonated in the minds of all Believers yet only a chosen few had ever experienced the same. His unrecorded footsteps through spiritual wilderness often led him through his personal dry places to a secret oasis where he would carry his burdens and leave them there. The power bestowed upon him was never lost for the prayers of the righteous availeth much. Each tear he shed possessed his God given gift to break whatever mold it touched but it never destroyed the oasis, his secret hiding place with God. And so the vile itself had to be made from the sand at the oasis for it was Holy ground.

Only one being knew where that stronghold was. Queen Hadiat smiled frenetically and she took it as a sign that Believers were ready for their war.

"Quickly, pour them on my chains, I have to find and embrace my girls so that they can form fik-iri together." Queen Hadiat extended her hands up, "we will win this war. It's not over... we didn't lose!"

The T'Malak did as she was told and finished right as a blade was driven through her back out her chest. She smiled while falling because she'd achieved her goal. Queen Hadiat was free.

Hadiat stood tall and stretched her aching body, cracking her knuckles. She could feel her strength returning but she could also feel the crimes of perverted men all over her once beautiful skin. The anger swallowed her whole and she attacked. Fighting with every skill she possessed she moved the earth and drew fire from above. Demon after demon ran to her attempting to rechain her, but she refused to be detained. She unleashed a series of rage-filled excellence. Right as she'd begun to rescue herself a pained feeling jerked her back into her trapped mindset.

Shadows of dark wings caved in the roof and Tiago himself appeared before her. "Triplets, huh? All this time, we were looking for just one." His height grew with each step as his shadow faded and his face revealed. The calmness of his bright blue eyes was as intimidating as his name and power.

"You'll never lay one lying finger on them. That's my promise." She stood firm drawing in energy from whatever elements she could feel. "Tiago, I presume?"

He pretended to ignore her whilst stroking his short sandy blonde hair, "And as for the prophecy you speak of, what was it? One to lead, one to free and one to...? What's a fik-iri? Why an embrace?" He paused for a very brief moment, "No matter, it will not be fulfilled. I will not allow it."

"You have no control over my Father's will." Hadiat began sizing him up searching for a weak spot. He was unlike the other demons she'd faced. His weakness was not apparent. She tried to remember not to forget herself, her own strength, and her babies.

"I will kill all of mankind before I allow any of you to ever rise again. I've already commissioned the mass production of akrhh matter, every Believer's limbs are already bejeweled in them. Slaves is the proper term." Tiago began circling the Queen as he instantly smelled her fear. "I'll enslave every single last one of your people if that's what it takes, fickle-minded humans. It won't take much. Hell!

Most of them don't even require the shackles anymore. True Believers, huh? He had such high hopes in those who refuse to open their eyes. Faith, he said they'd have faith because he instilled it but they accept blindness and thus refuse Him. I must admit, tickles the hell right into me. I can and will continue to disenfranchise every single one of them with and without chains. My prophecy, best prophecy I've ever heard. That's my word. MY WILL! I'll teach them all everything they need to know, just like you have, Sarah. And you're such a quick learner too!"

"All a part of the prophecy. You play a necessary evil in all this. I do not fear you, nor do my girls."

"Ah...Hadiat, my dear sweet Hottentot. Did your husband fear me? You don't have to fear me to die, you should know that by now." His undisturbed tone never peaked nor plummeted, an arrogance that capitalized his power.

Hadiat's eyes lit up with fiery embers. The smart path was to escape, but her anger and pride bled over top her wisdom. The disrespect for her King was something she would not tolerate no matter who Tiago was.

Tiago knew he hit the right spot. "So! Let's make this easy...that is, if you want your little bastards to live. Where are they? Where are these triplets of yours? Tell me now or I'll send you to ashes with your husband. Some king he was. He could lead his army of Guardians but could not protect his own family? Hmph! Tell me now. And I'll show mercy and chain the little niglets right next to you so that you may watch over them for the rest of your days. I'll even raise them as my own. We can be a..... family, of sorts. What do you say?"

Hadiat attempted to bring him down but without her King she had no strength to draw upon. They exchanged hits however not even her hardest blows phased him in the slightest. Frustrated at how a mere demon could be so strong, she paused for air, looking over all her scars. The bruises from white women's decorative walking sticks. The scars from white children throwing rocks. The blood stains she couldn't wipe clean from debauched torturous rape. Her magnificent skin was once the glory of His image. Hadiat's was fighting too hard to recognize herself...her worth. All she knew was she couldn't allow the same for her heirs. Hadiat accepted that she could not fight Tiago and win. Yet, she wouldn't dare allow him to recapture her and read her mind to learn the heirs' identities. She also knew, she was the only one who could teach and direct her daughters in truth to their respective thrones. The time had come for the great sacrifice the old visionary once told her would come. The Queen chose their lives over hers yet again. Picking up the vile, she whispered, "Thine will be done" and drew a spell using afterlife protective symbols then drank the remaining of David's tears. Her soul departed from her body and fled to wander the Earth in search of her heirs.

Chapter 3: Seek and Find

Hadiat's spirit was growing faint from the weight it carried but she couldn't fail her girls. After a few days, she found the eldest triplet, Aida, amongst the Ainu in Japan under the protection and guidance of a gentle light bearing and legendary T'Malak named Hathor. Hadiat was elated because she knew her daughter by her voice. After several years spent in captivity the Queen was blessed by the sweetest sound of Aida crying out 'mommy' and overcome with tears she wrapped her baby girl in her arms and squeezed tightly, an embrace that would never let go. She looked over Aida ensuring that her child was unharmed and relished in His favor every single time Aida cried 'mommy'.

Hadiat was slow to remember her friend, so Hathor showed Hadiat her light to confirm she was good, a genuine Believer. Celebrated and upheld highly in the realm of Believers, Hathor was most commonly known as the protector of the divine feminine. Close friend of the throne and proud to serve, she'd dedicated her hand to Aida.

Hadiat spoke gratitude that echoed above the stars to show her baby girl just how much she loved her. The Heavens opened up as Aida embraced her mother's spirit and learned her worth and the angels rejoiced with them giving honor to a battle already won. But the search had only just begun and she knew she had to get to the other two girls before the demons. Hadiat was grateful to Hathor who swore an oath to protect Aida until she returned.

A couple days later, Hadiat found the next triplet being hid amongst the Amazigh in France. A warmness filled the air when Liya felt her mother's face because Hadiat knew her second-born child by her touch. One touch made Hadiat care less about every torturous scar on her skin, Liya was worth every bit of the pain she once felt. She'd been being protected and guided by a wise T'Malak, Seshet. A chuckle crept across Hadiat's heart when Seshet dropped her scrolls and fell to her feet surprised at the sight of the goddess Queen's spirit.

The Queen delicately grabbed Liya's beautiful face and kissed her forehead. The Heavens opened as Liya embraced her mother's spirit and learned her worth while the angels rejoiced with them for they were one more step closer. Hadiat was grateful to Seshet who swore to protect Liya until she returned.

For several more days Hadiat searched far and wide for her youngest triplet Zoya and when she found her, her spirit nearly ripped in fright. She knew her by her brilliant brown eyes.

Zoya had been kidnapped into slavery, no T'Malak in sight. She was on a ship heading to Suriname. Hadiat could not embrace her child who was covered in akrhh matter chains and instead showed herself to the Heir but Zoya didn't recognize her mother, blinded by the weapons of demons. In foreign lands filled with peril, fear and loneliness Zoya became filled with confusion. She couldn't embrace her for she too had been ravaged by colonizers and was forgetting herself routinely. So Hadiat never left her side making every attempt to rescue her child, from whispering freedom's song into her ears while she slept to lighting up escape routes through the stars.

Finally, Zoya revolted in Maroon warfare on the plantation at a tender age and defeated the demons but without proper knowledge and acceptance of her worth she couldn't remove the cursed chains. After court trials determined the slaves to be free, Zoya was placed on a ship marked Deuteronomy 28:65-68 to sail home to Africa. The Dutch Justice Department claimed to have kept the slaves in chains for "everyone's safety." In reality, the Dutch made a deal with demon pawns and sent Zoya and the Surinam Maroons to South Carolina to be resold into slavery never to return home again.

Zoya eventually became impregnated by colonizer blood. She gave birth to a beautiful baby girl then died.

Hadiat's spirit screamed out as she watched the light in her beautiful daughter Zoya's eyes extinguish after giving birth. "Thou has forsaken me! Did You forget your own promise, Father? How will my grandchild know who she is if her mother never embraced me and learned her worth? What about your promise! My baby is gone!!!" Hadiat's screamed so loud that it woke Heaven and a T'Malak fazed into Hadiat's presence and showed Hadiat her light so that she would know the T'Malak was good and true. Hadiat finally recognized the T'Malak's face and melted into her arms, "Sekhmet..."

"It's me, your Father sent me. Allow me to help." Sekhmet was the strongest ally to the throne. She'd often been thought to be an omen and cantankerous by most Believers. But she'd always had a special place in the King and Queen's heart, for they knew her and refused anyone twisting words about her. Sekhmet was rarely seen, only when absolutely needed, otherwise her presence was always a mystery. After a brief reunion amongst longtime best friends, Sekhmet hid amongst the slaves under the name Hattie, hoping Hadiat's grandchild would *see* her, but the child never did and Sekhmet grew restless over the years. "I cannot force her to see, but I can give her my strength." She confessed to Hadiat without a tear nor doubt. Looking at Hadiat's grandchild while she slept she whispered, "feligu tagenyumalachihu" then sacrificed herself to God after bequeathing the Heir her renown strength and powers.

As the years passed by Hadiat's spirit continued to cry out because every time a female Heir from the line of Zoya was born, the mother died during delivery adding stones to the ever-growing wailing wall dividing them from their throne with each generation. The Queen watched as her lineage was raped, slaughtered and terrorized. She screamed when would-be Guardians were sodomized, castrated and lynched. "Why can't they hear my call?! How will any of them know who they are?!" She cried out to the Creator wanting to ask for an amendment to His word for although she knew the importance of it all, her heart couldn't take anymore of the recyclical struggle.

Zoya's lineage never had the chance to embrace their worth. And because Zoya had never formed fik-iri with her sisters, all the sisters immortality faded with each generation. Just as Zoya died, so had Aida and Liya except their deaths were due to old age.

Hadiat knew her other daughters' lineages were safe with their T'Malaks so she remained with the line of Zoya. Then, it happened. A colonizer showed one of Zoya's grandchildren a picture of Sarah Baartman, the Hottentot Venus, and unknowingly told the heir who she was, Tiago's promise fulfilled. Covered in shame, the Heir accepted this standard and Hadiat's spirit dampened at the sounds of her chains dragging across wooden splintered floors. Hadiat blamed herself for not knowing how to stop Tiago when she had the chance. It seemed all hope was lost, but Hadiat remained and allowed the dreary tears to trace Nile rivers flowing north, whispering to Zoya's line of heirs, "you were born free," every night attempting to undo akrhh matter's curse. "Follow the stars. Go home already. Please go home. Come back to me... I need you."

One Hundred and seventy relentlessly tiring years later, the sign of tide's shift appeared. The year was 1984. The first commercial for Apple McIntosh appeared on the screen at the hospital during a special showing people walking the moon untethered. Three women directly lined as heirs through Aida, Liya and Zoya were giving birth on the same day at the same exact time to girls. Confirmation of His sign meant the prophecy was still real. Hadiat's spirit began to feel increase, for this moment was written long ago. Thunder and lightning caused the lights to flicker in and out in the hospital room of Zoya's lineage, but

Hadiat knew it was no mere storm. It was demons searching to end the prophesied Heirs. Confident in the fact that the other Heirs were protected by their T'Malaks and families, she feared not for them. But she was uncertain to how she'd protect the line of Zoya as her strength was depleting. While the mother was giving birth, Hadiat mustered up as much energy as she could and showed the doctor his worth with a simple blessed touch to his head and a whisper into the wind. To Hadiat's relief, he heard her and remembered himself, a Guardian. A healthy baby girl was delivered and the mother passed away, the curse of akrhh matter remained.

A demon heard the Guardian's wings being reborn and found them. The same demon killed the Heir's father in the hospital with an arkhh blade. When he went to attack the baby, the Guardian succeeded in protecting her and escaped with her by bursting out a window and flying away but he was now under chase with the demon tailing him.

The Guardian wrapped himself and the baby in his enormous white wings and barrel rolled weaving in and out of traffic dodging bullets and calamity. Hadiat did all she could to help, but the demon was covered in arkhh matter. While she distracted the demon, the Guardian hid outside an orphanage for a moment and hurriedly made a blanket patterned in royal signs for the baby using the feathers from his wings. The throbbing stings he felt didn't matter in comparison to the mission of protecting the baby girl's crown. He wrapped her in his labor of love, the blanket covered her majestic scent and she smiled cooing, completely unbothered by the surrounding chaos. "You are because He is," the Guardian spoke over her never removing his eyes from hers. He took comfort in the fulfillment his destiny. He then carefully opened a window and placed her in an orphanage crib and returned to join the Queen in battle where he died after being pierced with an akrhh blade.

Just as demons lost the baby's scent, so had Hadiat. Fully understanding and trusting God her Father, Hadiat returned to the other two Heiresses and decreed their families to reunite in Paris, France. Through the years, the two Heirs learned their history, purpose and great deal more as they remained protected by Hathor, Seshet and now Hadiat herself.

On their thirtieth birthdays, while all three Heirs slept, they dreamt the same dream differently; their view from the mountain top as a crown was being place upon their heads. It shook them awoke so hard that it felt as if a hand violently tugged at their chests luring them toward purpose. When they rose, a single star shined brightly over all three girls. It was time.

Chapter 4: The Great Unlearning

Aniah laid in her bed awake with her eyes shut. Her hair curtained her face providing a plush retreat from suffocating thoughts she longed to escape. The alarm on her cell phone would soon go off but she lay there squeezing her eyes closed tighter in rebellion against time. Her eyeballs rolled back and forth underneath her lids like they were trying to run away from the memories inside her head. The visions she kept returning to. Every time she tried to simply have a quiet moment to herself, all she ever saw was the pain in the eyes of all the people she'd helped. All the lives she restored to a second chance. She put her hand on her head hoping to ease the pain. Recalling their fears of unjust sacrifice and their reasons for risking themselves was her burden as well... a lonely burden. Gently, she caressed her temples with her thumb and middle finger tracing the images of beautiful people into her own, owning their infringed heart beats as one. Moments of the stories embedded in their tears, pressed her own tears against her eyelids that begged for escaping relief. She prayed the tear's purity would wash the memories from her heart. And her chest, it swelled with dutiful inquisition. Why did she have to be the one to save them? When would she be done? Would it always be this way? Did anyone know or care? Was anyone watching...listening...feeling the cause? Who is to hold her up when she felt rather faint? Who would understand? She was tired, not from the work but from the loneliness. The magnitude of her battles meant enduring deeper and more distant solitude. Outside her windows, the stars had begun their ascension while she drifted further into her sea of thoughts. The more solemn her tears grew, the louder a voice from within urged her to move forward.

A sea of soft and fluffy white bedding and decorative pillows that were always in perfect position never provided any real comfort. Sunken into their softness, she wanted to drown but was only able to breathe. The lavishness of the custom-built furniture in her bedroom was one that most dreamt to have, but she'd give it all away for anything authentic. Having lived life in her apartment amongst the skies meant nothing to her if she couldn't fly.

The alarm went off playing Aniah's favorite song. She sat up in a rush but only for the purpose of breathing different and allowing the tears to trace new paths. Being left without any family always meant she had to initiate her own story; she had to etch her own name in a history that may never be told. Only, she had no idea how legendary she already was and the prophecy that declared her royalty before she was born. She rose from her bed and folded her favorite blanket, hugged it for encouragement then placed it on the edge of her bed neatly. Slowly, she walked by and traced the stitching and embroidery gently with her finger she stared into the patterns in belief of its hidden revelations. Whenever she wrapped herself inside, she'd lean into each thread like she could see someone cared. It was the only thing that gave her a glimpse of what it felt like to be loved, only she didn't know why. Born into a parentless world and never being adopted would've left her cold if it weren't for that blanket.

Aniah kept the music playing loud as she went into the shower to continue her release of the day. Expensive peppermint soaps and fresh aloe helped to wash off the fatigue and muscle pains as she allowed the melodies to sway her. Afterward, she stepped out refreshingly renewed dancing carefree. She twirled, pranced and skipped in her robe all around her home gliding past tables and bracing walls. Happily she smiled and laughed at herself because every time she glanced at the mirror, her true hidden goofy nature smiled back. While she moisturized and styled her long black coils, she used her hair lotion bottle as a microphone and adding her own adlibs and runs.

In her black stiletto booties, black leather pants, a black crop top and her custom made black Tuskegee Airmen leather bomber jacket, Aniah was ready for the nightlife. She slowed her stride slightly as a spirit of gratefulness had overcome her. She looked up and gave thanks for the moment, acknowledgment to God that her work was not yet finished.

Aniah blew a friendly kiss at the front desk attendant and as she exited the huge double doors she smiled and gave a head nod to the valet, a tall Black man wearing a fitted Yankee cap. "Who are you going with for the win in tonight's game?", she asked him as he escorted her to her truck.

The valet opened her door, "The Nets been looking right lately, I'm going with them." He smiled and tossed her the keys to her brand-new custom fully equipped Escalade.

Curly kinks danced in the wind and Aniah inhaled deeply taking in the aroma from nearby restaurants while stepping inside her truck and readjusting her seat. She coasted off and turned up the music. Shortly after, Aniah arrived at a nearby tented community for the homeless and circled their neighborhood. She finally spotted her contacts just as the valet hinted; men wearing Nets fitted hats. The men walked over to her vehicle and began unloading the meals from the back of her truck while she handed out clean socks, underwear, blankets, and teddy bears for the little ones. The valet was actually a leader in his community that organized help and relief for his people. Aniah, the valet and few others worked together in an underground capacity to give love to those in desperate need. Once the truck was emptied, she rode off to her job.

Aniah pulled up to the front of her club, parked and greeted the valet. She walked along the long line of people waiting to get inside and shook hands with her regulars and introduced herself to others. People smiled back in reflection of her warm invite and anticipated the good times awaiting them inside even more. Then she walked into the front entrance and caught a mere second of a glimpse of the security guard's eyes and saw how tired he was. He'd been struggling as a single custodial father to three kids, this was his second job and he was worn down. Aniah leaned in and asked him to escort her through the crowd. Near the bar she spotted the prettiest set of bright brown eyes on a sad woman. Aniah saw the woman's pain and her mind painted the picture; the woman had been in and out the hospital consoling her dying mother. Aniah playfully grabbed the woman's hand and went straight for the dance floor. She euphorically danced with the security guard and at the same time she twirled the pretty-eyed girl around until her frown turned upside down. Aniah left them on the dance floor in that moment together watching them escape into their forever.

Friday nights always ushered in large crowds. The club was packed wall to wall with people celebrating, taking shots and enjoying the three-year anniversary party. Aniah decided to do some people watching from her office upstairs to see if she could study and guess various walks of life. She thought she was making up stories about them all based upon the way they interacted and moved about. Her preference when in crowds had become seclusion. Often times she felt drained when she moved amongst clubgoers because life had already shown her more than she wanted to see, instead she watched over them instinctually.

"Hey Aniah!" Her business partner Victoria entered in the office and began shuffling papers around on her desk. She was wearing a form-fitted black dress with designer black heels. Her long reddish blond hair was wound tightly so her curls could last all night.

Aniah knew it as a style Victoria wore when she was really trying to impress someone. "Hey Vic, what's up?"

"Just finished posting the club on social media. Ran into an interesting story while I was on there. You hear about that woman who busted up the cops' sting in Chicago? Feds are looking for her everywhere. They can't ID her though...."

"Yea, I heard something about that. Weren't the cops baiting young boys into robbing a shoe truck by leaving it in the hood unlocked with back door wide open? Selling boys to the system again, I guess. Heard she exposed them and beat the cops' asses when they tried to apprehend her.... or something like that." Aniah leaned back in her office chair, propped her legs up on the low window sill and crossed her ankles waiting for the small talk to end.

"Yeah, the streets are celebrating her as some type of vigilante for thug justice. Come to think of it, I don't know many people that have hands like that. Maybe one?" Victoria waited to see if Aniah would confess. "No more than a terrorist if you ask me. Weren't you in Chicago earlier today?"

"Yeah, remember, I was there to look into properties for another club."

"Oh, well police said this chick is dangerous. She beat six officers and dodged bullets...something like a comic book or movie. They're stunned. Look at this!" Victoria pulled out her phone. "These four women witnessed the whole thing. Cops are looking for them too. There's a large reward for any tips leading to her arrest, not just money either."

Aniah wasn't about to take the bait. She'd already seen the news and knew everything before Victoria even walked in. There was a part of her that wanted to tell Victoria all the details about how she planned the whole thing. She wished she could exhale the truth about how it felt to land each punch and kick corrupt cops in their ribs. How redeeming it was when they finally felt what it's like to gasp for air and be in pain wanting but being refused every single breath. She made it back to Columbus before they could even checkout the emergency room.
Aniah wanted so badly to tell her long-time comrade about all the other wrongs she righted as well. Like, how she exposed the child trafficking ring in Michigan, or the inhumane body harvesting operations she busted up in California and how she sent proof to the news and media outlets about judges selling young Black kids to various government and private systems in the south. But Victoria wasn't the same person she grew up with in and out of foster homes and county children services. She was no longer the same woman who took shots with her after they stood before a judge emancipated themselves at sixteen. They had grown apart. They were suckled by the same teat but split apart by reality, reminiscent of the Black women that nursed White kids only for those kids to grow up and let hate win. The two opened their club as friends calling themselves sisters. However,

Victoria started hanging around a different crowd two years ago; the type of crowd that paraded in white hoods and sheets at night then went to work as teachers, doctors, celebrities and policemen by day. Their partnership was no more than Aniah's play at keeping her eye on her enemies. Aniah was now accustomed to being alone and understood being solo wasn't a punishment but a recognition. However, she prayed fervently for genuine bonds.

"Do you like the strippers I hired for tonight's occasion?" Victoria continued her intrusion of Aniah's space walking over closely to her, placing one hand on Aniah's shoulder and pointing with the other.

"Where did you find them?" Aniah stopped herself from letting out an exhaustive sigh while she slid her shoulder away from Victoria's hand.

"Eh...various college campuses, pimps and promoters. All their twerking and ass clapping definitely brings out the crowd and dollars. I think it's alright just for the night, don't you? Or, maybe they can be a more permanent fixture. I don't even understand what men see in their fat butts and gyrating but if it keeps our pockets fat, I'm with it. I was thinking we should add cages with poles in them for the monkeys, I mean girls."

"Didn't you just have an Afro-Brazilian ass injection surgery, or....?"

"Huh?"

"Did you order enough food for VIP? Looks like their running out." Aniah pointed to the section to draw Victoria's attention away from her obvious attempts to upset her. All the strippers were young Black girls, the exploitation hurt Aniah in ways she couldn't quite explain.

"Oh, there's more in the kitchen. I'll go grab it and mix it up with the crowd. You coming?"

"Yeah, I'll be down in a minute." Aniah waited until she saw Victoria enter the kitchen from their office window, then she took the back stairs down to the basement, picked up a flashlight underneath the stairs and went into a dark and isolated part that only she would ever visit. A shelving unit at the end of the hall had various items such as a jar full of nails, a tool bag, some manuals, blueprints and other miscellaneous items. Aniah pulled a book by W.E.B DuBois and triggered a trap door which opened a hidden room sheltering five homeless families she'd been secretly helping. She helped them hide because the fathers, heads of the families, were accused of felonies they hadn't committed and Aniah knew they were innocent but didn't know how she knew. After she ensured they had enough food, water, and blankets she sat down with them for a moment and listened to stories of how their day went and caught them up on how they were fairing legally. Innocence proven didn't guarantee freedom or lives worth living, so Aniah worked with them to create and achieve the milestones, detailing true paths to real freedom. "Well, I'll come and check on you guys tomorrow morning when the club is empty and everyone is gone, lock the door behind me." She rubbed one of the kid's heads gently, then they did their secret handshake before Aniah left.

Aniah headed back upstairs and walked around the crowd making sure things in the club were running smoothly, checking in with security and bar staff. Out the corner of her eye she saw the four women who witnessed her intercept the crooked cops plot in Chicago that morning. In all her dealings no one had ever caught her. Then she spotted Victoria talking to a few men in suits and pointing her out. Aniah moved quickly to get away right then and there and wasted no time going through the kitchen and out the back exit. She walked out the back door only to find three more suited men waiting for her blocking one direction of the alley way.

"Is it her?", one asked the others.

The darkness of the alley wouldn't protect her identity much longer. Aniah turned to go the other way but stopped in her tracks. The four women who witnessed her earlier filled that passage. Aniah stood there in between them all unsure of what she should do next, she needed a miracle.

"It's them! Go! Go get help and call Tiago! We'll hold them here." One of the suited men yelled.

"Aniah, get ready!" One of the women called out to her.

"Wait, how do you know my name?" Aniah heard movement over her shoulder and dodged a blade right as it flew past her head. The witnesses simply stepped to the side as the blade continued past them. Aniah fully turned in enough time to see the men reaching out to grab her and so her real fight began. She was a skilled street fighter and could easily take down any number of men without ever being scratched so she fought with that confidence until one of their punches actually landed. She'd not been caught with any fist since her days in foster care. Her back was toward them but from over her shoulder she was able to see the witnesses still standing there. Angry at the loneliness, she turned around and fought harder giving hits as good as she got it until she was able to subdue the men. She panted for air after their lifeless bodies hit the ground. Behind her, she could hear the women approaching. Aniah turned in enough time to see the women taking off their jackets and pulling out various weapons, she couldn't make it all out as her vision is blurred by the onset of rain. She lifted herself off the ground and turned to run only to see more suited men than before and this time, with guns and swords.

"Aniah! Get down!" One of the women called out.

Aniah squatted down and watched as another jumped over her head and into action. She knelt there poised as she watched the four women take on the men. They too were excellent fighters.

"Are you gonna help out or just sit there?!" One yelled out seemingly overwhelmed by her attackers.

Aniah started in the opposite direction but before she could commit to abandoning them, a hard blow of conviction took over her entire body causing her to stop. Aniah heard a distant voice call to her yet again screaming this was her fight and the sound of own beating heart took over her lung's air. She looked back at the fighting women who were struggling as more suited men came from nowhere. "They watched me fight and didn't help, why should I help them," she said to herself and her heart answered immediately. Aniah joined them in battle. This time Aniah was able to fully see the men's faces. They weren't men at all, their faces were stretched and disfigured and their eyes were completely black, no light emitted for proof of a soul. She fought harder, stopping only once all of the men were scattered across the ground.

"We must go!" One of the women plainly stated. "Tiago is coming and she's not ready."

"Who are you?!" Aniah gasped out, "what the hell is going on?"

"Come child!" Another reached out her hand begging Aniah to grab it. "We don't have time, please!"

Aniah didn't move so the woman stepped forward and grabbed her. Within a split second they were sucked into a blueish-green watery vortex, then seconds later they reappeared inside Aniah's home.

"Quick! Where is your T'Malak?"

"My what? What the heck is a...wait! Who are ya'll and how did we get inside my home?" Aniah struggled to catch her footing as the she began to recognize where they were. She clutched the edge of an end table and the vase on it shook but didn't fall.

"You don't have a T'Malak?" One asked Aniah, then turned to another woman, "I thought another was sent to her? Are you sure she's an heir?"

"Why else would the demons go after her? They wouldn't waste time nor that many resources if she didn't bare worth." Another responded almost ignoring Aniah's presence while staring right at her.

"Those things in suits that we killed are demons? Wait, this can't be real." Aniah straightened herself tall after everything stopped spinning from the transport. "Alright…boom…so, I was just at…okay, and so this morning when I woke up I…but last night my dream and…" She paced around her living room trying to make it all make sense.

"Allow me. I will try to explain quickly as they will find us soon. My name is Hathor and I am a T'Malak; the Child of an Angel."

"'Scuse me, a what?"

"This is pointless! She can't be an heir. We're all protected by T'Malaks who taught us who we are after our ancestors embraced their worth. If she has no T'Malak nor anyone to protect and train her, how could she possibly be an heir? She has no sense of worth!" Another interrupted slamming her fist on a wall causing Aniah to stare at her disrespect. "We're wasting time!"

"Seshet, do you sense it? Sekhmet is here…it's Sekhmet's strength, I feel it! Could never mistake it!" Hathor closed her eyes and blocked out all the noise to listen. Sekhmet was known throughout the universe for her legendary strength and valor. Sure enough she'd heard the fallen T'Malak's presence in Aniah. "It's her! I feel Sekhmet's spirit calling to her, strengthening her still, the power is so raw, unfiltered and untapped." Hathor walked quickly to Aniah. "Listen, this is Seshet. She is also a T'Malak. We chose to protect your ancestral lines many years ago. Those two over there are your sisters, Khailia and Ebelle."

"I don't smoke weed," Aniah's disbelief continued, "nor do I do drugs and I only had one glass of wine. That's it! Vic put something in my wine. She poisoned me. I'm seeing stuff. This is yet another wild dream. Wake up Niah! Wake up baby girl! Snap out of it." She spoke to herself while clapping in between every other word. "No one in their right mind would punch a wall, table or anything in my home. This is definitely a dream." Aniah spoke slower to bide time as she spotted her black high top tennis shoes she left near the couch from earlier that morning. She took off her booties and changed into something more appropriate for defending herself if necessary. She stood back to her feet scouting the room.

While Aniah finished sizing everyone up, Hathor went to grab Aniah but not quick enough. Aniah blocked her grasp and pushed her back. But she was still slightly woozy from the transport and Aniah didn't catch Seshet in enough time.

Seshet gracefully placed her index finger to her thumb finger then placed it on Aniah's forehead in an attempt to share the truth. After a few seconds Seshet snatched her hand away. "Child, how are you…how did you just…why…" Seshet's loss for words stunned the others. She shook her hand hard like it was stinging.

"What meaning does that hand gesture carry for you? In which way were you intending to..." Aniah calmly asked, "I saw..."

"They're here!" Hathor announced while searching for an exit. "Aniah, we must faze again."

"Faze! What's a faze? And who's here? Just wait a damn minute!"

"It's how we got here. It's our form of travel." Hathor stretched her hand out hoping the heiress peacefully latch on.

"You mean that thing that has me feeling like I'm suffering three hangovers at once?"

"Yes. And demons. The demons. They're here. We must go." Seshet glanced over her shoulder into Aniah's room and saw the blanket the Guardian made for Aniah and realized why it took so long to find her. She grabbed the blanket then glided over to Aniah and fazed them so fast that Aniah could barely blink or breathe. "Open your eyes Aniah. Look at your inheritance." Seshet released her arm to investigate Aniah's being with her eyes trying to research the answers standing before her, a truth.

Meanwhile, Aniah struggled to focus on the view of the world from the mountain top. Once she realized their height, she gasped for air. Unsure of her footing or herself in the world, she couldn't cling to anything she knew to be real. She tried to hide her panic but the world wouldn't stop spinning and nothing was making sense. The moon was up a few seconds ago but now the sun was shining brightly on the mountain. They were atop a green mountain along the backside of a walled city and a gold temple. The tiny pebbles slid with ease under her feet. Trying to find balance on stable ground, she stretched her arms out and took steps back landing her into Seshet's chest.

"How is it that you don't know what a T'Malak is nor do you know who you are, but you have a blanket made of Guardian feathers?" Seshet prodded on slyly as she twisted her cocoa eyes away from Aniah's glare, "who made you this blanket? Where is he?"

"What feathers? That's my baby blanket. I was wrapped in it and left at an orphanage only a few hours old according to the nurse there." The pestering of questions ushered in anxiety. Aniah panicked for familiarity, searching the room straining her eyes. "What is all this?"

"You don't know the man who made this?" Seshet continued with her questioning completely ignoring Aniah's condition. She pulled her silky hair back into a ponytail.

Noticing her new sister was in no space to speak, Khailia put her hands up begging Seshet to stop. "Relax sister." Khailia, the only one that had been silent, finally spoke. She walked slowly but surely toward Aniah, "Steady your breathing, relax your mind. There is no need to fear what is already yours." Subtle mercies guided her hands to grace Aniah's shoulders. "I'm so happy to finally meet you," then she pulled her sister in for what seemed a mere greeting.

An immediate peace stabilized Aniah's body and filled her heart as she wrapped her arms around Khailia and pulled her in tighter. Aniah had been desperate for the feeling they were sharing, securing a safe spot for their bond within. They both took deep breaths and spent what felt like their whole lives in a single moment. When they hugged, their eyes filled watery blue with jubilance and immense placid knowledge. A light shined brightly around them and the air elevated their growing love for one another. Aniah had heard the word 'sister' be used countless times but the sense of belonging she now felt gave life to the title. Before a tear could fall, she absorbed glimpses of Khailia's life as though she'd been there all along. Everything from her favorite color being green to the French foods that turned Kahilia's stomach, Aniah now knew. The scar on the back of Khailia's knee from an unsecured arrow while riding a horse and how she learned to speak Spanish fluently at the same time, Aniah was seeing it like she was there when it happened. She saw Khailia as a teenager when she dreamed of life outside of fulfillment, flirting with what it looked like to veer off God's path, Aniah saw it all.

Khailia spoke to Aniah's heart and listened at its echoes in return. She too now had an understanding of Aniah and all the things she'd seen in her life. She heard her sister learn to fight by standing outside a martial arts studio. She laughed at Aniah's interpretation of kung-fu and hood hands. From how Aniah learned to wear a formal dress and getting her nails done for the first time with her face turned up, Khailia heard every emotion. Then the laughter turned into hurt as she listened deeper. Life had been unkind to the heiress. All the running, the outcries against loneliness, and fears of never knowing love to its fullest capacity.

Aniah took a step back from Khailia and stared at her in awe while trying not to smile so hard. She'd never felt a kindred connection to anyone and it shook her harder than the faze. "What was that?" Their veins mimicked roots tracing the ancestry glowing beneath their skin. They both smiled at their friendship and stared at their hands. Turning them from one side to the other, their eyes followed the glow to their arms pulsating with their newfound strength in each other.

"Commonly, it's known as a bond between blood. You and I are now aligned as sisters. However, when we embrace, God's promise becomes fulfilled through us. A bond between heirs is called a fik-iri. You feel it too?"

"Yes...I...," the tears streamed down Aniah's face and her smile continued to vibrate between them. She saw Khailia's dreams and read her soul. Aniah watched her being molded into the woman that stood bravely in front of her and understood how she longed to take her place at her throne. As a loving sister, she wanted nothing more than to witness her Khailia's increase of power and ascension to her throne. "We look nothing alike," Aniah tried to laugh off her true emotions. She wiped her eyes then returned her stare to Khailia's high yellow skin tone. Khailia was a few inches shorter, with fuller curves and her hair was wavy and rested on her buttock. It took a few seconds, but finally Aniah noticed they had the same almond shaped eyes and although their lips were different in size, they were the same in downward turned shape. The more she stared, she even saw similarity in their oval face shape and cheek bone structure. The more she looked, the closer their kinship grew regardless of growing up with an ocean between them.

"I heard you and you saw me." Khailia smiled warmly welcoming her sister. "I am sorry we did not meet sooner." Khailia heard all the pain from Aniah's past. It was hard to hear all the silent screams for love, all the ripping tears her sister suffered in solace choked Khailia's voice for the first time ever. She opened her mouth to continue speaking but had not the words and it scared her as she frantically turned to Hathor for help; the fear was unknown.

Without any further scripture to define their hug, they know what each other meant to one another.

"Fik-iri can only be experienced by royalty as it can't be explained to a common understanding." Hathor gently spoke up. "Oh, the exultations I feel for you as God's kingdom reunites right before my own eyes. I smile from within. God is pleased."

"Well, I guess it's my turn. Let's get this over with...sis." Ebelle took a step forward to bond with her sister, but Aniah took a step back.

"Oh! She's stronger than we thought!" Hathor covered her chuckling smile. "You can't rush fik-iri Ebelle. She can sense your being disingenuous. I can sense it by merely looking at you."

Aniah's eyes twitched as she looked Ebelle in the eyes and struggled to find kindred heart with her, opening the door for discontention between the two. While Ebelle was easily the most beautiful woman Aniah had ever seen, something inside her had yet to catch up to her outward appearance. It wasn't difficult to see the almond shaped eyes are a feature all three have in common. However, Ebelle's skin was as smooth and deep brown as polished tiger eye stone. Her nose was slightly wider and while her lips held the same size as Khailia's, the shape was different from both sisters. Ebelle had a more slender frame but was firmly toned. "This is all so much, this can't be real." Aniah tried her hardest to make sense out of it all wiping tears from her face with the backside of her hand. "Why can't I wake up."

"This blanket you have," Seshet walked toward Aniah and handed it to her while Aniah took a seat on a boulder. "When is the last time you used it?"

"I sleep with it every night."

"This is why your mother could not find you. As long as you wear it, you're covered in Guardian blessings. They shield and protect royalty in the strongest way possible; no demon, weapon, spirit, man, not one single creation, absolutely nothing can penetrate Guardian feathers as they are pure extensions of God himself. The line of Guardians is dormant now, that is, until their King returns. That's why it's important you tell me who gave this to you. You're truly an heir. It took a Guardian an enormous amount of energy to pour out of himself in order to do this task. And this is threaded immaculately. He would never have done it if he didn't understand your worth. Plucking his own wings is a painful task, not to be taken lightly."

"Wait a minute!" Aniah stood to her feet sharply gently putting her hands up at waist level, "Back up a sec. My mother? I'm an orphan, I ain't never had a mother so what do you mean I have a mother?" Her heart rate began to rise again as the words unbelievably continued to slowly spill out her mouth and tears began cascading. "She's been looking for me? Where is she? Am I going to meet her? Is this what this is about?" She turned to Khailia then Hathor trying to remain tough. "How do I look? Do I look okay? What does she look like? Do we look alike?" The longing was easy to see all over Aniah's caramel-graced face. "I've tried dreaming of her face so many times. I don't know how she looks. Is she here?" She tried to straighten her clothes and wipe debris and dirt off then fluffed her hair praying her curls were still intact.

Seshet felt every word like a knife. Her own blade. She had only experienced a tiny morsel of Aniah's story and couldn't bear to hurt her any further. She watched Aniah's slightly erratic movements as her speech hopped around without a care for proper response.

"Aniah, you are an heir." Hathor began to explain.

"An heir to what? Wait, damn that! Do I have a mother? I got a real mommy? I want to see her, please? I need to..." Aniah couldn't understand if she was being rewarded or punished. Her hands shook unsure of what to do.

"I can show you better than I can tell you." Hathor reached out to touch Aniah's temple.

"Allow me." Another voice spoke gently. "Come child, bring forth your eyes." Hadiat appeared and walked closer and closer to Aniah. Her long silky purple robe opened with her outstretched arms and the wind rode every seam.

Aniah backed up some ready for a fight. She'd never encountered a spirit nor ghost.

"It's alright girl, I'm not here to fight. I wouldn't dare dream of harming not the tiniest hair on you." Her form became solid as she cried standing face to face with Aniah. "Now, let me see your eyes." Hadiat moved forward and grabbed Aniah's face. "I see my Zoya all in you!" Hadiat stumbled over the words, "You are most certainly my heir." She smiled with trembling lips, "Come! Embrace me and learn your worth."

"My worth? What could any of you possibly know about my worth or who I am? And who the hell is Zoya? Ya'll got me confused with someone else after all this?! Matter of fact, who are you?!"

"Aniah, you're out of line! Respect your ancestor! Our ancestor." Ebelle's discontention grew fiercely. "I knew this was going to be bad. Do we really need her? She has all that Afro-American hostility seething all through her."

"I'm hostile but you're yelling?" Aniah mocked her, "yeah okay."

"We don't have time for this! If she has to stay with us, we're just going to have to drag her along and put a muzzle on her." Ebelle fell out of touch with reason in the moment. She lacked any empathy for Aniah.

"Please tell me you'll be the one to try?" Aniah smized menacingly.

"As you wish!" In anger, Ebelle picked up a long sturdy stick from the ground and swung it at Aniah's face but missed.

"Ebelle, stop!" Khailia tried to intercede.

"No, sometimes sisters must gain an understanding of one another before they can embrace." Hadiat stood firm with her shoulders erect, "Let them fight."

Ebelle swung again but was unable to land anything because Aniah was too fast. Sensing Ebelle's anger and hatred, Aniah couldn't place her finger on where it was coming from. However, she knew that hurt people, hurt people and therefore refused to harm Ebelle, that was until Ebelle finally landed a hit. Aniah was triggered. Before Ebelle could blink, Aniah tripped Ebelle then grabbed her by her throat mid fall and slammed her into the ground.

"Enough!" Aniah didn't want it to go too far. "I don't even know why I'm here and you're trying to fight me! For what? Stop! This is crazy! I don't even know you and you don't like me. You don't even know me not to like me. Go chill out somewhere!" Aniah lifted herself from over top of Ebelle then stepped back with caution.

"Aniah, please...allow me to explain. Ebelle means absolutely no harm, but she's right. We're on the clock and running out of time. We don't have time for misunderstandings and foolishness which is why I don't understand hers." Khailia gently lended a hand to Ebelle helping her off the ground. "The three of us are of the throne of God. Queen Hadiat over there is our ancestor and by all rights, our mother. Have you ever heard the story of Sarah Baartman?"

"Yeah, the African woman whose body marked mine for constant harassment. The world's first known stripper or something like that, right?"

"Only if you believe the lies. The truth is Sarah sacrificed herself to save her triplet daughters. Sarah's real name is Hadiat, goddess Queen to the throne of God, our extra great grandmother. Her, right there." Pointing at Hadiat, Khailia smiled to calm the storm. "Because my lineage has embraced Hadiat, we form a trust that led to my ancestral line's understanding of our worth. In order to understand your worth, you must embrace your ancestor too. Your divinity lives within your heritage."

Aniah looked around at everyone and saw their calmness, a sense of safety. "Okay, I trust you Khailia. So show me."

"I cannot show you, you have to accept your truth through her. Hopefully you'll let her embrace you as it is key. But I can share what I have. My gift is my voice, I will sing and you will see."

"Okay."

"Come, sit over here." Khailia extended her hand to her sister and Aniah accepted.

Aniah looked around at the faces staring at her and saw various looks of concern, peace and disbelief. She braced herself and sat back down on the boulder relaxed her shoulders. Khailia sang a beautiful psalm telling the story of Hadiat. She sang of her greatness, power and resilience. Learning how nations revered her and respected her while she fought hard for their right to Believe. Khailia got teary eyed once she made it to the part of her sacrifice and search for her heirs. By the end of the song, without any of them knowing, Aniah sensed their pain and urgency after having looked into Khailia and Hathor's eyes. She equated it more to the people she's rescued in her vigilante efforts than she did as an alignment because she has not experienced fik-iri with Ebelle nor embraced Hadiat.

"I'm so sorry Hadiat. You lost your husband, the King, your girls and gave up your own life, how painful." Aniah locked eyes with Hadiat. "How are you doing?"

"You know child, you're the first person to ever ask me that. When you're a goddess, people make assumptions; No one ever thinks that you're not okay. I never got to give him a proper burial, my King. My love has been lost to me for many years now, but his spirit is very much alive. I searched for him from time to time when I wasn't training your sisters or looking for you. Someday each of you will know what it means and how it feels to love your King. I pray you never lose him."

Aniah took an overwhelmed loud deep breath exaggerating with her cheeks. She didn't know if she wanted to know anymore, but she knew she couldn't go on blind. "So, what's this embrace thing all about, Hadiat? Or shall I say, Queen Hadiat."

"I've waited for this longer than you know child. You're not insignificant. Ebelle *feels* it. Khailia *hears* it. Can you *see* it? Will you *see* it? You will *see* it! The three of you are the embodiment of God's promise to always be here with His people. To always protect his creations. You are the keys to His divine legacy and upholders of His greatest will, love. Aniah, heiress to the line of Zoya, the visionary, the seer. She who sees. You have your Father's eyes, what He created you build upon. What demons fictiously destroy, with a single blink you quake their lies. With one tear you purify nations, when the embers of your pupils flare, you set flames for evolution's path...Yes! Your Father's eyes they reveal glory, not just His. They're your eyes too, your truth most of all is His air in you, an Heir to His throne, The Throne of God. My blood pulsates through you, the King's blood lives because of you! No story can be finished without acknowledging the very essence of you. Daughter of the line that refuses to be forgotten; the spirit of my child envisioned you. My sweet baby. My Zoya. MY Aniah. Come to me. Remember who you are."

Aniah never learned the customs nor traditions, the uneasiness in her eyes led her to do what felt like a natural inclination and knelt down before Hadiat catching her sisters off guard and they chuckled. However, the T'Malaks and Hadiat took note. Hadiat decided to accept her just the way she was by kneeling down with her to embrace her. The moon and sun shined bright, the elements rang out and in the distance, Angels prepared their horns. As they embraced,

Aniah's understanding of her worth began to emerge. Yet almost as soon as she began, she was blocked. All stood still and remained silent in shock. The Heavens wanted to rejoice, the sun and moon yearned to share space at the same time and the elements eagerness for recognition calmed all at once, even they respect God's patience. Hadiat understood that it was because of the blood shed of Aniah's lineage that embracing was seemingly obstructed. Although it would be difficult, it was not written as impossible.

"Hadiat..." Aniah lowered her eyes searching for the reason she couldn't perform.

"This has never happened to me before, Aniah. You don't trust me, not excited to know me. There is a disconnect with the line of Zoya. No rest for the weary." Hadiat stood to her feet and looking toward the path heading to a hidden door along the backside of the walled temple.

Aniah stood and tried to shake off Hadiat's disappointment. Failure on her first day felt like failure forever in the moment.

"A disconnect I'm afraid we'll have to resolve while on our hajj?" Seshet reminded them of their lack of time.

"We're going to Mecca? Wait, for the most part I'm a Christian, am I allowed? I wanna go, just to see it, but am I allowed?"

Everyone laughed at Aniah which solidified her self-doubts.

"My child, you have a lot to learn. A hajj is a journey to one's self or uniting with the God in you. Your sister's lineages learned their worth many many years ago so they knew this day would come and have been preparing for it, but they couldn't go without you. Your destinies are intertwined as three must share an inheritance." Seshet slightly turned her nose up and tried to look down at someone with whom she stood eye to eye.

"Oh really? That's wild." Aniah toughened up to their laughter to hide her insecurities.

"Yep, like it or not, and trust me, I don't, our destinies are tied to one another, therefore we need each other." Ebelle chimed in.

"This won't be easy as all three of you have not bonded, but we'll have to make do with what we have." Hadiat smiled then turned to face Aniah. "Now! In order to learn one's self, you must fully understand where you come from. To understand where you come from you must be willing to serve. Afterall, to be a goddess Queen is to be in service to His greatest will, that we love. Aniah, on our hajj, we must visit some essential tribes, people, characters," she smiled harder thinking of all that was in store. "Each will have a lesson for you to learn and a gift for you to receive and you will learn what services your people need."

"Do we become some sort of Queen after that?"

"No, my dear, it doesn't work that way. I cannot answer as to when each of you will become a Queen, which depends on when you're ready. On that day, when it happens, it will be undeniable."

"Are you going to tell them the part of the prophecy you kept from the triplets?" Hathor interjected, "I think they should know sooner rather than later."

"I kept it from them to avoid a fight, jealousy or hatred. I've seen entire nations and tribes be ripped a part for less. I won't even begin to list the number of regicides I saw in ancient Egypt or Gaul back in the days. Literally one after the other. Watched tribes turn into Sodom and Gomorrah due to lack pure leadership, killing anyone claiming the throne, just sheer confusion. But whatever is to come will come. All three of you will become a Queen, one to free…one to heal…and one to lead. All three of you will rule your territory by birthright, but only one of you will reign over all. I am unsure which one of you that will be as my Father never disclosed that to me. We have tried for years to decipher which is more important, the one who frees, the one who heals or the one who leads. Truth is, we don't know which of you is which until you embark upon this journey. We will all learn this together."

Chapter 5: The Sentinelese Treasury

Nostalgia sadly evaded Aniah. Even amongst her family, there was nothing or no one she could lean on for confirmation that everything would be okay. To her knowledge, there was no joint history amongst them that would allow her to reminisce on a similar time when everything turned out alright. She was so used to being in control of everything around her, however she found herself in a predicament. Her shoulders sank and she lowered her head to hide her shame, crossed her arms to comfort herself. She felt more alone than she ever had before. Overwhelmed with the feeling of defeat, Aniah looked over into the nearby trees and hoped her tears wouldn't fall. She buried her face in the palms of her hands then rubbed her temples as she turned away still wanting it all being a really messed up dream and nothing more. She felt isolated in world with a burden she carried but couldn't quite understand. She went from finally having a family to being rejected in a matter of what felt like seconds. From out of nowhere, an invisible nudge graced her chin and prompted Aniah to hold her head high because in all Aniah's life, fear was never an option for her and 'the nudge' wouldn't allow it to be fearful that day either. She had nowhere else to go and with demons surrounding her club and home, she hadn't the slightest idea of where to pick up the pieces. So she stayed. Aniah figured something different was less psychotic than going back to her void.

    Queen Hadiat held her hands out and began to lead them all along the passage to solitary door along the backside of the walled temple. A monk dressed in a long red robe with gold trim opened the door and showed them inside. They walked in silence to respect the worshippers praying inside the monastery while wiping their tears against the golden columns. They looked around and took in the large deities, elephant statues and vibrant colors in the draperies. Seas of yellow, orange and red sheers flowed gently with the wind barely making a sound. A monkey ran through Aniah's legs and startled her which drew attention to them. Patrons gazed while others acknowledged Queen Hadiat, the T'Malaks and by pressing their hands to their hearts. Their presence in the temple meant danger to the innocent lives visiting, so they moved quicker through the streets and to the front entrance. They made it to the grassy side of the mountain and began making their way down a stone trail with Aniah at the tail end to create distance between herself and everyone else.

    Khailia sensed an energy shift through Aniah's lagged movement and chose to remain by her side. Khailia couldn't abandon their bond in any form no matter what. In love with her big sister duties, she slowed down and placed her head gently on Aniah's shoulder and they walked together. "We're atop Mt. Popa," Khailia informed her. Aniah's need for love was now Khailia's priority and she placed it above all else because she could resoundingly hear God in her baby sister. Now that her family was finally all together, it was time to carry out their purpose in this world, a task Khailia was groomed to and trained for. But nothing trained her for the bond she felt between her sisters. No matter how many rehearsals she had to prepare her, when it happened, the words, footsteps, and proper poses, any protocol, went out the window. "Over there is the Taung Kalat monastery. It's known for monks and monkeys like the ones running figure eights around our legs, but many people come here to learn about the Nat, or the gods that dwell within," Khailia smiled looking Aniah eye to eye. She slowly grabbed Aniah's blanket from her hand and wrapped it around her shoulders pulling her close. Khailia yearned for completion, so she reached her other hand out to Ebelle, but Ebelle shrugged the gesture off and pushed herself in between Seshet and Queen Hadiat. Khailia welcomed the gentle startle of a kiss upon her forehead from Hathor who sought to ease the obvious tension. Khailia's gaze followed Hathor to the other side of Aniah and she smiled with soft laughter as Hathor pulled them both into her embrace.

    Seshet felt a jolt in energy through Ebelle's discontented touch and looked around to find the source. Once she spotted Hathor, Aniah and Khailia behind her she understood and turned her nose up. In all her years of rearing the line of Liya, Seshet warned them against divisiveness from within. She then returned her attention and goals to the Queen. Seshet nudged Ebelle's shoulder subtly to let her know not to worry and motioned for her to adjust her disposition. Her reminder caused Ebelle to regain composure. Seshet gestured toward a few rare red flowers along the path encouraging Ebelle to scoop them up for later, a guise in order for her to take a moment to shake off her foul mood. She then guided Ebelle to stand back up using her hand to push against her spine then tapped her shoulders and winked to queue her to hold her neck straight as though Ebelle was wearing a crown not yet placed on her head, practicing for the day it happened. Seshet nodded for Ebelle to look over her shoulder so after placing the flowers and dirt into a small bag, she glanced back at her sisters then rolled her eyes. Seshet raised Ebelle and her family under the idea that westernized Blacks were the absolute worse. No sense of self, no pride in heritage and no recognition of anointing. Seshet engraved her beliefs into Ebelle and Khailia during heavy battle training and nonstop lessons on tradition and ancestry only to have to start from scratch for an arrogant angry American, the Black kind. Ebelle wasn't looking forward to any part of life with Aniah.

"The first tribe we'll visit are the Sentinelese of the Andaman Islands. They're an elder tribe and are a people of vast wisdom coated in simplicity. There is a piece of wealth being stored in treasury for you. But before we go, the three of you must learn to faze." Hadiat stopped walking to fully address her heirs. "We can't suckle you throughout this whole process, your crowns weren't meant for us to carry." She waited for everyone to gather around.

"I've been waiting for this one!" Ebelle stretched her arms wide as though one touch will teach her.

Hadiat laughed, "In order to faze, you must respect the value of time, in duality and wholeness." She grazed Ebelle's arms and tapped them to let Ebelle know to put them down.

"This time in English, please." Khailia chuckled softly. "Or Patwa, French, Spanish. Your choice, just make it make sense."

"With pleasure." Seshet stepped forward, "May I have the honor, Great Queen?"

Hadiat nodded in anticipation of their first lesson together.

"Each of you heirs must live in opposition and agreement with your past, your present and your future." Seshet looked at all three heirs seeming to calculate a response in their heads and tried again. "To simplify it, you must accept both good and evil of the things you've done, where you stand now and where you see yourself being." This time when she looked at them, she could see them searching their minds.

Khailia fazed first, Hathor followed her scent to ensure she arrived at the right place. The next to faze was Aniah, Hadiat asked Seshet to follow her scent and she did as requested with much difficulty due to the blanket. Ebelle remained, eyes still closed squinching them as tight as she could.

"Tell me what is stopping you?" Hadiat asked Ebelle.

"I'm confused."

"Oh? My genius heir is confused? Well isn't this a turn."

"Don't make fun, I'm serious."

"Try not to be too sensitive girl. I've been waiting for this for almost two centuries, I'm going to enjoy this part of my existence, dear. What are you confused about?"

"I'm confused about the difference between good and evil. It's just that some things are assumed evil that are really for the greatest good."

"Trust me, I know all about it. What separates the two is what's called the purest sacrifice, you'll understand that better by and by. What the demons meant for the worse, will turn out to be for the best, but only through the three of you. You, my dear, are a necessary part to it all. Close your eyes heiress. Stop trying to narrow yourself, your beliefs, and your actions by the labels of this world. It will jade you. Accept yourself without limitation. Let go."

She closed her eyes once more, Ebelle inhaled deeply, but before she could fully exhale, she fazed. When she and Hadiat appeared before the others they were laughing and cackling like little girls.

"What's so funny?" Khailia inquired when Ebelle and Hadiat finally arrived.

"Your sister has fazed nearly all around the world before she could focus and get us here! On one stop, we were standing on elephants in a parade!"

"What? The genius is laughing at herself?"

"Correction, I am laughing with myself. It's a duality thing!" Ebelle laughed confirming hers and Khailia's bond wasn't impacted by Aniah.

"Well, alright! Shall we proceed ladies?" Seshet smiled in unison with Ebelle's, conceding that Aniah's presence wouldn't come between the years it took to solidify Khailia and Ebelle's bond. "That island across this beach is where the Sentinelese live. They are indigenous to the island and do not like nor approve of uninvited guests. Foreigners are killed swiftly and they will make an example of their protectiveness by displaying the dead body to ward off any other curious wanderers. They are the world's most isolated tribe. No one but them even knows their true population nor intellect which has been the key to their tribe's untainted traditions. They are some of the most pure of people."

"They are extremely fierce and very protective of that purity," Hathor stepped beside her, "with great reason. They have been waiting for you and preparing for this day for their entire lives. The gifts they will bestow are more pure than they. And it's yours. All you have to do is be."

"A sister tribe of my lineage!" Khailia's spirit lit up, "Aida was hidden amongst the Ainu. The Sentinelese and Ainu have recognized their kinship. They'll accept me, right?"

"You're correct. However..." Hathor was cut off.

"Wait a minute, that doesn't make any sense. Aida is the daughter of Hadiat. Hadiat's spirit fled in 1815, the Japanese didn't occupy the Andaman Islands until around World War 2, right? So how did the Sentinelese people end up in Japan prior to the war or vice versa?" Ebelle tried to make it all make sense.

"Correct, Ebelle!" Hathor agreed. "But…"

"Madagascar split from Africa millions of years ago. India split from Madagascar several million years later with traces of African civilization cave paintings that are carbon dated in pre-historic Pangea like era…. 'modern' Africans reached the Andaman Islands 80,000 years ago, then Australia, China and Japan within that span so it's not impossible to…"

"Yikes, is she like this all the time?" Aniah interrupted. "Can we just refer to the spread of Africans throughout the world as the First Great Migration, in the spirit of time?"

Ebelle cut her eyes at Aniah in return. "I forgot, you Afro-Americans would rather not learn anything about your roots."

"If that was supposed to be a jab at me, you missed…. *sis*! I'm very aware of theory of mitochondrial relation between the Ainu of Japan and the Jomon and Sentinelese of these islands. Oh, and let's not forget the traces of the Eve gene found in the Aboriginal of Australia and Tasmania, The Maori in New Zealand and the Miao in China, the Mani in Thailand, Funan of Cambodia, Papuan in New Guinea, the first Koreans, Laotian, Vietnamese etc…all very San or Bushmen looking with various spins on the same ancient African customs, religions and practices, right?" Aniah stepped forward toward the coast with her gaze fixed on the water, "Once again, take note, I'm not the one to test. However, in all your yammering you're missing the eyes watching us."

Everyone slowly looked forward in the same direction as Aniah, they saw the camouflaged warriors standing near the water's edge.

"Oh, and don't turn too fast, but I count four behind us." Aniah slowly tied her blanket around her body then stretched her arms wide, showing there was nothing in her hands.

Ebelle did the same as Aniah, it only made sense. But Khailia stood firm and waited. The four Sentinelese warriors behind them approached quickly and looked everyone over, but when they got to Khailia, they understood who she was as if they heard the tranquility of her heart.

"I am Khailia. Heir to the line of Aida, the eldest heiress of Hadiat."

The warriors kept silent. They pulled a boat from the bushes and helped the ladies aboard. They paddled toward the island along water so clear that the bright colors of coral reef and fish appeared vividly, without distortion. The sea breeze filled their nostrils carrying them to a space of grateful intrigue. The sound of the oars splashing into the water could be heard against the quiet contemplation of the group.

Close to shore, the warriors got out of the boat and pulled the ladies onto dry sand. Everyone listened as the warriors spoke in The Great Andamanese language, understood only by Hadiat, Hathor, and Khailia.

Khailia's gift began to sharpen rapidly. A quick gasp escaped her mouth as she grabbed her ear and winced at a sharp pain. Having formed fik-iri with both sisters, she heard the annoyance and confusion in them and began to hum. As the soft melody could be heard, intertwining with the warriors' words, Khaliah blessed her sisters with the gift of translation. They could now understand the languages in every nation, tribe, and Believer.

"That one knows the song of the Queen." One of the warriors acknowledged and stared intensely at Khailia, "come, it's time for you to meet our Queen."

With Hathor in front and Seshet in the rear, the group followed the warriors from the coastline into the jungle. The T'Malaks continued to keep a watchful eye over them as the jungle's gigantic leaves partially blocked out the sun.

All three heirs took in the splendor of untouched creation as the jungle's life peeked out in testament of the prophecy's fulfillment. Neon colored birds with four-foot wing spans and greater, plants that were intelligent enough to observe them as well and animals, some with multiple sets of eyes, furred and hairless, the likes of which the sisters had never seen nor heard of. Ebelle reached out to gently graze the life of the island and feels its warmth and vitality. Khailia adored the sunlight dancing through the tree leaves while she listened to dew drops land softly on flower petals. Meanwhile, Aniah skeptically followed along unable to enjoy what old views struggled to observe.

They traveled to the middle of the island where a wide clearing opened the skies back up to them, a place none other than the Sentinelese had ever been. As they inched closer to the Queen, they heard laughter and drums. They gathered at the center of the island staring in awe at the beautiful Sentinelese people staring and smiling back at them in adoration. The people giggled and placed vibrant leis of Poinciana, red water lilies, and various orchids around their waists, heads, necks, and wrists. Blessings were poured upon the group as they walked through the crowd. Khailia knelt before the most beautiful little brown-eyed girl holding a wooden bowl filled with white paint. The girl painted the symbol of the sun using her fingers onto Khailia's forehead, then blushed and ran to her mother's leg.

An array of Obsidian, Onyx and Black pearl skin tones with perfectly placed highlights of Axinite and teeth whiter than the sand opened their home to the group. They wore strings of delicate flowers and tribal face paints, a strip of clothing here and there for ceremonial purpose. They stood proud and as fearless as the day they were born. The Sentinelese were proof that the true gems of the world had always been His people.

The Sentinelese Queen stepped forward, "Queen Hadiat! It's been a long time my friend!"

"Merina? Is that you! Oh, look at you!" Hadiat hugged her friend Queen Merina, "this is where you've been this whole time? Ahh! You crazy woman!"

"Yes, I see your spirit holds strong!" Returning the sentiment Merina rocked her dearest friend back and forth. "I heard of your misfortune and I knew the time was near, so it was written, so shall it be done. I've been waiting here for this day!" At another glance, she noticed the Heirs, "Come, let me see the walking talking prophecies." Merina's excitement grew further when she spotted the remaining travelers and then she paused. "Are those the infamous T'Malaks, Seshet and Hathor?"

"Yes, it is us." Hathor spoke up. "How are you sister?"

"You two are a sight for old sore eyes!" She continued to walk amongst her guests. "Ahhh.... the heirs! All of you are so beautiful! Let me guess. You! You're from the line of Zoya. What is your name heir?"

"No ma'am, I am Ebelle, line of Liya. Thank you for welcoming us to your island."

"Does anyone ever get it right?!" She laughed and looked them over further, "Oh, this island does not belong to me, it belongs to the three of you. And you, I could feel you from across the water, it must be you that's from the line of Zoya. What is your name heir?"

Aniah looked from side to side, "oh, you mean me. My name is Aniah, nice to meet you."

"Ahh... You have yet to embrace your worth, eh?" Merina began making inaudible noises that only the other T'Malaks responded to. "What are you waiting for child? Why do you block us out?"

"I'm not sure that I'm doing anything ma'am."

"And you, Aida's own. I heard you long before you arrived, how beautiful you sound, a voice that can make nations tremble or unite, understand there is a time and place for both my dear. And when the time comes, you must be ready for both."

"Yes ma'am. I'm Khailia by the way."

"Yes, I know...." She smiled and then winked at her, "come, you must all receive your inheritance. The demons are searching for you, and they are not far."

Merina guided the women to a large hut-like throne room with no walls. The hut's woodwork appeared simply designed from a distance, but upon a closer look, there were nine pillars holding it up, each decorated with ornate engravings and symbols. She took off her shoes off and planted her feet into the soil. "Ground yourselves so that you may fully receive."

The sisters slid off their shoes off and planted their feet into the earth. The cooling sensation gave them an adrenaline rush. A slight glow began to emanate from Ebelle's hands, Aniah's eyes, and Khailia's ears and throat. When they stepped up the stairs and onto the stage-like platform of the hut, the pillars too began to activate and glow.

"Heiresses to the Throne of God, welcome to your treasury. It brings me great joy to lay eyes upon you all, together, at last. I cannot lie, I wish I had more time with you. But it's His word we fulfill. I want dearly to give you everything I possess because I know the road you embark upon is not one that many would choose. You are going to face so many different obstacles and hardships simply because of who you are and who you are is not a choice, it's a birthright." Merina wiped tears from her eyes, tied her long wavy hair into a ponytail, and tried remaining as strong as the pillars. "However, it is your choice to accept it, and for all the sacrifices made simply because we believe, I pray you choose to live. I pray you choose to fight! And most importantly, I pray you choose to win." She stood in front of Khailia, Ebelle to the right of Khailia's shoulder and Aniah off to the left. "You will make time for what each lesson brings, but often we forget to make time to celebrate the air in our lungs."

Several women of the tribe entered the hut and knelt before the heirs. Their painted faces couldn't hide the bright smiles of their hearts as their tribal clothing made sweeping sounds across the floors. Outside the hut, men in loincloth and painted symbols gathered around with instruments while children rushed to whatever spots were available, eager to observe.

Merina lifted her arms and looked toward Heaven as her voice began to carry into the clouds and echo. "Before any demon ever had a chance darken hearts, minds, and bodies, your people, our people knew who we were. Hadiat and the Great King made sure of it and they taught us our story through dance.

Yes dears, dance is a way to communicate love, joy, meekness, patience, kindness, goodness, faithfulness, gentleness and temperance, the nine pillars around you that hold the very foundation you stand on. It's where we laugh freely and cry with understanding that any emotion can mean a great sort of any nine of the Fruits of the Spirit. Dance is a labor and appreciation of all nine." She lowered her head and voice to reconnect with the Heirs. "Right now, the eldest tribe and I dance because the battle is already won, for you three are here. God's promise has kept us for eons. And now we see, we are permitted to witness." She stretched her arms out wide and nature stood tall sending all their energy to the Heirs.

The Sentinelese hadn't aged since the birth of the prophecy. They'd been on the island century after century training and protecting a sacred gift for the heirs. The men surrounded the hut and started to play the song they waited a lifetime to perform. Each hand played its conviction and rang out their own unique testimonies. The women inside the hut allowed the rhythm to use their beings to celebrate the celestial union of the heirs.

Merina stepped closer to the heirs. "We're not so isolated that we don't know what's happened in the world around us. We just couldn't move on it because we know our role in God's great plan, never needed anyone to adulterate it for us. We know how Hadiat danced to conceal your existence. We know that demons lied to the world regarding why and how we dance. They perverted our story. We don't dance to satisfy falsehoods, we dance with honorable meanings."

The heiresses looked around at the men playing their instruments. Some with the biggest smiles and others with stern faces but most with tears. They watched the women dance as tears streamed down their faces, some watched the heirs and others with eyes closed. They all moved together, not missing one queue nor beat regardless of how their hearts interpreted the moment. The children on the side mimicked their favorite parts of the celebration. One child jumped up to mimic the heirs and another sense of responsibility fell upon them.

"These dancers led former slaves across the Red Sea. They have ushered royalty down the Hall of the Kings. They have prepared nations for war…. and now they dance for you. Join them."

Khailia and Ebelle learned the choreography as children and joined immediately. Aniah's eyes chased footsteps attempting to find the eight counts. Yet another part of the story she was afraid to fail.

"Close your eyes young Heir, a dance for you is yours. Listen to the drums not for the beat but for their meaning. Feel the breath of the dancers around you and put your empathy to use."

Aniah calmed her fears then closed her eyes and Hadiat stepped up behind her lifting her arms. The touch caught Aniah off guard and she re opened her eyes. She looked around as Khailia and Ebelle were fully caught up. Their eyes were lit up with fiery chakral colors. Around the hut blue flames were attempting to ignite.

"Listen, young heir, do you see the call?" Merina whispered gently in her ear.

A gentle breeze closed her eyes once more and Aniah listened for it. Finally, she saw herself within the rhythmic beat and although she was never taught the dance, she knew each part. Hidden within the hidden corners of Aniah's mind she found words scribed encouraging her to be free. She opened her eyes and the fire around the celebration fully ignited. As they danced, the heirs watched the stories happening within its flames. They saw Hadiat and the Great King slaying demons together while riding large-winged birds amongst enormous battles. They watched as their ancestors use herbs to feed and to heal. Their footsteps agreed with the nations standing firm in belief of the purest form of love.

The nine pillars holding the hut lit ablaze and from each pillar came different geometrical shapes of light. All nine lights merged into one great light and grew wildly then slowly. Then, it became smaller and more tame, finally it grew calmly into one true light. When it matured, it separated into three lights then entered the heirs' chests lifting them off the ground. Every inch of them was lit on fire, yet their skin and clothing remained intact. Once the light was done becoming a part of them, the music stopped and dancing slowly ceased. All were able to bear witness to the moment they learned God's truest intent for His people.

"Gifts from God himself. The world has taught you what each of these gifts mean. You may have experienced them either in receiving or giving. However, to wear your crown rightly, you must learn the balance of them is in laboring through them. Service, crown daughters, is the way to enlightenment. Fulfilling your destinies of gifting mercy and grace to His children, your people."

Their feet returned to the earth and their gifts began to ascend. Khailia heard every breath differently, she could hear that the Sentinelese knew something she did not. Ebelle felt the eery clouds so thick that she struggled to inhale. Aniah saw a collective bow. She knew their own lives were no longer their concern as the Sentinelese rejoined their families and braced for what was next.

Aniah tried finding the words to protest what was coming because she wanted no part in being the reason for their deaths. Before she could find the words, Khailia spoke up.

"It's all starting to sound very arduous. This whole fulfilling destinies through service, I've never heard it this way before."

"It is." Merina smiled warmly at all three, "But, will you love only when its easy? Are you faithful to your crown only while others watch? Should you express kindness to the enemy? Do you know when it's time to let all things happen? As a Queen, you possess all the gifts and can blunder your inheritance if you can't discern which is applicable and how much of it is needed at any given time."

"Okay, so what's the proper measurement? And what are the signs that alert us to which is needed when?" Discernment was a struggle for Khailia because her heart was larger than all the oceans combined. If she could, she would hug each and every person there and hear them out to map out a plan for their survival.

"I don't have that answer...you do. Discernment, my dear, it's important you learn it Khailia. Aida struggled too, but when she learned it, oh boy, was she dangerous."

"Forgive me," Ebelle interrupted. "I don't mean to come across as impatient but we have demons searching for us. Are we here to learn the Bible? If so, me and Khailia learned Biblical lessons and several other religions as children. I can't speak for Aniah so feel free to keep her, but if it's all the same to you, I'd like to move on to our next stop."

"She can't speak for me either," Khailia shook her head, "her mouth isn't big enough to fit my feet as well."

"Is she eager or forthcoming?" Merina asked. "Has she accepted her task at hand or is she full of hubris?"

"She's full of something alright," Aniah mumbled while walking by.

"Girls." Hadiat smirked, "He told me three girls and I asked 'are you sure God? One female can start an argument in an empty room, you want to give me three...and at the same time...to rule *Your* kingdom? Are You sure God?'" Hadiat laughed aloud and the T'Malaks joined her.

"So, are you ladies excited to meet your husbands, your Kings?" Merina's excitement consumed her curiosity.

"Husbands? No one said I had to get married!" Aniah was still trying to adjust to the all the newness that occurred in the last hour.

"Right! African American women don't need a man, or so they think," Ebelle walked by Aniah bumping her shoulder hard.

"Aniah, on this journey you will meet your husband." Hadiat diverted the fight, "I don't know when nor do I know with whom. This is not arranged, this is destined. And when you do, you will become your greatest self."

"So, are you suggesting that I need a man to complete me? Are you saying the only way I'll achieve greatness is through a man?" Aniah bypassed Ebelle bumping her back while she approached Hadiat.

"You are an heiress, created with greatness in mind from His first thoughts of you. One day, you will be a Queen. Your King is not meant to define you. By yourself, you are powerful. However, with him, you will fully experience the greatest power...love. You cannot fully understand what you protect and defend without experiencing the form of love that will come from your man. For it is within love, within yourself and him as one, that you will become your greatest self." Hadiat paused a moment to acknowledge the doubt and rejection in Aniah's eyes, "but as for you child, you need to see to believe."

"What makes you say that?"

"It's important that you keep up." Hadiat's disappointment from the lack of embrace was apparent from her tone, "As you know, Khailia is heir to the eldest triplet, that line's gift is their voice. Ebelle's lineage's gift is in their touch. And yours my dear is the gift of sight. Right now, there is a lot blocking you from using your gift to its fullest potential. However, the more you see, the more you believe. Someday you will correct that into the more you believe, the more you truly see. Your sisters have grown up honing their gifts with the assistance of myself and their T'Malaks. You haven't been so fortunate." Hadiat's comment slowed her own footsteps as she realized she wasn't being virtuous toward the heir and softened her tone.

Aniah cautioned herself to be careful not to respond in likeness to Hadiat. Frustration would only make it worse. "How do I begin?"

"My dear, you already have." Hadiat forced a half smile. "Our next stop on this hajj, I believe you may identify greatly with the tribe and learn a lot from them. Greek mythology hints at them by calling them Amazons, however, they were birthed in our culture. The truth about them is not written in any books you've ever read. You are getting ready to meet the Amanirenians."

"As in the Kushite Empire Queen Amanirenias?" Aniah's interest finally began to peek.

"Exactly, but not quite," Hadiat's energy felt a disturbance, "do you feel that?"

"They're here!" Hathor felt the demons as well.

"Go! Keep going, we'll take care of them!" Merina stood firm and pulled her bow and arrows from her backside.

"Aniah, grab my hand, we will faze together." Hadiat commanded.

"Why can't you just tell me where to go and I'll meet you there?"

"The demons might hear and because we're disconnected, you cannot see my thoughts. Quickly! We don't have time!"

Aniah was able to catch a glimpse of Khailia fazing. Ebelle and the other T'Malaks had already left. "Why are we running if we're destined to win?"

"I promise, you can trust me. Take my hand." Hadiat reached out and just as it seemed Aniah was going to receive her, an akrhh spear flew right between them. The spear alerted Merina and the Sentinelese warriors to jump into action fighting against the demons attempting to get to the heir.

Aniah's focus shifted from left to right as she watched bodies of warriors and demons flying about as blood painted the sacred grounds. An intense anger crept into Aniah as she watched a small child be murdered in front of her eyes. Snapping into the moment she started to join the fight but spun in enough time to dodge being hit by another blade. The quick action caused a half stumble in her step but she caught herself and then a demon appeared before her.

He smirked when he noticed the lack of trust between Aniah and Hadiat. He took slow steps in Aniah's direction, intrigued by her response at his presence. "You don't fear me? Don't you feel my power young heir. Which one are you? Which line are you from?"

Aniah straightened her posture and stood firm before the demon. "Who are you?" She watched as Tiago's wings folded into his back revealing more of himself. He stood slightly taller than her in height. Aniah noticed he wasn't like the other demons, his eyes weren't pitch black. He had bluish green eyes and slightly tinted white skin. His face could easily grace the cover of any magazine and cause the masses to swoon. He didn't rush in like the others, he investigated.

"He's a deceiver." Hadiat fazed then re appeared behind Aniah, "take my hand."

The demon didn't move. He knew Aniah had not yet accepted her worth, therefore he still had a chance at undoing the prophecy. "Sarah, so nice to see you. With clothes this time? From what I remember, you look better without. It's been a while! Does your spirit taste as sweet as your flesh once did?"

"What is your name, demon?" Aniah insisted.

"Tiago. What is yours heir?"

Aniah continued to stand firm without a word to see how much more he'd tell her about himself based on their interaction.

"Are you the healer? No, too blind. Let's see, are you the one that frees? Couldn't be, that line is more powerful than you. You must be she who's voice can move mountains, the leader, right?"

"How?" Hadiat didn't understand how he knew any portion of the prophecy. However, she didn't want to waste any further time. "Come, take my hand."

Aniah finally grabbed Hadiat's hand without ever removing her eyes from his. Tiago tried to stop them but Merina intruded on his attempt which allowed the heir to successfully escape.

"Merina. Overseer of the eldest tribe. I take it you're here to do your part in all this?" Tiago took time to toy with her as if he wasn't bothered by his encounter with the heir.

"I am no overseer. I refuse to share that title with your demonic understudies. I am a Queen." She quickly pulled an arrow from her back sack and readied herself for her final fight by bracing her stance.

"I could care less what you call yourself. You committed suicide long ago when you chose to serve the light, pure waste of divine semen." Tiago tilted his neck and loosened his shoulder showing no concern nor fear. He circled her as though he was having a casual conversation.

"Divinity in a fallen Angel? Yet you're still jealous of them, the so called lesser beings. You wreak of confusion." Merina positioned herself to remain face to face with him so that he couldn't attack from behind.

"None the less, since you believe in this nonsensical prophecy, you know what's next."

"If it is a lie or nonsensical, then why are you here?"

Tiago's anger became instant. He looked around at all the fighting surrounding them and tyrannically smiled as each body of the Sentinelese fell to the earth. "See how they fall? Your heirs have already failed." Tiago moved so swiftly that Merina had no chance at defending herself. He knocked her hand with the ready bow out the way, then slid his blade through Merina's heart, pushing the knife slower and slower inside.

"Then...," Merina pulled herself closer to Tiago causing the blade to move further in her and whispered in strength through pain, "Why are you here?" Her last words.

He yanked his arm back and watched her body slam to the ground. Then he stood on the battlefield in contempt of all the blood and fire. "I'll see you all back at headquarters," he ordered the other demons without ever raising his voice nor calling their names. With that, his dark wings spread as he lifted into the air and disappeared.

Chapter 6: Plots for Ascension

Headquarters was located just outside the city of Tbilisi, Georgia. Before Tiago returned, he needed to visit a relic shop in town. After having stood eye to eye with an heir, Tiago's curiosity drew him to quickly handle unfinished business. He retraced the steps through the city's historic streets that he'd taken many times, recounting each and every cobblestone. Over the centuries, the town had grown from at one time being overrun various monasteries all swearing sole truths, to a tourist destination. He recalled the monasteries and people being taxed by relentless raids from bordering kin of Mongols, Huns, Turks, Armenians, Persians and at times wished for the excitement of those days. The very earth under his feet held stories plagued with the blood of confused nations in allegiance to him without even knowing. There was once a time when he couldn't make it two steps without being recognized or revered. Now, he was disgusted by people's lack of reverence yet he also preferred no longer being known. Building facades now ranged from cobble and brick to glass and granite. Some devout Christians placed ornaments and trinkets outside their businesses to ward off the evil from the mountains and tourists. Tiago simply laughed for he understood symbols of crosses were often unaccompanied by faith, no more than empty vessels.

Tiago entered the shop and waited while the cashier finished with the last few people in the store.

The cashier gave him a long stare while speaking to other customers. Her beauty often kept tourists and usual customers' attention while she'd attempt to read their importance to the universe through various marks of DNA they'd leave on items they touched or cups they used while shopping. She was tall and runway model shaped. Her long dark blond-ish brown hair flowed past her buttock and her piercing eyes held thousands of years' worth of secrets. Y'Iscariah was a priestess, princess and warrior to a Scythian tribe long forgotten but her everyday purpose was to protect the secrets of the shop, right out in the open.

"How may I help you, sir?" She asked as if she hadn't seen him a million times before. However, she knew the ancient world still held secrets beyond her youth and wouldn't risk him being forge of himself.

"Kēme, please. May I read the Thoth sitting behind your register while I wait?" Tiago already read all the writings of Thoth centuries ago. However, the password phrase was one no one would ever think to speak. Without looking, he waved his hand to lock the doors so that no one else could enter. With another wave, he turned the store's sign to closed. Tiago flanked the back of his coat and it meshed into his wings. He took a seat at his favorite table careful not to mess up his expensive all gray custom suit, tie, belt, shirt and shoes. He was there to see the alchemist. Not just any alchemist, the first real student of alchemy, an Egyptian woman named Kēme.

Kēme entered the customer area where Tiago was seated patiently waiting. Although her age dated her in BC, she looked as if she'd just graduated college. Her hair was swooped in a shoulder length bob and her cocoa skin was as smooth as the chocolate fountain running in the shop's window. She gently sat two mugs filled with a tea elixir, one for herself and one for Tiago.

Tiago smirked at the cup as she knew he wouldn't indulge. He didn't need to. Although he frequented the shop and the women knew he was a powerful demon, they didn't know just how powerful he truly was. One glimpse through his DNA would cause unwelcome speculation, however, his denial of them proved his strength.

"The empty vile I brought to you some centuries ago, the one Hadiat left at the scene of her escape that once contained the tears of David."

"Yes, I have completed what you asked. It is now encased in a precious metal and warded to your specification. I finished it a few weeks ago." She sipped from her cup as eloquently as she spoke, "what do you intend to place inside?"

"Any new messages for Draisien?" Tiago refused her small talk. He was very aware of her contrived effort and never made the mistake of entertaining her.

"The last heiress has been found, I assume that's why you're here." She attempted to bait him into a reply, "her name is Aniah. Very pretty, wouldn't you say?"

"What else do you know about her?"

"Nothing yet. I'm sure word will come soon, everyone is feeling immense pressure. Once word comes, where can I find you?" She placed the small vile down on the table.

Tiago continued to ignore her attempts because Kēme knew as well as he that he was not to be sought after, he always found who he needed. Tiago waved his hand and the vile lifted and came closer to him. He inspected it to ensure there was no unwanted scribing on it or inside of it.

"You still don't trust us? The throne belongs to us. You know this. Will you stand in our way once we reclaim it?"

"If it were really yours, would you need to ask or proclaim? When will you objects learn the value of not having to advertise?" Tiago placed the vile inside a velvet black cloth without touching it then stood to his feet.

"Something is new with you? To what do you owe this new intrigue about yourself...or to whom?" Y'Iscariah asked. Knowing he wouldn't answer. She softly pledged herself to service again, "When it's time, we'll be ready."

With nothing left to say or hear, Tiago spread his wings and disappeared then reappeared at castle headquarters.

Upon his descension onto the estate grounds, Tiago refused to be bothered. He ignored the heinous stares of evil creatures, marked spawns and indebted human souls. The bows from lesser demons surrounding the headquarters meant nothing to him once more. He knew they held ill repute for him as he arrived without the heads of the heirs. What they didn't know is that he could kill them all with one snap of his fingers and he didn't want them to know, it wasn't his time yet. He walked inside the castle and continued his enraged stride.

"Sir, where are they heading next?" One of his reports tried to pry info.

Tiago walked by the imp inquiring and completely ignored his existence. He continued down the Versailles inspired hall that looked just like Louis the 8th's famed hall and entered the room at the end after two guards speedily moved to the side. His boss, Draisien, seated at the Romanesque demonic throne sat up with much disappointment as Tiago inched closer.

"I don't see three heads with you Tiago, another fail?" Draisien inquired while standing and to swing his long red Nordic braid. "Tell me, where are the girls now."

Tiago knelt down with hesitance, "Forgive me, my lord. They escaped with the assistance of Merina and her Sentinelese warriors." He stood to his feet disgusted with himself.

"And were The Sentinelese full powers restored to them?"

"No sir. They fell easily."

"Well then, they have not yet come to their full power. We must stop them before they do, otherwise you know what happens, but I'll remind you. Should these heirs of Sarah come to full power, every Believer will begin to remember themselves and come into their own gifts and powers as well. We can't have that mess ever again."

"Yes sir, I will take my best."

"Oh, will you? I've grown tired of your repeated failures. There is another who seeks to take your place as my marked hand." He motioned toward a guard, "bring her in." The guard exited the side entrance and reentered with a woman wearing a dramatic white veil and a long white gown.

Tiago took a step back to see what was coming his way.

"Tiago, meet Victoria. By the glare in her eye, you'd swear she has no soul.... she's working on it. The final heir that was found today, she knows her." He removed her veil and held her hand out toward Tiago.

"Her name is Aniah. We grew up together." Victoria snared then gestured a bow.

"Would you believe Tiago, one of the lineages was under your foot the whole time? Right there! Mixed in the general population of slaves. AND YOU MISSED IT! SHE WAS RIGHT THERE IN PLAIN SIGHT THE WHOLE TIME! You had the power to kill the prophecy this entire time but you and your worthless army decided to let them live for your own ridiculous exploits that you could've enjoyed after we killed them all." His anger caused the entire building to shake. "Victoria has shown me many things about her former friend, the heiress they call Aniah. Come, let me show you."

Tiago moved closer. Draisien placed his hand on Tiago's head and allowed Tiago a glimpse at all Draisien saw through Victoria's mind and Tiago fed him a response with a fatigued glare as if he was over the mediocrity of his surroundings.

"Now, if I were a mother, frantically worried about the safety of my children where would I go?"

"Somewhere to hide them?"

"Correct. But if I were a Queen protecting the heiresses, where would I go?"

"The Amanirenians."

"Not so stupid after all, eh?" Draisien sharply turned his back and went to sit on his throne. "Hadiat will want them to learn their true strength right away."

"But the Amanirenians are nowhere to be found. We lost them after we apprehended Hadiat."

"Would you like me to solve this problem as well?"

"No, allow me." Tiago mocked him with a bow.

"Good. Wake your brothers you'll need them. While you're doing that, I'll train up your potential successor here, Victoria. She may possess the key in defeating one of the heirs and dismantling the entire prophecy. They call us confused but it was He that created weaklings and loved them more."

Victoria's arousal heightened as she scanned over the room enamored by all the power. She noticed she was in the lap of luxury and had thoughts of being involved in a threesome with Tiago and Draisien, wanting to be both of their favorite. Her eyes undressed them as her hand slipped up her breast and she started to slide her sleeve down her shoulder.

Draisien prepared to participate in the show and snatched off his shirt, meanwhile Tiago looked at her as though she'd been rummaging through sewage for months.

Tiago looked her in the eyes and stated, "Keep your thoughts to yourself! Not even with a stolen dildo would I ever." He walked out the room with no desire to fathom the thought of her.

To his knowledge, he was the only demon to encounter the final heir and live. He and all the other demons learned the other sisters' identities at birth and kept tabs on Ebelle and Khailia via spies and fake Believers. But Aniah, no one could find. Tiago didn't simply want them dead, he coveted their favor and position with God and he wished to insert himself as their king. He stepped outside onto the terrace to spread his wings and disappeared.

Chapter 7: Amanirenian Sanctuary

The hajj had only just begun. Already, the Heirs and T'Malaks were faced with the feeling of having lost one Heir. A grief not yet earned began to creep in on Ebelle and Khailia. The two of them had fazed safely, but where were Aniah and Hadiat? Khailia looked to the Heavens, searching beyond the clouds for relief. She thought, surely, gray skies couldn't be the ending, especially not on a sunny day. She only needed to remember there was no need for a forecast when the prophecy was fore written. The time was now and their win was foretold. A story foretold couldn't end this way but the doubt strayed into Khailia's heart, carrying years' worth of 'not yet' in tow.

Khaliah frantically paced the flat lands of scattered trees as she tried to figure out what to do next. Her sister and Hadiat had not arrived and she was forbade by Hathor to go after them. It was unlike her to worry. Worry was never included in her training but nevertheless it encroached her spirit. "We have to go back and get them!" She screamed out with tears streaming down her face, Khailia threw her hands up in the air exhausted from worrying. "I, I mean we...we just got her..."

"Look! There they are." Hathor pointed at the shift in the air making way for their faze, reassuring Khailia they were alright. She had never seen Khailia act out that way before. Usually Khailia was as serene as the coy ponds. "But Merina..."

"Merina, what about her?" Khailia asked.

"Merina is dead." Seshet spoke up in a somber voice.

"How do you know this?" Aniah tried to shake off confusion from the news and dizzying swirls from the faze, "I just saw her."

"When one good T'Malak dies, all other good T'Malaks feel it." Khailia placed her hand on Aniah's shoulder and pulled her in for a quick hug. "I'm glad you're okay, I thought we lost you again."

Aniah had never seen worry for her in the eyes of another woman. Being on her own for so long, she'd seen more betrayal than affection in her life. A deep sense of accountability fell over her. Not like the vigilante justice she previously figured her purpose to be. Not like how she once felt for Victoria, something much stronger. The need to not be a worry.

Ebelle confronted Aniah and attempted to pierce through her gritting teeth, "What took so long?"

Aniah quickly adjusted to the counterbalance of emotions and simply sized Ebelle up and walked away. "What do we do when T'Malaks die?", she asked Seshet.

"You mean, how do we memorialize them?" Seshet's lure of Aniah grew a slight bit more.

"Yes."

"We are not memorialized. It is our duty to protect the heirs." Seshet stepped closer to Aniah, "We do this in secret and sacrifice and we are well aware of how it ends for us. Merina knew when and how she was to die and she celebrated your arrival yet and still. You, specifically, are the cause of her death. Something you would do good to remember."

"Merina died to protect me and Hadiat. We're not going to acknowledge her sacrifice? Respectfully, martyrs are honored by some means. Not giving her at least a moment to be remembered doesn't rest well with me." Aniah turned to Hathor, "what was something she loved?"

"Uh… She loved the orchids of Madagascar. She used them for décor and medicinal reasons. She kept them everywhere." Hathor smiled softly understanding Aniah's heart in the moment and that she was trying her hardest to come to terms with a lot all at once.

"Orchids, especially from palm trees, are very potent and powerful. I could brew you some to heighten your intelligence." Ebelle added more of her relentless sarcasm. "Please! Let me brew you some."

Hathor sidestepped Ebelle's taunt at Aniah, "Those orchids played vital roles in how she was able to protect her tribe for so long."

"Ebelle, come to me." Hadiat stretched her hand for Ebelle to join her. "Khailia," she stretched her other arm and Khailia walked over. She simply looked at Aniah as though to boast of the trust established between herself and Aniah's sisters. Aniah took the stabbing hint and walked over and grabbed Khailia's hand. "Close your eyes and feel for Merina." Hadiat waited for a moment until she saw in the girls' expressions that they were on one accord. "Now, open them."

A gentle breeze blew and centered in front of the heirs. Into the breeze, from the left and right, flew in pink and violet orchids. Aniah looked over to Hadiat and saw she controlled the wind.

"You too will control air once you learn to trust me and accept your worth." She lowered her arms and tried to hide her fatigue. Hadiat never looked Aniah's way, but Aniah knew the message was for her. It took a lot for Hadiat's spirit to draw energy for even the slightest display after she used so much of it having watched over the line of Zoya. "You want to establish memorial without learning tradition. I can teach you both to establish yourself and all about tradition."

"And I will help." A different voice entered the conversation. A gentle looking woman swayed her way into the small group. She was absolutely stunning with beautiful burnt sienna skin tone accompanied by subtle hints of hazel that flirtatiously danced with the sun. Slender but toned, her hair braided in long twists with beaded and stringed jewelry on various strands, her long red dress floated above the ground perfectly.

"My friend. It does my heart good to see you." Hadiat let go of her control and placed the orchids at the girls' feet.

"Oh, likewise my Queen, likewise. How much I've missed you, you wouldn't know!" The woman spoke up with slight laughter and solace as they hugged each other tightly. "Hathor and Seshet, still hanging in there, eh?"

"Queen Nefertiti, still as beautiful as ever." Seshet embraced her in guilefully.

"Thee Queen Nefertiti? The Egyptian Queen Nefertiti?" Aniah's mouth dropped wide open, "the lost, missing, never heard from since ages ago Nefertiti?"

"In the flesh, my dear." She took a subtle bow. "And you ladies must be the heirs. Hadiat, please, let me try to guess which is which. Has anyone ever gotten it right?"

"Not really," she laughed. "They miss it every time."

"Okay, you. You must be from the line of Zoya?" Nefertiti pointed at Ebelle.

"No ma'am." Ebelle stepped forward. "That would be that twerking ball of confusion and ego over there," she pointed at Aniah. "I am Ebelle, line of Liya." She shook hands with the Queen.

"My name is Khailia, I am descended of Aida." Khailia smiled and pulled Nefertiti in for a hug.

"Aniah, the confused twerker." She raised her hand then waved.

"What is a twerker?" Queen Nefertiti asked causing all three to laugh. "Kids!" Queen Nefertiti smiled while trying not to look Aniah in the eyes but couldn't help it. "I guessed wrong as well. Hadiat, how did you do it? How could you tell them apart?" She jerked herself away from Aniah's stare, she wasn't ready to face the guilt she'd long harbored.

"It's their gifts that separate them. And a mother always knows."

"Well, Heirs, let me be the first to welcome you. I watched you from the falls over there. I was meditating when you fazed in. Hadiat, I wish they could've seen you in your full glory! They would know that display of moving flowers is nothing compared what you did while you reigned."

"Oh Nefertiti, you shouldn't."

"Heirs, your great great great and many more greats, grandmother was amazingly powerful. If you think that little gust of wind and the flowers were something, you should've seen her in battle! She could cause a hurricane with no water. Could take the air right out of a demon's lungs with the lift of one finger." Nefertiti paused and remembered herself, "When I heard you gave yourself, I almost died with you my friend. And the Great King…"

Hadiat stopped her mid-sentence with a gentle lift of her hand, "Thank you."

"I've waited many long years for you girls. I am elated! The worlds have waited patiently for you." Nefertiti smiled and walked firmly beside Aniah who noticeably caught her every word as Nefertiti knew she would. Nefertiti wanted Aniah to ask about 'worlds vs. world', but when Aniah didn't question it aloud, Nefertiti knew she was not dealing with a careless heir. She was tickled and relieved at Aniah's existence and wanted nothing more than to dive deeper into any moment with her. Nefertiti tried to hide her heart's smile but pieces of it snuck out through her eyes as she looked over the heiress. "Come, follow me. Come and meet the Amanirenians, my tribe and the greatest army of women you'll ever lay eyes on."

"Wait. What do you mean your tribe? History books place you as either Egyptian or Syrian. Yet we're here in Ethiopia judging by the Blue Nile Falls back there, and you're stating your tribe is here?" Aniah's interest in Queen Nefertiti sparked humor in Nefertiti.

"You catch everything, huh? Young heir, those history books are never quite able to tell whole truths. Walk with me, talk with me." She led the heirs on a hike back toward the Blue Nile Falls. "Let me start by stating that creation is purposeful. That bush right there…bears flowers. Those flowers heal intestinal inflammation and eczema. However, tourists pass by it every day and call it beautiful. Yes it is beautiful but its more powerful than it is beautiful. In ancient times and to this day, I'm adored for my beauty, I was even able to use it to persuade people to look in whichever direction I desired. And when they looked left, I went right. They never knew my true power even though I used it in front of them daily. Afterall, Queens can move in ways Kings cannot, but when your

King is gone.....," she caught herself before her words could pierce Hadiat and changed direction. "To this day those 'historians' are looking for me. Searching for the truth in my existence and death. Am I Kush, Nubian, Arabian, Syrian? Meanwhile, I found joy in mystery, happiness in my discretion and honor in my duties."

"So then, who are you?"

"I am Queen Nefertiti my dear." She smiled remembering the good ol days with Zoya.

"I thought you called Hadiat your Queen."

"And that she is! I was regarded as an earthly Queen and that I am. However, within our realm, I am general to the Queen's personal army and her very best friend, that is if you don't count the King. I am a many things, I wear many titles and have done many deeds. Please, try not to define me. And for Heaven's sake, don't allow anyone to define you either, Heir. In owning all that you are and all that you will never be, you will find joy."

"That sounds more like finding peace." Ebelle impatiently intruded.

"Peace is the stillness in which what one sees, hears, touches, smells or tastes. Joy is the choice to appreciate those experiences. It's in the laughter of smelling a fart. Or the in smile from a loved one's kiss."

"Still sounds like peace to me." Ebelle continued to argue stance in challenging Nefertiti.

"You possess both peace and joy but lack them at the same time." Nefertiti stopped in her tracks and gave Ebelle a slightly scolding stare, "Is she always like this?" She joked quickly at Ebelle's expense.

"Huh?" The joke went right over Ebelle's head.

Khailia chuckled at Ebelle.

"So, my dears, have you learned to faze yet?"

"Yes ma'am!" Khailia's excitement refused to be hidden any longer. "I'm so ready to learn from you now! I read all the stories of you fighting side by side with Hadiat and those stories kept me warm at night. I've waited for this for so long."

"I see. You're ready to gain something from me, but what are you ready to give? What price will you pay for something you've waited your whole life to get?"

"Queen Nefertiti, my gift was never meant for me. Anything you invest in me is what you invest into His will. I freely give to His people, I have no right to keep it, doesn't belong to me. You give your light, I fragment it in arrays."

"Spoken like Aida herself." Queen Nefertiti stopped again to face Khailia, "How refreshing. Aida, oh that sweet girl, she always knew the right words even when she felt she didn't. She wasn't afraid of any truth." She stepped back to address the crowd. "It's a two and a half hour walk to Lake Tana. I'm happy to walk it with you, however, you ladies look like you've been in a few fights today. How about fazing there?"

The new normal was now established without any of them stopping to recognize. Khailia gazed over the rips in her sleeves and a stretched collar worn like everyday clothing. Ebelle had dried blood trails coming from her shin. Aniah didn't even realize she was holding her stomach where a pain was thumping from being caught off guard by a demon earlier in the alley way. It felt like several days happened within several hours but the road ahead was still long and no time to waste.

"Aniah, are you familiar with Lake Tana?" Hathor placed her hand on the Heiress' shoulder again and Aniah nodded. "Well then, shall we?" Hathor extended her hand and Aniah accepted it as they all fazed.

When they appeared, Hadiat's contention with Aniah was highly visible as she herself couldn't reach her own Heiress. She was angry that her own bloodline preferred the outside over her. Feeling betrayed, she still understood Hathor's meaning. A gentler touch was needed, one that Hadiat had yet to explore for her own. Hadiat remembered not to let her thoughts linger as one slip and Khailia would hear or Ebelle might feel her anguish, she shifted her thoughts to her Heirs' amazement with Lake Tana.

The sun was beginning to set but it was still bright enough to take in the splendor of the green water. The monasteries mounted on islands with rich trees with trunks wide enough to tell the whole story of time. Most of the people there were packing their things for their journey to wherever they came from, however a few stood at attention. There was no visible village or residency to explain their lack of rush to beat the sun.

"Oh my, listen. The birds, how sweet they sound." Khailia lifted her hand and a green parrot with a yellow head landed alongside a Black-winged lovebird.

"Different kinds of the same species." Ebelle's genius level IQ for nature quickly became enamored with them almost immediately. "Did you know they're both rare? Lake Tana is not as big as it once was so evolution's course makes the native birds wander to where its more plenteous sometimes, but this will always be home. No matter how they change, they always return home."

"How do you know all this stuff?" Aniah's perplexed stance at how common Ebelle spoke about things that didn't matter to most caused her to forget Ebelle's dislike of her.

"It's called a book. I'll make you one with pictures and smaller words to help you along the way."

"We have to know about all the things we protect, Aniah." Khailia rolled her eyes at Ebelle for the insult. "Ebelle and I have had to study these facts since before I care to remember. Our families groomed us for this stuff for many years. Ebelle loves nature. It's helped her hone in on her gift. Plants, animals, it's sorta her thing. She can literally write books to fill several hundred libraries on the various topics that fall under nature. My gift is found within my love of the arts. I've studied cultural arts in this world and ours, from modern cultures to tribes with erased records, it's what helps me control my gift."

The idea of having to catch up to her sisters was an overwhelming thought. Aniah read about things she took interest in but never bothered to pick up books on animals. She mostly read about history and politics or ideologies that confronted her while meeting random people. Knowing a person's origin helped with understanding the very essence of their being, but she didn't think she could fill one book, let alone several hundred libraries. Nefertiti could see the Heiress felt isolated and sped things up some.

"Aniah, your eyes my dear, time to see. And Queen Hadiat, your army awaits." Nefertiti moved her hands and whispered "we are light for thine path" in an ancient tongue, revealing a hidden-in-plain-sight view of the warrior women at work. They were gardening and playing with children. Others were eating and drinking wine. They seemed like normal average women going about their day. They were all astoundingly beautiful with untarnished skin and not a hair out of place. Silk dresses across their bodies hid their nature. "Aniah, I'm willing to bet no one has explained the existence of this forgotten realm of Believers to you. As a part of this Hajj, you, my dear, now exist within two worlds which used to be one. There's the common world, you've known it all your life. Then, there is the realm of Believers which you've been a part of all of your life. In short, Believers aren't as in the open as we used to be. After losing Queen Hadiat and the King, we've had to hide a lot in plain sight. Non-believers cannot see what we see, they walk by or through all the time. However, now that you are all together, that will change soon and all will be exposed and merged as one."

Hadiat stepped forward and deeply inhaled a deep breath of air while Aniah was taken back at how an entire busy city appeared that wasn't there a few seconds ago. However, Khailia and Ebelle were very unimpressed. Their expectation of what they'd read their whole lives was very underwhelmed by the mundaneness of it all.

"Is this the Amanirenian Army? Who are they fighting? They look like I could take them all on with my pinkie finger." Ebelle's impatience grew, it was all too basic for her approval.

"Oh good! A challenge! I haven't seen one in a while. Please, pick one that you can take on with your pinkie finger."

"I don't think…" Hadiat tried to stop it from happening.

"No, my Queen, they must learn." Nefertiti permitted herself to continue, a stance only Hadiat's best friend dare take.

"The stories I heard about the Amanirenians painted them as warriors with great strength. They were brutal and unforgiving." Ebelle kept firm in her belief. "Precise with any manner of weapon. They're tall with muscles and athletic builds. Armor of impenetrable metal crafted from God's own being. They had scars to prove their survival. I doubt these women have ever even had a splinter or chipped nail!"

"Have you picked yet?" Nefertiti's intrigue took on a menacing smile.

"Does it matter?"

"Oh good! Grace! Please step forward." Nefertiti waved one of the women over.

A very beautiful and petite figured woman steps forward with a small child. The woman was wearing a yellow, long and wide pant outfit that looked as tender as she. Placing the child down beside her, she removed her head wrap allowing her long braids to hang down, then retied them into a ponytail. Understanding what was getting ready to take place, the child stepped in front of her mother ready to fight in her stead.

"Big Grace please, little Grace might kill her on accident." Nefertiti laughed. "Grace my dear, you have a challenger."

"Big Grace? She's all of 5'2. She's not ready to fight me, she was just playing with and feeding little Grace. I'd rather not do this, I'm an heir after all. I've been training my whole life for this and I've studied in your art of combat, I know it like the back of my hand."

"Grace. Ilum!" Nefertiti backed out of the way with a smile that could've wrapped around her head twice.

Without blinking Grace took on a defensive stance. It wasn't swift nor sturdy looking. She didn't look capable of defending the leaves on the trees around her.

"Fine. Grace is it? You seem like a very nice woman, I don't want to do this, especially not in front of your child, but I have a point to prove. I apologize in advance." Ebelle put her fists up.

"Tewagu." Nefertiti gently commanded Grace to fight.

Ebelle threw the first punch and Grace dodged it. She attempted to trip Grace, but it was as if Grace floated over it. Ebelle concocted a six-move combination strike and not one time did she come near Grace.

"Ch'ewa." Nefertiti whispered slowly.

With one hand behind her back, Grace came from behind Ebelle and placed her in a choke hold then tripped her to the ground, catching her before she could fall face first then gently laid her head on a stone. Then she backed up.

Ebelle grew angry and continued her attack on Grace, however Grace never harmed one hair on her body but embarrassed Ebelle repeatedly.

"Didn't we just inherit peace?" Aniah whispered to Khailia.

"Yeah, but I guess Ebelle isn't appreciating it right now. Looks like she got herself into a lot of trouble by not appreciating God's gift of peace." Khailia softly laughed.

"Never learned to eat all her fruits, huh? Should we help her?"

"Nah, I appreciate my peace. You?"

"I'm appreciating all this joy in my heart right now." Aniah smiled and crossed her arms as she watched Ebelle try again only to end up on the ground. "I'm filled with so much love and happiness right now."

"Ebelle, are we done young heir?" Queen Nefertiti inquired. "Have you learned to widen your perspective on women of strength? I gather you haven't become as smart as you are by only reading books with standard covers?"

Ebelle stood up and wiped the dust off her clothes then let out a gentle smile. "I think I'll go stand next to Khailia and wiggle my foot out of my mouth using my pinkie finger."

"Fast learner, good." Queen Nefertiti glanced at the other chuckling heirs, "please, follow me." She led them past the women on guard. The heirs smiled at how modern and simple yet advanced the homes were, nothing like what they were expecting. To describe it as Harlem Renaissance meets nice suburb doused with Imperial Gebi would be the minimal. There were corner shops, libraries, parks, commercial businesses and sky scrapers. The smell of halal meat on the grills filled the air causing the heirs stomachs to growl. Various modes of transportation from people bicycling to driving cars or riding horses, no one was a stranger but the Heiresses.

"I wish mine could be here too," Khailia watched as the horses passed by. She started to reach out but remembered herself instead.

"This is crazy! These people look like me. They dress and smile like me. They speak like me and yet it's still culture shock for me. The nature, the warmth and cooling, it's a home away from home that's been waiting for me to come home. So weird." Aniah looked around curiously at first not even realizing she was speaking. Her excitement led the way. She caught herself before she could ramble any further and tucked her feelings back inside.

Queen Nefertiti grabbed Aniah's hand and gently chuckled, "We've been waiting for this day a long time. And just wait until you taste the lemon pound cake that's for dessert!" She continued her walk while greeting the onlookers that stared as they walked by. "Now that the heirs are together, my tribe's full powers will be returning soon. They won't need to hide behind several layers of mirage, I won't have to move my hand to reveal our home anymore. We'll be out in the open. Trust me, they are all so very excited to see you and even more excited to be with you. Make sure you take the chance to wander around and learn about yourself. Look, over there, that's an apothecary. And there, that's a museum. You'll want to spend a lot of time there. A lot of the elders frequent that museum, you can always catch a good story with that crowd. This is probably one of the most diverse places on Earth, as all of the Amanirenians come from all over the world. There are a few Americans here too. Brazilians, Australians, Panamanians, Persians, Russians, Canadians, beautiful Sudanese, indispensable Congolese. You name it, we have them. There are about five thousand soldiers here, but one of them equals 5,000 men in any other army easily."

"Nefertiti, there are men here. I thought..." Ebelle was unable to match the fable to the reality.

"Aht aht, remember darling, no more narrow perceptions. We love our men. We wouldn't know our strength without them. These soldiers are wives, mothers, sisters. I would never separate any soldier from themselves. Families have always been welcome here." Nefertiti took the long way home walking through parks and streets showing the heirs all the bakeries and several boutiques. They finally reached a palace in the midst of it all seeming wonderfully misplaced. There was no gate, mote or exaggerated distance of a driveway. The palace stood high amongst other homes, significantly larger but not away from it all. "My palace is your palace." She opened the door to her home and invited them all in. "You ladies could use a bath and change of clothes." She called to a woman nearby.

"Now this is how heirs should live and be treated! Can you ask your servants to bring me a drink as well?" Ebelle asked while looking at the high painted ceilings.

"Servant? I've never seen a servant here. These are my sisters in battle, we don't practice conscription amongst Believers. Not one mankurt in sight. They may help me around my home but please understand, they are warriors. Please, stop trying to define them." Nefertiti reminded her yet again. "Follow her to where you will be staying while you are here. Seshet, Hathor, Queen Hadiat, please follow me."

"Wait, we've never been without protection. What if demons attack?"

"Khailia, you have your sisters. You will be just fine." Nefertiti turned away before further protest and the Queen and T'Malaks followed.

"You don't have to look and smell like what you've been through." The woman stated while motioning the Heiresses to follow her down a long hall with gold statues and into a room. "There are clothes in the closet, they will fit if you wear them right. They aren't your normal clothes, they're made from ālebabesi. A special linen woven by our ancestors but threaded by us, always timeless. They bend with your mind. You put on the garment and it designs based upon your mood and thoughts, so guard your thoughts accordingly. The bathroom is that way." She pointed it out then exited the room leaving them alone.

"I'm ready to faze back to the Sentinelese. They knew how to welcome the Heirs...and Aniah." Ebelle walked to the closet to look for something to wear. Everything looked more like drapery than any accustomed clothing. She shook her head as she thumbed through trying to find the best colors to compliment her deep mahogany skin.

"Aniah, why are you so hesitant?" Khailia sat down on a bench beside Aniah as they took their shoes off.

"Khailia, you grew up with an understanding that I didn't know even existed until today. You call it hesitance, but I think I'm doing a great job with all this stuff. A few hours ago, I was doing what I normally do, by myself. Now look! I haven't even known you for 24 hours yet. Heck, I accepted that this wasn't a dream roughly thirty minutes ago."

"I understand. I apologize if I've offended you."

"No offense taken. You've been very kind to me. I genuinely believe you'd never purposely hurt me. It's not in your nature."

"Oh yeah, what makes you say that?"

"I've met so many people, some of the worse you can imagine. And I knew their hearts or lack thereof. I saw their thoughts and stories...not literally, but I just know them. It's hard to explain. Well, I guess now I'm to understand my visions were real after all, being gifted with sight. Anyhow, when we bonded, I knew I had someone other than me that understands. I continue this hajj, so to speak, because if you're just the beginning, I want to know what else there is out there. It's like you lifted something in me."

"Well, good. I'm just happy we finally found you. I hope you and Ebelle can form a fik-iri soon. One blatant and the other stubborn, can't tell which is which myself." Khailia laughed to soften the truth "No pressure, just the fate of the world relies on it." She stood up, "let's get cleaned up."

Aniah walked around the room to take in its splendor. She didn't want to gush over the lavishness in front of everyone else when they first arrived but she was astonished by the size of the palace. It had 10th century architecture, with high arching halls and doorways. But it was also a modern version of the past as though it had been kept intact through multiple centuries and splashed with current comforts. The room she and her sisters were staying in was bigger than her entire apartment. Two large fireplaces accented separate sides of the room with unscorched firewood in them. There were three beds spread about in various corners with curtains draped over them. They would flow when a gentle breeze came through the high arching windows. Around each bed, plush hand-stitched rugs rested on the marble floor underneath each bed. Upon a window she stared out onto the city. She was amazed at how the people lived and although she was used to entertaining herself by making up stories while people watching, this time she could relax and watch the stories happen right in front of her. Children laughed while men sat around tending to grills sharing traditional customs of each own's country of origin. They were comparing marinades and wines. At another glance, she noticed she no longer saw any of the women. The men and children were still out and about, but the women were gone. She looked for one but there were none in sight. She closed the curtains and backed away slowly.

"Hey, you wanna go freshen up already? Haven't you made us wait long enough?" Ebelle emerged from the bathing area wrapped in a towel and pat drying her hair.

Aniah looked over at Khailia who's trying to figure out what to wear. Then looked back at Ebelle, flicked her off and walked away to bathe.

After the ladies were finished bathing and dressing, the woman reappeared and asked the heirs to follow her. The woman stared at Aniah who was the only one wearing sleek training apparel as though she was ready to fight, everyone else wore long gowns. She led them to a dining hall where Hadiat, the T'Malaks, Nefertiti and a room full of women wearing silk and linen gowns were waiting.

Aniah didn't mind being dressed differently, she'd been out of place now for several hours. Better to protect herself than impress other, she thought. While everyone else stared and whispered she went about as though it was all normal. She'd felt judged a million times before.

"Young heirs, please, come in and take a seat." They looked over at the table with Hadiat and Nefertiti but didn't see any open seats. No matter where they looked, they didn't see any table with three open seats.

"I guess we'll have to sit a part from each other," Ebelle whispered to Khailia.

Khailia looked at her in disagreement. "Come with me." She walked over to a table and asked three of the women if they wouldn't mind moving. The three women snarly obliged.

"Well, if you're all settled in and comfy now..." Nefertiti paused and stared at the heirs, "Welcome to your home for the next few how-ever-long this takes. The ladies with whom you have the pleasure of dining with are soldiers, queens and warriors. Only one of you will command them. Not sure who it is just yet, but until we know, all three of you will share command. What these beautiful women have had decades and for some, centuries to perfect, you must learn in a matter of weeks. They are experts in the skill of war with various specialties. Simpletons will have you believe that war is only physical, however you will learn that it's more mental and emotional than it is physical. Also, you will learn not only how to use every weapon known to man, but you will also learn how to command those weapons out of sheer thought, something only Hadiat and her heirs can do. For now, shall we eat?"

Dishes of goat meat, chicken, vegetables, fruits, breads, and legumes were brought out and placed in the centers of each table. Everything on the table was less African and more European and American.

"I was really looking forward to some Beyainatu. So what's your name?" Aniah asked the woman sitting next to her on the left.

"Melaine," in shock that one actually finally spoke to someone outside their circle. "The best Beyainatu in the world is made here in Nefertiti's home. We're all from everywhere. No telling what'll be on the menu. Happy to know you're well rounded."

"Melaine, beautiful name. Melanesian? Where are you from and what's your weapon of choice?"

"Let me guess, the blond hair, blue eyes, brown skin gave me away? I was born on the Island of Vanuatu but raised in Sweden. I can use any weapon here, but I'm my best with a bow and arrow."

"A fellow archer?" Khailia joined in. "I'm Khailia by the way."

"What about you Ebelle? You are Ebelle, right? What's your specialty?" Melaine interrupted Ebelle mid bite.

"Yes, I'm Ebelle. Guns my dear. I can shoot any gun and hit any target. I also fancy Turkish daggers."

"And you, Aniah?"

"I've never been trained to use any weapon. Never really been trained to fight at all."

"What do you mean you've never been trained? We were told you all have above average fighting skills."

"Don't be fooled. Aniah took down two demons with no help. We also saw her take on six men bare handed." Khailia stepped in very proud of her sister.

"How long had you guys been following me?" Aniah almost forgot about ever being home that day.

"Watching you fight in Chicago was our first time seeing you. We were listening to a Fed tap. Some of those agents either work for demons or are demons themselves. Vigilante by day and club owner/shelter provider by night drew a lot of attention and speculation around you being an heir. No one could take out as many men and demons as you have without drawing that type of curiosity."

"Not to mention your little business partner Vic. She ratted you out for a large lump sum of money and the feds promise they'd kill you so that she wouldn't have to worry about your revenge. She told them all about your life growing up in foster homes." Ebelle took another opportunity to rub anything in Aniah's face, "some choice in friends you have!"

"Wish I could choose family too!" Aniah rolled her eyes, "Besides, I haven't considered her a friend in a long time. I was just tired of being alone. Not that you would know anything about that having lived all protected with your T'Malak, family and friends."

"You blame me for your misfortune?"

"Not at all, but don't pretend to know me either." Aniah got up from the table, "you only know what I let those feds know about me. You only know what I allow you to see." Aniah walked off in search of a trash can. While she moved around she studied her environment. Eventually, she found a secluded corner where she could watch everyone from a distance without being bothered. She watched the women move around the room conversing about next steps and being in disbelief that it's finally happening. But what was "it"? While she grew curious about many things, holding her immediate attention was the handful of women who left and had yet to return, soldiers are dismissed and they weren't, so where were they?

Nefertiti watched as Hadiat's heart ached for the line of Zoya. She knew Hadiat wanted nothing more than to reach out to her child and embrace. She worried that the centuries of blasphemous teachings had created momentously rigid and impossible terrains between Aniah's heart, mind and purpose. Looking at Aniah was difficult for Nefertiti too, however she felt like she'd been given a second chance and an opportunity for retribution as well.

"I wish I could've taken Zoya's place." Hadiat mentioned to her best friend. "I don't know where to begin with her." She took a deep breath to disable her tears. "Zoya was a daddy's girl, he knew how to deal with her, he'd know what to do. I saw what they did to her....She...she...my baby couldn't even...I didn't..."

"Even the pain is for a reason." Nefertiti placed her hand on Hadiat's shoulder. "It too is a part of the plan. Don't fret, Zoya is very much alive in that one. She'll be just fine." She turned to address the army and heirs. "Ladies, it is time to train. Amanirenians! Illum!"

The women stood at attention. Not forceful nor overstated, but gently with poise.

"My dearest heirs, before you leave, myself and the Amanirenians will help you perfect your fighting skills. You will be able to wield any weapon of your desire. As heirs, you possess unique talents and gifts that we do not. Once you come to fully understand your worth and form fik-iri with one another you will be able to command any weapon. Back in the good old days, Hadiat could shape any weapon from her own being. Hadiat, do you mind?"

"I would love nothing more. However, I must reserve what strength I have left for something greater."

"Understood. Heirs, imagine yourself being able to merely think of a weapon and then producing it from your thoughts through your veins and out your hands.

That is one of many powers you all possess. Also, once the reigning Queen is united with her King, the Amanirenians will regain our full armor. Yes, we are strong now, but stronger once led."

"Forgive me Queen Nefertiti," Ebelle interrupted. "I understand the reason in getting started as quickly as possible, however, we are tired and need to rest."

"Ebelle, my sweet Ebelle. You and Khailia have had the privilege of training at a protected capacity. However, your enemy cares not for your level of fatigue. It is not time to rest right now. The time has come to fight. Amanirenians, please escort our guests to the sanctuary."

The heirs followed several Amanirenians down a long wide hall. Columns three stories high with small dimly lit torches stood on both sides as they walked. The hall was filled with legendary images of battles they saw in the fire while dancing with the Sentinelese and other images they were seeing for the first time. Vivid paintings looked as if they came to life once they passed, as if the stories were speaking for themselves.

Aniah felt Queen Nefertiti staring at her back then a pressing feeling came over her. She looked to her left and right and noticed the Amanirenians next to her made no effort at eye contact causing her to question intent. She slowly looked down to the right and noticed the Amanirenians clothing was changing from long gowns to form fitted gear. She looked ahead to see that Khailia and Ebelle were being guided the same way; by an Amanirenian on the left and right making no effort to look their way. Out of her peripheral, Aniah spotted the Amanirenian to her left glance out the side of her eyes in the direction of the wall where a woman was hiding. A trap! Aniah, thinking quickly, didn't want to give warning that she was aware, instead she knelt down to pretend to tie her shoe. Khailia heard the sudden movement then turned to check on Aniah which disrupted Ebelle right on time. As Ebelle turned to scold Aniah yet again, she caught Aniah's glance toward the wall. Instead of remaining calm, Ebelle jumped right at the hidden Amanirenians separating herself from her sisters feeding right into the Amanirenians plan. Their training had begun.

Khailia quickly placed one of the Amanirenians in a headlock then turned using her as a front shield while loosening the woman's blade. She threw the blade at one of the women next to Aniah causing her to move in order to protect herself. When Khailia moved, Aniah tripped the other warrior standing next to her then jumped up to spear the other woman who had been escorting Khailia. Khailia turned the woman loose who she had in a headlock then stood back to back with Aniah.

Meanwhile, Ebelle was off on the other side of the columns; she struggled in a fight with the two other women. The women split up on each side of her and ambushed her at tandem and were wearing her down.

"Khailia, go to her." Aniah panted out, "I can handle this, go to her."

"Are you sure?" Khailia was afraid to leave her.

"Go." Aniah ran off in the complete opposite direction from Ebelle and drew six of the women with her.

Khailia got frustrated but ran over to Ebelle to assist. Khailia and Ebelle fought hard but were unable to subdue the two women.

Nefertiti commanded the Amanirenians to halt. When the fighting stopped they looked down the hall and saw Aniah laying on the ground with Nefertiti standing over her. "She held her own for as long as she could. The two of you struggled one on one with an Amanirenian, imagine six to yourself." Ebelle and Khailia ran to Aniah quickly and knelt down to check on her. "This is what happens when you get too comfortable or don't fight together." Queen Nefertiti stepped back to allow them the opportunity to pick up Aniah. "Aida, Liya and Zoya deserved the chance to grow together and rise, their separation gave them no choice but to stand alone. Be the difference, learn from your ancestors."

To Khailia's relief, Aniah opened her eyes, "Hey, you okay?" She pushed Aniah's hair from over her face awaiting a response.

"You may go rest now. See you ladies in the morning when your real training begins." Nefertiti turned her back, "I trust you'll find your way back to your room," she walked away.

"Why didn't you both just run toward me?" Ebelle inquired. "We could've fought them all together."

"Not now, Ebelle." Khailia helped Aniah to her feet. "Let's just go get some rest."

"You were stupid to run off on your own, Aniah!"

"You struggled with two. There were eight women total. You wouldn't have had a chance if we brought the other six your direction. And what gave your genius ass the bright idea to just strike out like that in the first place? No plan, no attempt at a communication, you just started fighting trained militia on your own! I took hits for you, dumbass! I been taking hits all my life for people like you. You don't know anything about that though, huh? The words you're looking for are 'thank you.' I'll draw you a picture book about manners for your convenience." Aniah straightened herself up, snatched her arm away from Khailia, wiped the blood from her lip and limped away with no assistance. She held her side with one arm and raised the other hand as high as she could to flick Ebelle off.

When Ebelle and Khailia arrived back to their room, Aniah was already there standing outside on the balcony with her blanket wrapped around her shoulders glaring out into the distance. Khailia didn't need to use any powers to hear either of her sisters' thoughts. There was an anger inside Ebelle that swelled up by the moment. And instead of Aniah getting closer, she veered off to herself where she found comfort. Unsure of whether she could say anything that wouldn't simply make matters worse, Khailia looked back and forth at between Ebelle and Aniah and prayed. With tensions so thick between the two, Khailia began to doubt they were the ones of whom the prophecy spoke. Maybe it was to be the next generation or the one after that? Khailia's shoulders sank into the bed while heart shattered into silent tears.

Chapter 8: Kandake-Mino

The next morning Khailia woke up in high spirits hoping to unite her sisters. She turned to the direction of Ebelle's bed, she was still laying there with her back turned to everyone else. Then Khailia turned to Aniah's bed, she wasn't there.

"She never came inside," Ebelle muttered. "She stayed on the balcony all night."

Khailia stood up in a panic and raced to Aniah's side. Her eyes fluttered while staring at the loner laying on a hammock wrapped in her Guardian blanket, eyes wide open. "Did you sleep out here?"

"Yep." Aniah kept her gaze on the distant horizon.

"Aniah, that was really dramatic of you." Khailia welcomed herself by sitting ledge staring at her sister. "Why didn't you just come inside?"

"How did you sleep, Khailia?" Aniah sarcastically chuckled at Khailia's hypocrisy. She found it funny that she was being called dramatic by someone being very dramatic.

"I slept well, thank you." Khailia caught her overarching posture once she heard Aniah's thoughts and relaxed her shoulders.

"The Amanirenians have been up and moving around for the past hour or so. I'm going to go freshen up and go down for breakfast."

"How are you feeling? Are you up to training today?"

"Our purpose isn't checking for our health, correct? Did you hear Nefertiti? It's supposed to be now or nothing for us. I'll be alright." Aniah slowly got up and folded her blanket then walked inside and gently laid it on the bed that was meant for her. Once she dressed, she went down to the dining hall, grabbed some fruit and oatmeal, then found an empty table and took a seat. Before taking her first bite, she noticed a woman approaching out the side of her eye.

"Hello, my name is ZaQuaysia." The woman joined Aniah at her table. She had silky dark skin with long wavy hair, strikingly beautiful deep brown eyes and was holding a medical kit. "Heard you had a lil fun yesterday before going to bed. I never get invited to any of the good parties."

They both chuckled a bit.

"You missed a good one." Aniah finally looked in her direction. "Where are you from? You look Taureg."

"I'm American, just like you." ZaQuaysia grinned, "But my peoples are definitely Taureg, good eye. Those who were once slavers became slaves, that's what Kingdom descension looks like. So all over Africa many of us Believers were swept into slavery by our own. And you, the heiress with the luminescent eyes. More to you than what meets the eye, huh?" She opened the medical kit and motioned for Aniah to place her leg on her lap. "All of us Amanirenians are from different places. We're an elite group of warriors. The world's selected few, chosen to be a part of the Queen's army. The best of the best from various corners of Earth." She pulled out an ointment and showed it to Aniah before rubbing it into Aniah's leg then wrapped it in aloe cloth. "Pull your shirt up, let me take a look at those ribs."

"So how did you come to know about all this? This whole 'realm'," Aniah stood up from the table slowly and lifted her shirt up as requested. "I would've thought we Americans are so far removed, but you're here and you're a part. How?"

"My parents groomed me for this. My great great great great grandfather was a Guardian. My dad always talked about his wingspan and the way he handled his sword. My great great great great grandfather was known worlds over for his bravery and care for the homeless. I've heard a million stories about his cooking and baking. Heard it so much I could almost taste every bite. He always told his kids stories about Guardians and the prophecy. The stories got passed down generation after generation. My grandparents said they kept us during slavery, although no one believed us anymore. Still, made us feel powerful and regal. They wanted to pass the honor to all the males of the family. Wanted them all to become Guardians. But once the Great King fell, the Guardians faded into history. I wanted to redeem my family, you know, carry the torch. So I decided to pick up and carry on the tradition of protecting the throne." She smiled. "Out of a few hundred girls back home, I was selected by Queen Nefertiti to come here and train to be an Amanirenian, the first in my family."

"Why did she choose you above the others?"

"Honestly, I'm unsure." ZaQuaysia started to rub ointment on Aniah's ribs amazed at how Aniah didn't flinch because from the look of the bruise, it had to hurt. She pressed a little on it to see if Aniah would even take a deep breath, but nothing.

"What's this stuff you're putting on me?" Aniah lifted the bowl of oatmeal off the table and began to eat.

"A little something I concocted that helps blood circulate which will allow you to heal more quickly. It also repairs damaged tissue in a matter of minutes. And this one here that I'm about to put over the other one promotes cellular repair. Your ribs aren't broken, but it was close. And this one will relieve the pain." She opened another jar and rubbed in the cream then wrapped Aniah's ribs. "As for your busted lip, use this balm. You should see results in about an hour or so. Additionally, for the impurities in your body, drink these herbs. The food you'd been eating is highly toxic, even the 'safe' stuff." She pulled out an elixir and hands it to her. "I couldn't find a seeded grape anywhere back home! Anywho, the more seeded fruit and real veggies you eat, the more your body will cleanse and balance out within your soul's alignment. You're an heiress, so for you, that could mean something more powerful than it does for everyone else here. You'll need only speak to, or touch, or see yourself healing and it will be so."

"Are you a doctor or something?" Aniah pulled her top back down and took her seat.

"No, I'm an architect but Melaine is a doctor. We all teach each other everything we know that way we better our chances of legacies thriving. You and your sisters should try it."

"How long have you been here?"

"Since I was twelve." ZaQuaysia sat back in her seat after she put her equipment away in the kit. "Introverted much? Why are you sitting over here alone?"

"I'm observing." Aniah looked up at her sisters who were sitting amongst the other women.

"What have you observed, bright eyes?"

"A little of this, a little of that...," Aniah smiled.

"The one who sees, eh?" ZaQuaysia took Aniah's juice assuming she wouldn't need it since she had the elixir. "How many of us have you read so far? Tell me, what is it that you see?"

"Heirs!" Queen Nefertiti stood in the front of the sanctuary interrupting all conversations. "Kandake-Mino is the style of fighting we use no matter what the weapon may be. It is a technique that combines both femininity and fearlessness in battle. It's based upon making the enemy think you're on defense, all the while, you're leading them into their death." Queen Nefertiti walked to the middle of the room and nodded to the Amanirenians while she placed her infamous blue capped crown upon her head. "Khailia and Ebelle grew up learning the Kandake-Mino way, however, based upon yesterday evening, they need a lot more work. You,

Aniah, will begin from the beginning. I thought long and hard about how to institute your training. Originally, I meant to separate you from your sisters to catch you up. After last night, I change my mind. You will all three learn together."

The Amanirenians staged the room by moving the tables to the outside walls and placing the chairs on top of them. Once they finished, they formed a human wall around the room. Queen Nefertiti tapped the crown on her head and the room completely shifted into a training camp of sorts. The ceiling opened up in the middle of the room to allow sunrays inside. The solar energy changed the room even more into what resembled a dojo. All of the Amanirenian were in fierce armor that was threaded with ālebabesi. There was scripting in each woman's armor but none of it was the same, blessings from each woman's tribe in their tribe's language.

"Welcome to the sanctuary! When I reigned as Queen of Egypt, this is what my training room looked like, fighting mats and gold columns everywhere, I figured it befitting for the day." Queen Nefertiti continued to speak to keep the attention. "Aniah, when I say Ilum, it means to get ready. Tewagu means fight."

"What does ch'ewa mean?" Aniah's clothing changed into something more loose and comfortable for training, sweat shorts and a midriff sweat top, her favorite. She'd already read Queen Nefertiti's eyes for the glimpse the Queen allowed and saw today would be basics. Aniah saw Ebelle rolling her eyes and smirked it off.

"Ah, you caught that yesterday! Quick learner. I was telling Grace to be gentle with Ebelle. Not because she's an heir, but because Grace is one of the strongest fighters here and Ebelle was not ready to spar with someone of her caliber."

Aniah walked slowly over and stood firm in front of Queen Nefertiti, not with arrogance but with interest.

"Today I will help you perfect hand-to-hand combat. Heirs, with me!" She turned around quickly and got into her first stance.

Ebelle and Khailia joined Aniah in the middle of the room. Khailia's clothing changed into traditional training wear of her lineage; dark emerald green form-fitted gear with Nibutani patterns. Ebelle kept on her gown to prove her pride.

Nefertiti had her back toward the heirs, "watch me." Her movements were more like a dance than a defense or fight. "With each step and movement, you're leading your opponent to where you want them to be. No need to foresee a strike if you know exactly where they're going, setting up your stage as such." Nefertiti felt their attention resting on her as she continued going through the movements, "As a woman, you always hold the power to mystify your opponent. You do that with both elusion and intention." She moved around with so much grace it was hard to imagine there was any boldness nor strength in any part of the moves. "At any point, I can strike. At any point, I can subdue or kill. While I move, I am watching the entire field with purpose. I'm lining every sister up for a win. I can push an enemy in the way of his own teammate's bullet. I can pass him or her over to my sister to use as a shield. I may not have created the battle or battlefield, but I won it because I was created to create that win." She stopped to see their faces then continued after sighing at Ebelle's foolishness regarding her attire. "These are your basic movements. No matter what, always remember and refer to your basics. Now, with me." After going through the motions with Nefertiti a few times, she walked in between them correcting their posture as they continued. "You must be both gentle and strong, tighten your arms." She tapped Khailia's forearm. "Your legs are meant for moving, learn the value of a lighter touch," she nudged Ebelle's leg with her own which made her stumble prompting Ebelle to reshape her attire. "Watch but do not become so fixed that you cannot truly see," Nefertiti placed her hands behind her back and moved as an opponent between Aniah's movements. "Again! We will repeat these movements until they are etched in your spirit."

The Amanirenians remained at attention the entire time. The Heirs repeated the movements for hours until Ebelle broke the monotony.

"At some point today, will we spar?" Her posture showed both fatigue and boredom.

"Alright young heir, I'll reward your level of patience today. We don't have time to invest in gentle introductions anyhow, so you will start with three of the strongest here." Queen Nefertiti called out, "Melaine to Khailia, Grace to Aniah, and ZaQuaysia to Ebelle. Ilum!" She moved to the side, "remember your steps heirs. Tewagu!"

Over the next few days the intensity of training increased. Every day the heirs faced a different Amanirenian warrior. They learned just how strong and beautiful each woman was through their gifts. Although the Amanirenian movements were graceful, they were also very disciplined and incredibly strong. Every one of them held different styles and impacts of the same movements. Some start strong then finish fast. Others kept the same force throughout their entire match. Intensities and styles varied with each warrior.

At night the heirs returned to their rooms exhausted and bruised having gained a deeper understanding that the journey they must continue together would not take it easy on them. Some nights they received little to no rest as Queen Nefertiti wanted to ensure the element of surprise and that fatigue wouldn't be their downfall; Amanirenians attacked them whether resting or bathing. Soon the heirs learned to work together to defend themselves and plan for surprises. They perfected changing their clothing by mere thought and were able go from pajamas to athletic wear in a matter of seconds.

After having suffered multiple injuries, the heirs learned to apply various ointments and wraps on themselves and each other. The exact chemistry of each ingredient was easy for Ebelle as herbal remedies was a growing gift that she fell in love with daily. Her concoctions of roots and herbs would get the heirs up and running in no time, whether broken finger or scraped backside. Aniah didn't trust her, so she learned how to make her own through Melaine and the books she'd been given by her.

Each Heir's gift continued to grow. With growth came immense pains and the continuous random disruptions were annoying at times. Ebelle's hands would feel like they were on fire while she tried to block an Amanirenian fist. She meditated day and night to control her gift only to find that letting it be what it's meant to be increased her defensive capabilities. But she needed more. She learned to feel energy shifts and react much more swiftly. For the most part, Khailia had a very peaceful spirit. Her lineage trained her to know peace wherever she may be. Yet, when her ears rang, the subtle jolt would throw her off balance. Her problems with discernment were becoming more visible as her gift grew. For the time being, she learned to feed off her sister's gifts, hearing Ebelle's energy shifts and listening for Aniah's rhythmic heart. Aniah wasn't so fortunate. Her headaches from her gift forced tears that sometimes would block her sight. So she learned to fight blind instead of acknowledging the pain.

Ebelle and Aniah had yet to bond but they were at a truce with one another for the time being. Although Ebelle's impatience toward Aniah increased by the day, it only took a few concussions before Ebelle sought her out for advice in hand-to-hand combat.

Aniah had also taken her fair share of hits but she gave ten times as many and had earned the respect of the entire city and army quicker than anyone expected. Aniah showed Ebelle and Khailia the artistry of reading an opponent in hand-to-hand combat, the way she taught herself. "You have to notice their habits and force them to play into that habit deeper and deeper, making your opponent lean into their own understanding. People's falsehoods and arrogance are the easiest weakness. They create foundations built upon conceited lies and vanity. Respect their strengths and be patient in exposing their weakness. They'll show it freely and you won't have to do much." She stood in front of Khailia and took a fighting stance. "I'm learning to see. My gift helps me with not only see where I need my opponent, it helps me understand who my opponent is. Your hearing, try listening for anything out of the ordinary like the rhythm of their heart changing or someone holding their breath. That means they might be building energy for a hard blow." Aniah walked through the Kandake-Mino steps with Khailia quickly and aggressively. "Use your gift! I read Khailia all the time to see what's going on with you too Ebelle. Your hands, you're holding back for some reason, maybe unknowingly. Your pains aren't from the Amanirenians, they're self-inflicted. Try absorbing versus deflecting and see if that helps with the power in your delivery." An onset of pain caught Aniah off guard and her eyes trembled as she shook it off. She grit her teeth to hold the screams inside not wanting to show any vulnerabilities to anyone. As hard as it was, she stood firm until the headache softened, then pretended as if nothing happened.

Khailia knew she was hurting but opted not to confront Aniah's ego. Instead, she went on implemented what she'd learned from Aniah immediately. Ebelle pretended to ignore her but eventually gave in and tried Aniah's methods after a few more hits finally rang a bell.

After a few weeks of hand-to-hand combat training the heirs had become almost unstoppable by any combination of Amanirenian; regardless of how many attacked and when, the heirs subdued them each time. That was until Nefertiti exposed their weakness. They couldn't win without Khailia. Nefertiti held Khailia to the side one day during training and made her focus on choosing between right and wrong through a series of puzzling debates on morals and ethics with Seshet. Kahilia's struggle with discernment meant the scales of justice often tipped back and forth nonstop, overthinking was both a vice and virtue for her. Yet, Khailia the only heiress to have fik-iri with each sister. Therefore, only she could communicate with them through gift. Aniah and Ebelle were lost without her because every time one tried to read her, they only received her confusion.

"Divisiveness will cost you." Nefertiti's warning was proving to be a theme through their hajj. "Khailia, your indecisiveness has cost all three of you." Nefertiti jabbed at her after noticing she looked stressed out after a long day of what ifs. She motioned over her shoulder where Ebelle and Aniah were laying out to rest, their faces full of blood. "Now, it's time for you to become experts with the bow and arrow." Queen Nefertiti moved on. "Not just any bow and arrow, our bow and arrow. You see, our weapons have been anointed and created in a very special place by a tribe you don't want to meet. Rare indeed, they only work for those who Believe but they can be vicious and often require great payments for their craftsmanship." Nefertiti pulled out a glove lodged in the waistline on the back of her pant and slipped it on her left hand then pressed her index finger to her thumb and quickly lifted her hand to the sky when a bow appeared. With her right arm she made a motion as though she were playing a guitar and an arrow appeared. She placed it on the bow and pulled back the string to let loose the arrow which Khailia caught with her bare hand then spun into a low defensive position. "Good. Khailia, let's walk everyone through the basics. First your form. Do you see how Khailia's feet are pointed and spread a part? This is key! Her legs are more sturdy than an oak but she's positioned for quick rapid movement. She can shoot, climb a horse, remain steady, run, do whatever the situation requires based on her foundation. Next, nock your arrow then draw back, aim, release and follow through! Khailia makes this look easy, but there was one key step I did not mention! Khailia?"

"Breathing, breathing is the most overlooked yet critical step. And when you lead, you must believe."

"Finally!! There's the decisiveness we need, Khailia! Excellent! Kandake-Mino is to be applied to every weapon. You lead your opponent to the truth! You lead your shot, your kill. Khailia, you can't hesitate to kill. Someone can get hurt while you're deciding or discerning about whether or not to kill. What you kill are demons. The host body's soul is gone long before the battle. We no longer deal with demons who invade bodies. People willingly and knowingly choose their demons nowadays. You come to the table with your truth and principles. Believe in yourself. Trust your truth. Understood, young heir? I see how hesitant you are in training. And Hathor has told me about your lack of kills when fighting demons. You knock them out but won't kill. They are no longer human! They chose their path!"

Khailia nodded but lowered her head. The nod weighed heavy on her neck and both her sisters could sense how much she truly disagreed.

The heirs stepped up to the task without fainting or crying and received their archery gloves. What would typically take most years to command, Aniah had to learn in a matter of weeks. Khailia was beyond excellent with her bow and arrow and not one person there could match her skill. It was the one thing she was confident about. So she spent most of her time training her sisters and teaching them all she knew about using every corner of the bow and arrow. Since Aniah already formed a bond with Khailia, her bow and arrow skills grew rapidly. She understood the weapon as she understood her sister and they spent hours training, even after others had long gone to sleep. Ebelle's familiarity sharpened and she even learned how to see shots from different angles while secretly watching Aniah.

In an attempt to initiate a genuine bond amongst all three, Khailia commissioned matching finger guards made for them. They were engraved with an Ainu proverb that Khailia's father taught her on a trip to Lake Akan when she was a child. On the palm side, from the tip of the middle finger to the wrist, read 'everything in this world has a role to play'. Khailia taught her sisters how to say it in ancient tongue: 'Kanto-orowa-yaku-saku-no-arankep-shinep-ka-isam'. Once the words were spoken into guards it lit up and helped them guide the arrow with truth into its intended targets.

To celebrate and keep Khailia lifted, Hathor fazed her horse, Shinsei in to the sanctuary. Khailia hadn't seen her horse in months and rode him gallantly while showing Aniah and Ebelle how to shoot from horseback. Her ability to stand, flip, switch sides and lean in multiple directions made Aniah's mouth drop. For Khailia, learning to ride a horse was something she mastered before she turned ten years old. It was tradition in her lineage and a rite of passage.

After only a few days, Queen Nefertiti graduated them to gun fighting. Ebelle shined with every lesson. She took an interest in guns as a young child and became an expert marksman by the time she was twelve. Her mother taught her everything she knew about any and every gun. Their catalogue could easily put a military to shame. Khailia did very well also but Aniah didn't care for guns. She used one well enough but preferred to get closer to her targets for hand-to-hand combat. She knew how to dodge bullets and mislead shooters from her vigilante days. However, every once in a while, a bullet would graze one of them and it burned immensely. Ebelle showed her sisters how to hit a moving target while they themselves were moving. She also taught them how to lead a target to the shot and snipe. Taking Khailia's lead, Ebelle had special holsters made for the three of them. They were designed in an Amazigh pattern that signified a holy person. She left it on their pillows so that she wouldn't have to give it to them directly, avoiding Aniah.

"Alright heirs, now let's incorporate the bo staff and spear." Nefertiti started them on balancing their weight with the bo's.

While Khailia preferred the bow and arrow, she was deadlier with the bo staff. She'd even perfected using both at the same time in a synchronized manner.

After having suffered several bumps and bruises during training, the heirs finally remembered to keep with their Kandake-Mino movements, the basics. Once they applied it, they conquered the bo and spear.

"And now, my personal favorite, the blade." Nefertiti grinned from ear to ear.

"Oh, hell no!" The words escaped Aniah's mouth as she pretended to walk out the training room jokingly, but Melaine stepped in to turn her around and laughed at her. The two had formed a great kindred in their trainings and had become the best of friends.

The sanctuary had a slight adjustment that day. In the middle of the room was a long table filled with swords, daggers, knives and various other blades.

"Alright Heirs, choose your weapon...or weapons." Queen Nefertiti watched carefully.

Queen Hadiat, Seshet and Hathor joined the training room as well. Selecting a blade was ceremonious and they didn't want to miss it. The heirs' selections could tell them a great deal about who they are.

Ebelle stepped up first and confidently chose a Turkish kilijis and two daggers which was what her father trained her to use. While Ebelle chose it for comfort, her choice told Hadiat she preferred a quick and precise kill. It also informed Hadiat that Ebelle is an advanced protector with expanse in mind. Khailia chose the changdao which was what her mother trained her to use. Although it was not a traditional weapon of her lineage, Khailia was not brought up to simply be traditional. She was raised to break barriers. Her choice revealed that she preferred to deal with her enemy at a distance in order to protect her peace. It also spoke to Khailia's ability to connect with people who seemed too far out of reach. Aniah approached the table and stood there for a while. A world of choices and no idea about how any of them worked. After staring long and hard, she finally called upon her eyes and she selected two katanas. Yet before she could walk away the row of khopeshes caught her eyes and wouldn't release her, and a headache began. There were a few with rare and priceless stones in them and one with simple engravings that had a manual extension on the rod. She chose the one with engravings and strapped it on her back underneath the katanas then whispered, "'kifuni ātifira, ānite ke'inē gari nehina. My comfort, His shield," And her headache ceased.

Hadiat tried to force herself to believe it to be inadvertently selected because it was the King's khopesh. An unsettling feeling nestled itself in her heart. She began to gasp for air and tried to figure out how Aniah could know not only her husband's weapon but his words. Hadiat pulled Nefertiti to the side demanding to know how it got there. Nefertiti explained that after Hadiat was kidnapped, the girls were found next to the King's khopesh and brought to The Amanirenians. But when Hadiat inquired as to how the girls ever got separated, Nefertiti had no exact explanation. All she knew was that while she was out searching for Hadiat, the girls were removed from the Amanirenians care in a decision made without her knowledge. There were contradicting stories as to how the girls were taken, but most all the stories stated seeing Esu, an Orisha Gatekeeper on the grounds that night.

The heirs continued their training. They kept their basics in mind and became experts with using their sword but it puzzled everyone that Aniah never withdrew her khopesh, she simply kept it on her back in its non-extended form and used it as a protective shield. When anyone would attempt to attack her from behind, she'd tap the khopesh with her elbow in whatever direction necessary and the attack was defended. It hooked swords and deflected daggers with ease due to its shape. One night after training, she redesigned her sword holders so the khopesh could turn more freely. This allowed her to both defend and counterattack without looking at her opponents. The Amanirenians joked at how she never accidentally grazed not one strand of her own hair, they called the khopesh her second set of eyes. The weight was heavy but it didn't slow her down one step, it balanced her, making Aniah the most dangerous heiress with a sword. Still, the Amanirenians and her sisters preferred fighting her with a sword rather than hand-to-hand, as she was also the strongest hand-to-hand fighter they'd ever witnessed.

Nefertiti and Hadiat thought it'd be best to allow each heiress command over soldiers who matched their specialty. Ebelle took the majority of Amanirenians since most were expert with sniper and sharp shooter skills. Khailia took on the archers. Many of them were from the Eastern part of the world and already possessed bo staff skills. Aniah took on the sword fighters. Although their specified skills separated them, they all trained together to maintain unity and continual growth.

Tired after a day of intense training, Aniah decided to take a minute to herself and sat alone on a high beam. She watched the comradery amongst the warriors and thought to herself how grateful she was to belong. Then she spotted an Amanirenian by the name of Meeran mimicking her sword fighting style. Aniah jumped off the beam to join her in laughter but a dagger flew at Aniah and cut the left side of her clavicle. She looked in the direction it came from and saw Ebelle looking directly at her trying to smother her laughter. Aniah ran at her full speed prompting Ebelle to throw another dagger which missed. Then Ebelle pulled out her pistol and shot at Aniah and missed her by less than an inch. When Aniah made it to Ebelle, she faked a left punch and put all her strength behind the right fist but Nefertiti appeared, locked Aniah's elbow with her own and stopped the blow from connecting. She was fazed by Nefertiti to a garden inside of her home where she released her, then backed away slowly. Aniah was steaming hot and her chest and shoulders moved hard with her agitated heartbeat. She looked over Nefertiti's shoulder as though she was going to blow right past her.

"Aniah, calm yourself. You cannot kill your sister, you both need each other." Nefertiti's heart rate picked up, her words weren't affecting Aniah.

Aniah fazed back to the sanctuary, spotted Ebelle and headed in her direction. She pushed everyone who tried to stop her out of her way.

Nefertiti fazed back and stood in front of Ebelle.

Seshet fazed in after having sensed Ebelle's heightened panic. "You dare come after my liege!" Seshet removed the cover from her rod and revealed her spear tip. "If you take one more step I'll kill you myself this time."

"ENOUGH!" Hadiat fazed in, "WHAT IS THE MEANING OF ALL THIS?!" She looked around at all the warriors and furniture Aniah had tossed to the side trying to get to Ebelle. "What happened to you? Why are you bleeding?"

"I accidentally hit her with a dagger." Ebelle's lie earned the disgust of several Amanirenians and Khailia. "If she would've paused for a second, I was trying to apologize.

Hadiat calmed her stature, "Well?"

"Aniah, you came out of nowhere. I shouldn't have been toying around with my daggers." Ebelle's words were accompanied by a smirk from Seshet.

"Ebelle, you are the most proficient here with daggers. We all know you have no accidents." ZaQuaysia let go of Aniah's arm. Her shoulder hurt from trying to restrain Aniah, she rubbed on it as she left.

Everyone else turned to Aniah and waited for her next move.

"Move." Aniah continued her path to Ebelle.

"You will not harm my child!" Hadiat placed herself in the middle of Aniah and Ebelle.

Aniah's rage refused boundaries as she balled her fists. Before anyone could offer anything else to the scene, Nefertiti fazed behind Aniah, grabbed her then fazed once more back into the garden.

"You want to fight, fight me." Nefertiti loosened her sword holster and tossed her sword under a nearby tree. "Come on, you and me. Let's go! You angry? Be angry with me." Taking slow steps toward Aniah, the closer she got the more she saw her hurting. "Come on dear, take it out on me if you must. I can take it."

Aniah slammed her swords and khopesh to the ground and screamed aloud, "I'VE HAD ENOUGH. I'M DONE WITH THIS SHIT!" She turned to walk out the garden.

"You'll turn your back on them?"

"Hadiat, Ebelle and Seshet's backs been turned to me!" Aniah kept going.

"What about everyone else? Khailia? The Amanirenians? What about the eyes you can't stop seeing?" Nefertiti's words caused Aniah's pace to slow. "Even if you leave here right now, you'll still see their eyes. I know all about it. Zoya never stopped seeing their eyes." She knew she was getting through to her when Aniah completely stopped. "Are you walking away from them too? I can't stop you from leaving. And I don't know why Ebelle antagonizes you. I can't make her stop either. But I can give you something I never got the chance to finish with Zoya. It was helping her. Let me finish it with you. Let me help you."

Aniah turned around to face Nefertiti, "I didn't ask for any of this." She fought every tear from their escape as her rage turned into a more dutiful acceptance of divinity.

Nefertiti ripped the sleeve of her gown and folded it into a gauze shape. She placed the cloth on Aniah's wound. "I will help you heal this too. Come, sit over here with me." Nefertiti escorted her around a fountain and sat on the ground right in front of the tree. "You think you have a guard up, but actually it's a blocker. You're blocking yourself from experiencing your truth in its fullness."

Aniah sat down beside her, "They don't want me here. You saw how Ebelle, Seshet and Hadiat dismissed me. Like I don't even exist or like I was never supposed to exist. Like they would rather I not exist. I'm really trying. I swear to you I am. Even when it doesn't make sense I'm still giving and trying and I don't half ass anything, I never have. Why can't it ever just be simple? I'm tired of dumb shit! I'm tired of not understanding. Why can't I just be?"

Nefertiti couldn't look Aniah in the eyes, she knew she'd cry. The hurt Aniah was feeling and had always felt was seeping through. She dare not tell Aniah not to feel. A quick breath to evade her own tears and she quickly grabbed

Aniah's hand and kissed the palm, then cupped them into her own hands like the greatest treasure ever created. "It's alright to be frustrated. There's nothing wrong with addressing what's real within your heart. But don't you ever forget who you are. You are already equipped with everything you will ever need and as long as you Believe, you will be provided direction and support along your hajj. Your gift is not about them, never was and never will be. They don't understand it because it's not meant for them. If they understood, they would never treat you in such a way. Ebelle has issues that have nothing to do with you, so does Seshet and Hadiat, forgive them and don't let anger consume you and lead you astray. You were created for love and anything that isn't love, you will question and rightfully so. You my dear, must rise above it all because there are so many who need your gift. You were given sight with royal lineage because only you can bear it. And Believers and non-Believers, everyone is depending on you in ways they don't even know. I need you. I need you to live beyond this moment. It will get better, you will see. Do not fall into tricks and deception, you cannot become distracted. I know its heavy, but it's yours for a reason. And I Believe in you, my dear. Always have and always will."

Nefertiti ripped her other sleeve and handed it to Aniah to help with the bleeding. Then a memory caught her off guard and lifted her heart. She smiled into the wind and looked into the fountain as though she could see history from centuries ago happening right in front of her. "Zoya had three favorite hiding places. This garden was one of them. One day while I was passing by I noticed her in here weeping silently. When I asked her what was wrong she said I wouldn't understand. I begged her to tell me anyhow and she said that's just the thing, I don't know how to put it to words. I imagine if she could, she would've just shown me, but her sight was hers and often times it made her feel very lonely." Nefertiti paused to ensure she hadn't lost Aniah then continued, "So I taught her how to meditate. After she learned to meditate, she learned to compartmentalize her experiences in a way that kept her sane. Her gift was enough to drive anyone crazy, but even at a young age she discovered it was given to her for a reason and made the choice to protect it. That little goddess girl was a sponge. She grasped on to mediation quickly, but I didn't get to finish teaching her. She never got to her highest level of consciousness. She was taken from me. But if you'll let me, I will show you."

"You said she had three hiding places, what were the other two?"

"So observant." Nefertiti chuckled, "She hid within herself quite often and I don't mean in the hermit way. I mean she found her core. The last was within her father's eyes. I don't know how, but she would take on his sight and he would show her so many things, I imagine he showed her how to cope with or manage her gift, I don't know, that was their bond."

"Okay, teach me. I mean, I would like for you to teach me, please."

"You're just as fearless as she was." Nefertiti smiled and started to cross her legs but before she could get into the lesson, Hadiat fazed in.

"She's as fearless as who?" After she gave Aniah a look, Hadiat glanced to Nefertiti and was reminded of Zoya and Nefertiti's bond. She grew slightly jealous because the type of bond she longed to have with the line of Zoya was still intact, just not with her, yet again. "To apologize, Ebelle is going to patch you up. She needs medical supplies so you, her and Khailia will run a small errand to the town's apothecary together. The bonds that matter most is you all having fik-iri. Let's work on that happening so that we can get this over with." Hadiat fazed away.

"We better do as she says. Hadiat has never been the type to ask twice." Nefertiti and Aniah interlocked arms and grasped hands to help each other up off the ground.

....

At the apothecary, Aniah picked up some literature on natural remedies and the plants they derived from. It held the contents for understanding plants origins, purposes and rudimentary cures. Some, she'd grown familiar with, while others she'd never heard before. While Ebelle tended to Aniah's laceration, the herbal pharmacist there explained the rare ones to the Heirs and informed them of how he believed they were used while warning that the plants true purposes were recorded in lost scrolls written in a dead language, one that he only knew Gate Keepers and a few Mansa-Ibn knew. He cautioned the dangers in seeking them out.

Ebelle cleaned up after herself and felt a difference in the air and grew curious. Aniah had already walked out and was standing on the sidewalk watching people watch them. Ebelle and Khailia joined her. They walked slowly through the city and took it all in. The heirs got to see the Amanirenians outside of battle, a sight they hadn't seen since entering the city, except Aniah who watched them every night from her hammock on the balcony. Some of the people were tending to their everyday life but stopped to grant and wish blessings upon them. Suddenly, Ebelle's heart rate slowly climbed and Khailia suggested taking a break so they walked into a nearby bakery. The smell of fresh breads and desserts filled Aniah's lungs and she jokingly swore she'd now been cured by the whiff alone. Since all the grains used were as ancient as Nefertiti, it was all gluten free and non-dairy. One of the owners began to explain how gluten and dairy blocked alignment and centeredness to Aniah while pointing out some of the plants in her book, when she spotted Ebelle out the corner of her eye.

"Ebelle! Ebelle! What's wrong?" Aniah grabbed her before she could fall.

"I don't know. My skin is on fire and my heart is racing out of control. I think I'm having a heart attack." She faintly explained while gasping for air and clenching her chest.

A customer ran to her to check her pulse. Once he touched her, it happened. Her heart slowed down and Ebelle felt his heartbeat match hers. He slowly sank onto the ground next to her and pulled her closer to his chest. Unaware of what was happening, Aniah grabbed his arm and started to break it. However, she was finding it increasingly hard to do as his muscles grew right in front of them. Due to decades of learning their purpose, Khailia understood what was occurring and placed her hand on Aniah's shoulder to let her know everything was alright. Having fik-iri with Ebelle, Khailia knew this was a part of her destiny.

"Aniah, Ebelle and her king have found each other. He is remembering himself as though he has always been what he is to become. And she is adorning her crown. This is what happens when an Heir and her husband meet." She pulled Aniah close to her and lifted her fingers from the man's arm, "you can't see it, but right now, the two of them are actually within each other, not sexually, but intimately, a space that only they can share."

"Good, maybe now she'll stop being such a bitch. So what do we do now?" Aniah stood up and wiped the dust from her pants.

"Let's give them some time alone. Come, there's more to explore here."

"Can we explore a hospital? I don't trust her work," Aniah looked back over her shoulder to check on Ebelle as she was being guided away by Khailia.

While Khailia and Aniah wandered the city, Ebelle and her beau began their courtship.

Chapter 9: Iji mesit'eti

Customers walked in and out the bakery blushing for Ebelle and her new beau. They whispered about how grande they thought the wedding should be, ready to celebrate with the heiress and her king-to-be.

The love birds remained in the bakery falling into each other's hands. He held Ebelle's hand as though it possessed every secret of his heart. Taken with her beauty, he counted himself fortunate to be chosen by God as the husband of an Heiress.

As for Ebelle, she couldn't get over his smile. Seconds passed and healed her from some of the negativity she'd detained for so long. She knew she didn't have enough room in her heart for him and hate. It inexplicably worried her that she couldn't completely let go of or even identify all her hate. The choice to love as she'd been created to do was her favorite option, but the toxicity was her drug.

"Line of Liya, huh? Your reputation precedes you. You are literally thee absolute most beautiful woman I've ever seen. I've heard the stories of your beauty and I still wasn't prepared."

"You don't have to try to win me over, I was yours before we met. But if you must, please continue...." Ebelle smiled and took a sip of her coffee. After her sisters left, he lifted her off the floor and sat her down at his favorite table and ordered beverages for them. "How'd you get your name?" She didn't need to ask it, she learned it by his touch.

"My father and grandfather." He braced his cup in between his hands and started to speak.

"Queen Hadiat is summoning me. We should leave."

"Telepathy? That's sweet!"

"I mean, I can do that too but, no, it's the armored Amanirenians at the door are waiting to escort us. I'm sure she wants to meet you."

"Well then, let's not keep her waiting. Shall we?" He stood and extended his hand to her.

Their promenade through the city streets made them smile as they held hands sharing the first of many memories. When they arrived at the palace, Ebelle and her future husband were escorted directly to Hadiat. With her stood Seshet, Hathor and Nefertiti.

"Speak your name." Hadiat commanded.

"I am Hasan Ali of the Mansa-ibn tribe." He cleared his throat and straightened his posture in front of his illustrious audience.

"Etruscan or Amazigh?" Her face was stern and cold.

"Both, on my mother's side. Mansa on my father's." Being raised in a respected tribe, Hasan was well aware of protocol and kept his stance true and his answers short and direct.

"Interesting. Noble blood you have in your veins. Tell me about your family."

"My father is a high priest. Mother a mid-wife. I came here to visit my sister Grace, the Amanirenian, and her family."

"Well then clearly you are very familiar with the realm of Believers as well as non-Believers. Did you know the Heirs were here?"

"Yes ma'am, I was at the university library upon your arrival."

"You've been here a while?"

"Yes, I was supposed to leave over a month ago. However, I haven't quite been able to depart. Something kept holding me back, now I know what it was." His smile wanted to break loose, but he dare not lose composure in front of her majesty, the Queen.

"You've been away from your responsibilities for quite some time...no career?"

"I am a politician, an ambassador to be exact."

"Ebelle, where are you sisters?"

"We are here." Khailia announced her's and Aniah's arrival.

"And did you witness iji mesit'eti?"

"Yes, I did." Khailia spoke gently while smiling lovingly at Ebelle and gave her approval of her growing love for Hasan.

"And you, Aniah, did you witness as well?"

"What is an iji mesit'eti?" Aniah stumbled through the annunciation hysterically.

"It is what occurs when an heir meets her king. They surrender to one another for it is God's will. It would have seemed like a quickening to your eyes."

"Well then yes, I witnessed Ebelle being extremely dramatic and making a scene in the bakery.... I think she fainted for a moment too. Very damsel in distress looking..."

"Thanks sis!" Ebelle snarked in embarrassment while everyone else tried hard to hold in their laughter.

"And your bond, my dear?" Hadiat tried to continue.

"It is true and grows with every passing moment." Ebelle's rosy cheeks stretched across her face so hard it hurt with pleasure.

"Well then, we have a wedding to plan." Hadiat smiled and walked to Ebelle to hug her. "Welcome, my son. I have a son! Finally! A break from all this feminine divinity!" She laughed joyously.

"Thank you Queen Hadiat." He greeted the Queen by kissing her hand then respectfully hugging her.

"Considering time, Ebelle, you will continue your training. Your fiancé' may join you so that your bond may continue to grow and strengthen. In the meantime, myself, Seshet and your biological mother will plan your wedding. I'll have the Amanirenians send for her. The descendants of Liya will be elated to hear the news. Hasan, please call your mother, as I am sure she will want to assist in the planning of your wedding."

"Yes, your Highness."

"Khailia, please update your sister Aniah on all that is to occur and her role in her sister's wedding."

"Yes ma'am."

....

Khailia and Aniah walked back to their room. Once there Aniah uncovered her wound and rubbed it with ointment then left it exposed to the air for healing. Khailia joined her on the balcony.

"Tell me, why do you still sleep out here?"

"Have you ever had to lay in a room or home with a person or people who don't trust you and vice versa? People who don't love you or care about you?"

"No. I can't say that I have."

"No one would adopt me. So the private orphanage turned me over to the state. While the orphanage wasn't glorious, at least I knew the abuse wouldn't surpass a certain point. But when the state placed me in my first foster home I knew the bottom of loneliness. My first night there I paid attention to how scared the other girls were once the lights went out. It shook me entirely. So much that I couldn't sleep. Then I heard the steps. The foster father from hell. He came up the steps and the closer he got, the loud softness of whimpers from the other girls pulled on me. Then the others started to shift around and when he opened the door one pushed me closest to it. He reached for me and I jumped so quickly that it confused him. I remember smelling the alcohol all on his breath as he grabbed my arm tightly and pulled me toward him. I yanked my arm away and it broke his finger. He hit me so hard that I passed out. When I woke up I could only open one eye. The social worker came in the morning to see how I was adjusting and his wife blamed it on the other kids which made the other kids hate me. So that night they began picking on me and jumping me as well. A few nights later when he came up the stairs they pushed me closest to the door again. But before he could open the door, I ran and grabbed my blanket, slipped out the open window and went outside on the roof of the porch. He chose another and I slept on the roof with one eye open. I was eight. Eventually one of the older girls got pregnant and he and his wife were arrested, and we were placed in other homes. None better than the other. To say the least, I didn't sleep in a bed again until I was sixteen."

"I'm so sorry Aniah."

"All these years what really haunts me is that he chose another. God knows I didn't want to be molested, but I didn't want it for any of the other girls either, even though were regularly trying to beat me up."

"You learned to defend yourself."

"I learned to balance myself. Those other kids never really beat me up but I always ended up really hurting them whenever I applied any amount of strength. I wanted to learn discipline. So I'd stand outside boxing rings, dojos, martial arts schools, you name it. And I learned for free."

"Ebelle would never hurt you like that. She just doesn't know how to love you. She really is trying to figure you out."

"You do know she threw a dagger at me, shot at me and has tried to fight me multiple times, right? People who try to force a learned definition of love to fit into their mind or understanding are some of the most dangerous types of people out there. They make sense out of their confusion and label others as they see applicable, they really love to label us Black women back home crazy and unworthy, a tale as old as time. During and after slavery, Black women were raped and tortured by white men, then thrown into insane asylums for crying. Same white men taught that hate to Black men, who now call us crazy for any display of humanity."

Khailia's heart sank for a world of Believers unaware of themselves. She didn't know how to respond to Aniah feeling hated and wondered how deep her wounds really went. She took the ointment from Aniah and started to help her rub it into her scar. "Well, I'm hoping the two of you will form a fik-iri soon. Ebelle has tough skin but a very gentle touch. I was raised with her, I know her well. I promise you, she means no harm. Maybe you'll see it during the wedding prep."

"So what is my 'role'?"

"Ebelle is very traditional and I'm sure her wedding will be as well."

"What's traditional for her? What does that mean?"

"Crash course, let's see. In America, I believe you guys do a bridal shower, bachelor or bachelorette party, then a wedding, right?"

"Yes."

"Well, it's something like that but with a different focused intent. However, there are two sides to this coin. On one hand, The Mansa-Ibn tribe has their own customs and traditions of which Ebelle is already somewhat familiar given her line was raised amongst the Amazigh tribes in France. You may more commonly know the Amazigh as Berbers, but historically speaking, the term Berber is a Greek label and often taken as offensive. A traditional wedding lasts seven days. There is a lot of preparation, music, food, laughter, and dancing throughout the first six days. On the seventh, the wedding ceremony takes place. Ebelle and Hasan will be working hard not only to mutually build one another for the capacity to love each other, they must also honor each other's families. Meanwhile, our job is to ensure that Ebelle is provided with all the support she needs in becoming a wife and Queen. On the other hand, there is no forewarning, therefore the planning occurs immediately instead of over time. Iji Mesit eti, our marital bonds, much like our sister bond of fik-iris, form in different respects with time. And as if that's not enough, we must also continue our training. Lastly, there is the dance. The steps are very easy, I'm sure you'll learn it within an hour. Basically, it's like mixing a European Viennese waltz with an African drum. More intentional movement and better music. You'll see."

....

Caravans of various nomadic lineages arrived safely over the next few days. The Mansa – Ibn also trickled in and lit up the Amanirenian city with laughter and loud voices. Everyone came together creating splashes of vivid colors that reminded all of the first time they embraced home. As people entered, they were permitted to stitch a patch to a quilt that was to be a gift to the soon-to-be ``Believers weren't in attendance but the first heiress to marry caused a great sounding of joy throughout their nations...and drew curiosity from others.

The Amanirenians were on high alert because the more word spread of the wedding, the more word spread of their location. Their home was sacred to them but technically it was on holy ground, and therefore penetrable by demons and pawns. Though most wouldn't dare to go head to head with Amanirenians, it didn't mean they wouldn't.

The Heirs trained hard for most of the day and then raced off to prepare Ebelle for a lifetime with her king. They shopped in every boutique, bazaar, visited spiritual stores for stones and herbs, read books together and danced crazily. Every night Khailia and Aniah placed fresh rose and jasmine petals under Ebelle's sheets to permeate her skin with aromatic essence. Ebelle woke up to key lime spring drawn drinking water to purify her body and warm oils in her bath tub to soothe her muscles and soften her skin. Ebelle's hair was washed using aloe and grapefruit essence and her sisters put green clay mask made from plants freshly picked on her face after every training. It became apparent to all three that this type of self-love needed to continue throughout the course of the rest of their lives. To be fierce and ready for battle at the drop of a dime but always finding time to pour back into self in preparation to love. Meanwhile, Queen Nefertiti worked them harder. She sent Amanirenians to attack them in their sleep with every weapon known to Earth and Heaven but the heirs were mastering the art of becoming queens.

On the morning of Ebelle's wedding her bath was interrupted by the sound of Aniah playing music from a wi-fi speaker.

"What is that?"

"THAT, my dear, would be Jagged Edge." Aniah sang along with the music.

"No, you have to play Raveena." Khailia ran in. "That's who you play on wedding day."

"What is a Raveena?" Aniah asked while swatting Khailia away.

"You're both way off base, play Tekno" Ebelle got out the tub and wrapped herself in a towel. "Play *Be*.... that's my song!"

"Who?" Aniah laughed while twisting her behind to try and bump Ebelle while holding Khailia off with her hands, "what is all this?"

"See you Americans think you own music, listen to this." Ebelle jumped in front of Aniah to play the song.

"Oh, this is dope! Ayyeee...," Aniah started to dance while helping Ebelle dry her hair.

"Listen to the words, not a bit of disrespect! Not a twerker's first choice, I'm sure."

Aniah shook her head and walked away, "I can definitely twerk to anything, it's my gift, but you need to know we're not all disrespectful, some misunderstood mostly by themselves, but us Americans are pretty fucking amazing. And I guarantee, before this year ends, you'll beg me to teach you to twerk." Aniah chuckled softly.

"Again, with the cursing. You flick me off every day and curse to express a point?"

"Yes. As a matter of fucking fact, yes! See, you're getting me. Fik-iri can't be too far down the way now." Aniah smiled and held up Ebelle's veil to the light shining bright through the window. "Not all the time, but sometimes you just gotta put the correct punctuation in place and a character ain't it." She danced back over to the radio, "now any Black person anywhere on this planet loves this." She changed the song.

All three jumped to attention and start singing in unison.

"Who doesn't love Prince!" Khailia yelled as they all danced around pointing at each other screaming I would die for you. The intensity grew as she watched Ebelle and Aniah finally getting along. She wasn't supposed to rush fik-iri but she was desperate. They only needed to touch so that Ebelle could feel Aniah and Aniah could see Ebelle. Khailia grabbed Ebelle by the hands and twirled her around in Aniah's direction. She let go thinking Ebelle would spin into Aniah but Hadiat fazed in between them.

"What is going on in here?" Queen Hadiat tried to remain formal but a smile slowly crept across her beautiful face. She knew to remain parental but also enjoyed seeing her heirs be roguish together.

The ladies straightened themselves up.

"Blame it on the boogie!" Aniah laughed as she walked back out to the balcony.

"Oh, play that one next!" Ebelle shouted as she sat down in the chair. The hairdressers and stylists entered the room to get the heirs ready for the wedding.

Ebelle's parents entered the room and their family reunion was touching to say the least. From outside on the balcony Aniah stared as they poured out adulation onto Ebelle. Draping Ebelle with gifts for her coming life with her king, they laughed and shared tears of joy. Then they greeted Khailia with much familiarity and took pictures with Hadiat, Hathor and Seshet.

Aniah wasn't jealous but unsure of where she fit into this scene. Her sisters had known each other and experienced each other their whole lives. Their bond wasn't made from urgency but genuine sisterhood which made Aniah wonder what life would be like had it not been for a history in which she never asked to take part. Would nations know how to honor her glory if slavery in the Americas never occurred? Would Believers worry about freedom had her lineage not been broken? She started to think, if neither Ebelle nor Hadiat could see her worth, did she really even possess it? Maybe Ebelle was right and Aniah needed to humble herself?

After fixing their hair and makeup just right and putting on their dresses, Khailia and Aniah left the room to prepare to usher their sister down the city streets and into the church. Nefertiti walked with them to a dimly lit room where they were anointed by an Amanirenian priestess to aide Ebelle through her new life as a wife. Aniah stared at the priestess and took in the décor of the dimly lit room. She noticed the candles burn with green flames that swayed to them. The closer her eyes got the more she saw the flames reach out for her begging her to step in and become one with the fire. She snatched herself away from the trance in enough time to hear the priestess finish her prayer. After the pre-ceremonious tradition, they walked out the room and there stood Ebelle. She was stunningly beautiful. Aniah and Khailia's mouths dropped and Ebelle's eyes released a single tear. Her princess ball gown was white and gold with a long lace veil. It was simple yet classic satin train that flowed endlessly. Within the details, each member of her lineage had sewn in their proverb and wishes for Ebelle. Blessings wrapped around every inch of Ebelle's curves. She wore them proudly with her head held so high she could cause a mountain to do a double take.

Khailia and Aniah took their places in front of Ebelle and proceeded out the palace and down the streets. On the way to the church people threw flower petals at Ebelle's feet after they whispered well wishes on them. Little Grace and her friends skipped alongside them tossing more flowers into the air giggling the entire way.

When they got to the church, Aniah and Khailia made room for Ebelle's father so that he could walk her down the aisle. They entered the church doors and took their stance on each side of the alter off shoulder from the priest, Hasan's father. Hasan waited for his bride with great anticipation and when the doors opened his heart skipped several beats and his niece little Grace laughed at him which snapped him out of his fixation.

As Ebelle made her way down the aisle, Aniah caught a glance of Nefertiti pacing outside the doors; she looked worried. Aniah understood the importance of the day and looked away so that Khailia didn't pick up on anything which would alert Ebelle. Looking at Ebelle's happiness brought a smile to Aniah's face. She looked over to Khailia who had tears slowly dropping around her cheekbones. Aniah reminded her of the tissues tucked inside her flower bouquet by motioning toward her own.

The priest took his time and to ensure the two understood their vows. Once he finished, they embraced and their hands glowed as they kissed. When their lips parted from one another Hadiat appeared and placed her hands on their shoulders. They looked toward Heaven and a medium-height princess tiara with yellow oval diamonds shimmered upon Ebelle's head and a simple gold crown with ancestral scribing took shape upon Hasan's; their union recognized. Aniah and Khailia followed the two down the aisle. As soon as they made it outside the doors, Nefertiti tapped Aniah on the shoulder and asked her to step aside.

"Demons are outside the city. We have no time to celebrate any further, it is time. Get your sisters and go to sanctuary to prepare for battle, now. I've already had the Amanirenians put the city on alert and prepare in case demons find them."

Aniah hurriedly did what she was told and Nefertiti spoke to the people in the congregation informing them of what was happening. As they had prepared to do their whole lives, everyone parted and went to their homes and tents to stand guard in case the demons breached.

"Where is Ebelle?" Hasan asked Hadiat.

"With her sisters preparing for their first real battle."

"I will go with her."

"You may witness, you may not join her on the field. You are not ready."

"I will not allow my wife to go fight without me. As her husband, it is my job to protect her."

"As a King, it is your job to live. You will not be your strongest until the reigning King is revealed. Ebelle needs you to live. She needs your energy to survive. Try not to worry. She's trained her whole life for this."

Hasan was extremely frustrated but he understood and ran to the sanctuary to help her get ready. His sister Grace tried to encourage him to go back to her house but he adamantly refused to leave his wife's side. He even marched with his bride to the battle field as far in as Hadiat would allow. Right before they went out further he grabbed Aniah and Khailia and stared into their eyes. Khailia heard him loud and clear. Aniah saw his concern. Hadiat fazed him to where she would stand watch over the battle, so he began to assemble his long-distance rifle. The heirs went and gathered amongst the generals and commanders and waited for Nefertiti's plan.

Lake Tana's waters were empty, not even a hippo in sight. They heard no birds chirping only lonely gusts of wind and water gently smoothing its way through reeds and lilies. There were enough demons to fill a football stadium and they were packed from the flat lands to the hills in the background.

"Interesting," Nefertiti spoke up. "I wonder how they found us." She looked around for unfamiliar reactions but none jumped out to her immediately. In a tone audible enough for their ears alone she reminded, "Heirs, this is not training. Every demon over there is waiting to kill you. You will not easily recover from any wounds caused by their weapons.... and their weapons are the only ones that can kill you, Akrhh matter. Remember, Ebelle is the only heir with a king. Therefore, she is the only one that can heal quickly, and quite possibly she is now the strongest among you as her energy source has doubled. Khailia is the only Heiress to form Fik-iri with both sisters therefore Khailia will take lead, communicate through her. Protect each other and protect yourselves. Zoya..., I mean Aniah, don't you dare go being stupid and die today, you hear me?" Nefertiti pulled out a map and began pointing at various parts. "This is our current formation and the demons have been spotted as far out and here and here. There are more of them than there are of us. This hill is where we may possibly spot their commander. Hathor, Seshet, Hadiat and I will stand back in case we're needed in the city. Kill every single one of them! How dare they stand outside my home with such disrespect!" She put the map away then joined her Queen and the T'Malaks.

The Amanirenians stood ready for battle. Over a century had passed since the last time the Amanirenians had seen any action of this magnitude.

Khailia heard the mix of the Amanirenians emotions in every breath so she stood firm on her power to give encouragement. She put on her glove and secured it tightly. She strapped on her changdao sword then held her hand high in the air "Amanirenians! Today is a day for statements! Today is the day we restate our claim to God's promise. We stand tall and give notice to all manner of injustice that we are here! Your weapons are anointed to render a sole truth. Demons have no claim in this world. They are more in numbers but we are stronger in purpose. Remember, today is the day we won centuries ago when they initiated their part of the prophecy. WE WILL NOT LOSE!"

Ebelle drew her pistols. Khailia struck air for her bow and Aniah pulled out her katanas. They allowed the energy to surge higher and higher through them then aligned themselves in battle formation.

"Ebelle, take your shooters with you to the flanks, take out their drones." Khailia continued leading, "Aniah, come in after I meet the frontline. Calvary to the front! Archers, on me!" Khailia got on her horse and rubbed his neck, "Shinsei my sweet and brave one, are you ready?" The horse lifted his front legs the stomped down hard. Khailia and her horse were one.

The sight of all three excited Tiago as he made his way to the front of the demon frontline. His unscrupulous voice was so loud he needed no microphone and he didn't stress to be heard. "Sarah's bastards! I'm assuming you've been training to fight.... Me? Amusing." He laughed. "And the infamous Amanirenians, and yet another slut queen, Nefertiti. And my word, are those the famous failures the T'Malaks, the weaker half breed of my kind? Seshet and Hathor? My blade has longed for your putrid light. I was feeling nostalgic, aye Sarah? Open battlefield, just like the old days. The ground is begging for blood nourishment. Just felt appropriate."

"Amanirenians, ilum!" Aniah spoke.

"No dialogue this time heir? What a pity. I thought we were going to be friends."

"Tewagu!" Aniah was growing impatient as she swayed from side to side with a slight hop, ready to fight.

Tiago felt he was too close for watchful eye, so he spread his wings and mounted himself atop a small hill alongside a few strong demons.

Khailia signaled her archers while Ebelle and her sharp shooters ran to the sides of the battle to draw out the drones. Khailia let out her first arrow officially starting the battle and the archers let loose theirs as well. Khailia took off on her horse shooting more and more arrows and her calvary followed her into battle. The demons launched their arrows as well and Queen Hadiat summoned the winds and caused them to go off track. Khailia's archers' arrows succeeded in piercing demon flesh, the anointing on the arrow tips killed them instantly. Ebelle and her sharp shooters took out not only the drones but other demons along the way.

Khailia jumped off her horse seemingly in one stride, pulled her changdao and continued to charge toward the frontline. Aniah waited as requested along with the other strong swordswomen. Once Khailia and her archers made it to the front and broke through, Khailia called to Aniah.

Anxiety lifted from Aniah's body. Aniah and her swordswomen flowed into battle like raging waters. Aniah caught up to Khailia and jumped high. Khailia sensed her and held her changdao out on the flat side for Aniah to use it as a spring board. Aniah pushed off the sword and landed right in the middle of a sea of demons. She got low and swung her swords and decorated the field in their body parts and blood. Thousands of demons fell to hundreds of Amanirenians.

Tiago's smile turned heavy as he watched the heirs take out multiple demons at a time with ease. He studied them fighting together and tried to figure out who is who with regards to the prophecy. He noticed Ebelle's overarching anger when she pulled out her daggers and began her overkill. Then Tiago grinned when he found Khailia struggling to finish kills due to the demon's human form. She knew they inhabited someone else's body and hesitated to kill at times. Then he spotted his opportunity to separate Aniah from the rest and pulled out his sword as a signal to all. He entered the battle with his stronger demons by his side causing Hadiat to panic, yet she remained as still as possible while Hasan sniped as many demons away from his wife's path as he could.

From the corner of her eyes Aniah saw Tiago and did not delay in going to the aide of the struggling Amanirenians in his path. Tiago was mere seconds from thrusting his Akrhh matter sword into the chest of an injured Amanirenian but was stopped as Aniah threw the head of a demon in its way. Before Tiago could blink, Aniah was before him to protect her injured soldier.

"The heir without worth, remember me?"

"You brought your pawns out to play, huh?" Aniah lacked any fear of Tiago, "study time over?"

"Perceptive. Aniah, right? You think you're ready for stronger demons? Let's see. Ilum, is it?"

Hadiat froze in terror. Tiago was no demon to play with. One of the most dangerous to her knowledge and she shook at the thought of how he swung her around like a rag doll centuries ago.

Aniah didn't know her worth, but she fought anyhow. Even without full strength she proved to be a problem for Tiago, that was until he decided to show her his real strength. She took a step back when Tiago spread his wings and spun knocking Aniah's katanas out her hands. Aniah looked over to Khailia, who heard it immediately and began fighting her way to her sister. Meanwhile, Aniah felt Tiago's fingers grab her by the throat with one hand. Lifting her in the air and pulling her closer with the other hand, he retrieved his dagger from his waist. Aniah struggled for air and her legs frantically searched for the ground or so it seemed, making Tiago think he was in control. She nervously looked over to Hathor who began to faze in to help, but Nefertiti stopped her and gestured for her to simply watch. Aniah placed her fingers around Tiago's causing his curiosity to peak at her will to fight. She noticed Tiago staring at her body as though to celebrate her demise but then he made a crucial mistake and looked the Heiress in her eyes with his dagger lifted high. Aniah cocked her head to the side then locked in her glare and looked him directly in the eyes and read his story.

He felt the strange energy from her and unwillingly opened his eyes bigger while he realized that he'd fallen for her trap. His body shook feverishly as he did and did not want her to see more of his story. He fought to pull himself away and at the same time, he needed her to learn more. His vulnerability attached itself to Aniah, something he didn't know he knew to do. He thought his fall stripped him of such grace.

Aniah fought past her nature to pity and continued to force his truth. She realized she didn't have to fight too hard, he wanted her to continue, he needed her to see how he fell. She found a good sum of his truths and would have continued but Khailia arrived to them.

In all his years, Tiago had never been caught by any weapon, but Khailia's arrow went right through his shoulder and jerked him loose from Aniah. As soon as he dropped Aniah, she ducked low and unleashed fist after fist, over taking him. He attempted to retaliate but he couldn't and his affixation confused him further. In anger, he spread his wings again and created space between he and the heirs attack. And just like that, he was gone.

"Are you okay?" Khailia gasped for air. "I got here as soon as I could."

"I'm fine."

"I bet he wishes he left those katanas in your hand. Your fists hurt him more." Khailia smiled and continued on with fighting the remaining demons.

Once it was all over, the Amanirenians and heirs stood over the field and reviewed their work. Although some escaped, there was demonic carnage everywhere. The injured Amanirenians were helped to their feet and headed back to the city.

"We need to burn their bodies," Ebelle announced. "Cover them with sage and burn their entire bodies. No return."

The Amanirenians moved quickly to do as the heir requested.

Hadiat and Hasan entered to ensure the heirs are unharmed and praised God for the victory in His name.

"Aniah, you read a demon." Hadiat's puzzled face requested a response from Aniah. "You read a very powerful demon, only the King.... not even I have done that. How?"

"Everyone has a story, even our enemies. I needed to know who I was fighting."

"Did he read you as well?"

"I had to give a little."

"So you let him in but not your own?"

Aniah gave no response, she simply fazed back to Queen Nefertiti's palace. The T'Malaks, Khailia and Hadiat fazed to the palace as well. Ebelle asked Melaine to continue with the cleanse and grabbed her husband by the hand then fazed to the palace.

"Aniah! I am speaking to you, answer me now!" Hadiat continued on Aniah's heels, "You can embrace an enemy but not your own. I do not understand this! You know the task at hand! Why won't you embrace me?!"

"Answer her or I'll shoot you right where you stand!" Ebelle's anger took her back to a dark place as she drew out her pistol and pointed it directly at Aniah's head. Her new found strength was one she had yet to balance with fruits of the Spirit and it scared everyone except Aniah.

Aniah wasn't about to ignore her disregarded dare. In a blink she pulled a dagger from Khailia's waist and threw it at Ebelle. The dagger flew at Ebelle's chest but Hasan stepped in the way and blocked it. He couldn't believe how quickly Aniah moved. Once Ebelle was distracted, Aniah fazed and reappeared behind Ebelle and placed her in a sleep hold while removing her pistols from her hands.

"Since you're so enamored with Afro American habits and culture, street rule number one with guns, never pull it without the intent of using it." Aniah squeezed tighter with every word.

While Aniah was naturally stronger, Ebelle was now able to draw energy from Hasan; his skin touched her while he tried separating the two. Before he could stop them from fighting, Ebelle elbowed Aniah hard in her temple and knocked her unconscious.

Chapter 10: Power in a Name

Ebelle felt no remorse. Knocking Aniah out had been coming since they met. She believed Aniah was ungrateful of her position and royalty, in willful disobedience to her crown. Ebelle paced back and forth in anger yelling at Khailia's defense of Aniah. Ebelle felt like the outsider even though she was the one who came into majesty fully aware of her worth. A firestorm brewed inside Ebelle and it was growing out of control.

"I've waited my whole life for this and look...look at who we're cursed with! As if we hadn't gone through enough growing up, now this! Now her! I'm over it!" Ebelle's discontent for her sister Aniah had never been a hidden one. "We were trained! Spent hours being groomed and days having to recite, remember, rehearse, and look at her! This is an heiress? This has to be some foul joke! Our God, Thee God, would send this to us?! As if having to save the world wasn't a big enough task all by itself. I can't do it with this.... this.... UGH!!! " The muscles and veins in each finger bulged as she threw her hands wildly in the air.

"You genuinely have no idea as to what she's been through. You should be thanking God she's still alive. If you would only let her show you, you would feel differently. We can't do this without each other, that includes Aniah and you." Khailia softly stated as she continued trying to revive her sister, rubbing Aniah's arm while softly patting her hand to her forehead. "You got a small taste of awakened power and look at you. Still leaning toward you own understanding. You're jaded! As smart as you are, you don't realize it." Khailia shook her head at Ebelle while accepted the rhodiola root soaked cloth from Nefertiti and pressed it against Aniah's head.

Before Ebelle could respond, Hasan placed his hand on Ebelle's shoulder calming her. A tear forced its way out. She grabbed her pistols, walked out of the room, and into the sanctuary to let off a few rounds.

At first, Hadiat pondered over what she could do to make Aniah see, but Khailia's words convicted her as well. Her regrets eased the tension in her brow and brought forth the compassion in her own eyes. Hadiat slowly cupped her hand over her mouth as she saw her sweet baby Zoya laying there on the floor inside Aniah. It was as if Zoya was holding Aniah, trying to keep the seams all together. She stared at Aniah's body and had never noticed the scars. They weren't from training, those scars were healed some time ago. She suffered nothing during battle, so where did they come from? She couldn't understand how an heir could bare scars that never healed. She started to stretch her hand out but the shame she felt created a barrier inside herself.

"Hadiat, join me in my terrace please." Nefertiti interrupted the growing concern. Her part had always been the one who held things together during the many transitions over the centuries. "Don't worry, Khailia can look after her."

For the distance to the terrace, they walked in silence. While they walked, Nefertiti meditated. She knew what needed to happen but understood the cost as well. They sat down in the middle of the terrace on a bench. The fountain's peaceful flow created an ambience for honesty. Nefertiti took a deep breath and inhaled the smell of the jasmine flowers that filled the night's air.

Hadiat took in the message of the fountains flow and allowed the memories to escape. "I remember when we, the King and the girls and I, would come here to visit. Those were the days when flowers were placed gently at the royal family's feet. The girls would come out to this very terrace to be themselves. Aida would sing for the wind and excite a gentle breeze that would carry her voice into the ears of Believers. And Liya, that girl was smarter than anyone I ever met. She just lay across Aida's lap researching truths in multiple books at a time, the universities didn't want her there. Those educators were so scared she'd realize they didn't know any truths after all. She knew those so-called scholars prayed she'd never feel anything from them. And Zoya, that little girl loved people, but never really too closely. She'd climb up that tree right there and watch everyone from the balcony over there. If it looked like they were about to fall, she would race over to catch them. If a child needed a friend to play with, she'd run them tired....She loved people. You remember that?" Hadiat's longed deeply for day's past and times. She desired a chance at living days she never had with her girls. At times she still felt the need to ask God why but didn't.

A mischievous humor slightly pulled at the corners of Nefertiti's lips, "I remember Aida used to sneak halva and chocolate to this terrace and pretend to be training her voice while shoving desserts into her's and Liya's face. I remember Liya trying to find ways to absorb a book's energy from her touch, she was too impatient to read until the end. And I remember Zoya always smiling at them, hugging them, grabbing her share of the snacks then ensuring them she'd stand lookout. Those were the beautiful triplets I remember."

"That Aida! That's where all my cakes went?" Hadiat laughed, "they were a handful then and an even bigger handful now. I guess I knew when they were up to no good, but they needed time for that too. When they were able to be curious in peace, they came back stronger every time."

"Indeed, maybe you should be mindful of that even today." Nefertiti winked at Hadiat trying to be as gentle as possible with a spirited Queen that had already endured too much.

"At least back then, they looked to me. We taught them Kandake-Mino in the hardest of ways. Those girls could almost take out an armada by themselves. And when lessons were done, they'd look to me as their mother. They came to me for comfort and understanding."

"Ah, not quite. True, Aida was a momma's girl. And Liya was momma's little rebel and personal bodyguard all wrapped into one. But Zoya, the one with the King's eyes, she was a daddy's girl through and through."

"Goodness! Zoya and the King, those two trained all the time. I overheard the King and Zoya one day, he understood her sight better than I did. She told him it hurt really bad sometimes to see the truth in people and have to prepare herself for an Heiress' response. She didn't appreciate her gift, even back then."

"She didn't appreciate it? Or did she understand the weight of the requirement? To see as He sees….can you imagine? We were hard on those girls, never really gave them a chance to be both innocent and Heir."

"True, but Liya and Aida adjusted just fine because they came to me for understanding, but Zoya…."

"Zoya needed her father. Aniah needs her father."

"What do you mean, you know he's gone." Hadiat nearly snapped into insanity but calmed herself by rubbing and pressing her hands feverishly on her lap.

"Is he?" Nefertiti knew she had to pick at the scab that refused to heal.

"That's enough Nefertiti. You know I searched far and wide for him. I looked for his spirit everywhere. That guilt sits on my shoulders to this day."

"Did you try searching within yourself? Have you healed what hurts most so that you can be ready for your King?"

"I can't do this right now, I need to go check on Aniah."

Nefertiti gently raised her hand asking Hadiat to remain seated. "He used to walk through the Hall of Kings holding your hand proudly. He deserves to have you say his name."

Hadiat gasped for air in disbelief of what she was hearing.

"No one dared contest his khopesh." Nefertiti continued her prowl, circling the scab on Hadiat's heart as its crust began to lift, "He commanded The

Guardians, an army greater than any other. Stricken from history books but never from hearts, say his name."

"I...I." Tears snuck their way out Hadiat's eyes.

"His name buried in Vatican tablets. Demons trembled at the very sight of him for they knew he held direct alignment with the Creator. For all his might and earned glory, say his name."

"He, he...." Hadiat's chest could no longer contain the pain, the scab on her heart was fully open.

"He reigned true; protected this earth and the fullness there of. He loved his Queen with every thread of his being and held her highest especially after birthing the promise. Flying sea to sea to secure his legacy, his works obscured vanity. Defined, his name is to love bravely. Never in vain, always with purpose. SAY HIS NAME!"

"Jasir." Hadiat's breaths softened as she realized she hadn't called love by its name for centuries.

"There is power in a name and his is to be spoken for the truth it bares holds weight unbroken and because he was purely molded. Say his name." Nefertiti stood firmly on the foundation laid at creation. She crossed her legs while seated as her hands began moving through meditative secrets until she rested in aang.

"King Jasir-Amare"

"Call to your King, let him know where you are. Tell him you are coming to remind the world to say his name."

Hadiat fought past her self-pity to close her eyes and she levitated in the middle of the garden. She drew strength from the mere thought of his return as the ground began to quake. Her heart danced in raging fires searching for his soul unscathed amongst the stars. Waters from vast distances ceased to roll as even nature silenced its prayers so she'd hear his cry. She opened her eyes to the truth. "Nefertiti, it's time to go back."

Chapter 11: The Fallen and the Façade

Tiago returned to Draisien's castle estate more confused than ever before. Aniah saw him and he saw her. He witnessed her unparalleled beauty and it torched his understanding of who he was. The hatred for God etched into his wings, he was unsure if it belonged. She was so strong that even though she read his whole story, he only had a glimpse of hers, a brutal carnality he held dear. He was now dependent on her and his thirst grew rapidly.

"Where are their heads?" Draisien entered Tiago's lair with pure disgust.

"This mission was purely to see their capabilities. Now I plan their demise." Tiago barely looked over his shoulder to acknowledge Draisien, he lost all interest in their lie. He was no longer the same. Aniah's eyes freed him from his disguise.

"How stupid are you? You were there. On the battlefield with them. They aren't even at full power and you still can't kill them?"

"It's not that simple." Tiago rolled his neck annoyed with wanting to go after her.

"One of your pawns said you had Aniah's neck in the palm of your hands. You didn't crush it? Why?"

"Although she hasn't embraced Sarah, she's still strong, stronger than Sarah at that." He quickly forced words out like he was reciting a pledge with words that held no depth.

"The other two?"

"Khailia is equally strong but differently, she is the gel. Ebelle has united with her king making her the strongest right now." His struggle to keep face was becoming more and more apparent. Remembering himself, without a blink he snapped back into poise. His eyes were still, shoulders erect and movements suave. He no longer cared to remain hidden.

"How do you know all of this? You observed all of that from a small hill?" Draisien noticed Tiago ignoring the question, "And as for the King's khopesh the heir parades on her voluptuous backside? The dreaded demon murdering piece of shit! Did it frighten you?"

Tiago offered no response, not even a raised brow hair.

"You failed me yet again. I'll send your brother to finish the job." Draisien tried to reassert his position of authority.

Tiago wasn't sure if Draisien believed his own lie. He possessed a need to figure out the conflict that was piercing a hole through space and time. He'd done many things in his lifetime and preferred to hide behind the veil of drunkenness as he scourged. Tiago was responsible for the rise of hateful regimes and distraught nations that were once moral; The black plague was something he created on his day off. So many years had been spent drawing energy from innocent souls brought laughter and riches to him. Every win was simply to mock God's understanding, desire, and reason for love. In all his deeds, he never looked back on them unless there were further greed to gain. All of that came crashing down around him with one glance into her eyes. Beauty is easy, knowledge is relative, but love he had yet to define. One glance made him remember everything he'd ever done, but this time to recollect and ponder the necessity of it all.

He wandered off from his lair and crept in on Victoria's training without her noticing. He could tell her focus wasn't the prophecy but killing Aniah. Tiago laughed at the hate that drove her soul insane and how she wore it with pride. A mere human may scratch the Heir but never would she be able to kill her; he shook his head and walked away. He continued down the hall and out to the pool where he found his brothers Tien and Trigon eating and being entertained by vixens.

"Ah, Tiago! Come sit with us loser!" Tien shouted to him while he smoothed his hands over his low-cut waves. He glanced over his shoulder at Tiago but locked his brown eyes' on his lunch. He sat up in his pool chaise ready to devour.

"Tell me you'll spare us by not getting in the water. No one wants to smell mangy wet animal." Tiago joined them. "You Inkanyamba types and your wreak....Ewww."

Tien was a p'irveli shekmna Inkanyamba who often disguised himself for the purpose of blending in with humans. In his human form, he was the owner of a large grocery chain and a billionaire. In his created form, he was a winged serpent-headed demon with a horse body and lead supplanter of deadly sins.

"Oh joy, you brought your sarcasm along with your self-pity and losing nature to keep us all warm." Trigon's hyena laugh scratched at the air. "Come, sit next to me. Tell me what you learned of the Heirs so that I may kill them all successfully."

Trigon was p'irveli shekmna kishi. He was very handsome and charismatic and took pride in being well-versed for the purposes of detouring Believing women from ever hoping again. He smelled the weaknesses of women from miles away, both their power and secret desires were his favorite weapons. He chose not to hide his p'irveli shekmna form in public, but people missed it due to being charmed by him. While on the surface he looked very human, behind the scenes was not quite the same story. It only took for someone to dig deeper and they'd see the hyena face beneath his long brown hair.

Tiago was a p'irveli shekmna roc. Many stories were told of his existence that made him seem as majestic and noble as the eagle. He resembled his own personal conflict through and through; a mirror couldn't paint a better picture.

"Another bottle of champagne? To celebrate my coming victory, shall we?" Trigon continued picking at Tiago. "Coach is putting me in. Try not to be too jealous at my victory when I return. And I prefer maroon rose petals be thrown at my feet. They smell so much sweeter than any other color rose. The smell of victory. You can place them petal by petal at my beautiful feet."

"You mean paws? And champagne is for pussies! Bring me hooch! Only the good stuff please." Tien laughed while he stood to flex his defined brown muscles then dove into the pool with a few of the vixens. He playfully pulled them under the water with him. After a few seconds the water began to bubble but no one came up for air. Tiago and Trigon simply ignored it.

"Now, tell me about the Heirs? What did you see?"

"Ebelle and her King have found each other, she will be the hardest to get to. He too is training and gaining strength every day. He looks to be from the Mansa Ibn tribe and he has hands that are decent with blade, he's good with a gun but better with persuasion. Khailia carries the scales of sin into battle with her and therefore finds it hard to hate demons enough to kill. She prefers peace but do not mistake peace for weakness. She may hate to kill but she will, nonetheless. Yet she may be easy for a professional to manipulate...Trigon. Aniah..."

"Leave Aniah to me." Victoria rolled her eyes and continued past the pool and disappeared down the hallway.

"You heard your wife! Leave the small stuff to her." Tien came out from the bloody water after devouring the vixen's vexed souls.

"Excuse me, my wife?" Tiago smiled. "She's not enough of anything for me. I wouldn't defile my dick that way."

"Draisien must not have consulted your holy testicles then. He's announced your wedding to Victoria as payment for her services." Trigon laughed uncontrollably, "I've been arguing with Tien over which of us will be your best man. Please tell us."

Tiago spread his wings and lifted off in his roc form, this time out of sight.

Chapter 12: A King That Findeth

The sound of the busy streets and waves that crashed upon the shores served to be lullabyes as Aniah remained unconscious. Khailia never left her side and Ebelle eventually joined as she feared the worse for her Aniah and the prophecy. The T'Malaks, Nefertiti and Hadiat kept busy by making a list of places they thought the King's spirit might be. Melaine, Grace and ZaQuaysia stood watch outside while Hasan spoke to the locals regarding their recent protests.

    Ebelle peeked outside at her husband who was sitting at the corner coffee shop debating politics versus morality. Although he carried four pistols on him, she trusted no one. She was fully aware that if something happened to him, she'd be lost. "I didn't even hit her that hard." She continued watching out the window while referring to Aniah, "she's just being dramatic."

    Aniah raised her hand slowly in the air and flicked Ebelle off.

    "Hadiat! She's woke! Aniah is woke!" Khailia yelled in excitement.

    "False alarm! I'm about to knock her back out." Ebelle shouted in retaliation of the middle finger still high in the air.

    Hadiat fazed in the room and the T'Malaks and Nefertiti piled in immediately after.

    "How are you, my dear?" Hadiat tried to peek around her shoulders to see her face.

    Aniah sat up and stretched her arms high and tilted her neck from side to side. "Ebelle hits like a girl." She laughed, "where are we?" She looked around the room and noticed they weren't in Queen Nefertiti's palace anymore.

    "We're here at Clifton's Beach in Cape Town, South Africa. We all fazed here while you were resting." Hadiat smiled while rubbing Aniah's leg in care.

    "Ahhh...hence the symphony of waves crashing, cars speeding by, and protesters regaling my ears. How long have I been out?"

    "Three days. Some girly hit, huh?" Ebelle walked out to go tell her husband the news.

    "Shows how smart she is. I happen to believe girls are very strong." Aniah accepted a cup of aloe water from Nefertiti. "Thank you. What are we doing here?"

"Thought I'd bring you girls here to see what it'd mean to you. This was the last place I was before it all..." Hadiat couldn't find the courage to face her own words. "Also...searching for the Great King."

"I thought he was dead."

"Absent from the body but definitely present amongst the living. I can still feel him."

"I hope that's a good thing. Why are we searching for him?" Aniah stood up and stretched her back and legs.

"Because *you*, in particular, need him."

"Okaaaayyyy.... but that's not what I meant. Why would any woman search for a man? Isn't that his job?"

Hadiat fell silent. She never thought of it that way before. All her searching may have caused them to miss each other on numerous occasions. What if she'd just been still and gave room for her King to be King. "That's actually very perceptive insight." Hadiat sat down beside Aniah and smiled. "Well! This is you girls' hajj. What would you like to do?"

"Can we go to Sarah's memorial site? It's in Eastern Cape, right?" Khailia asked excitedly.

"I never stopped to see my dead body." Hadiat bowed her head in shame, then in one deep breath gave in, "well, alright."

"We don't have to..." Khailia regretted her words immediately and reached for Hadiat's shoulders. She leaned into Hadiat and squeezed her tight while gently rocking her from side to side.

"No, we'll go at once. Go grab everyone else so that we can faze. At least Aniah is woke this time. She can faze someone with her.'

"I've never been to Africa until all this. I understand we're in a rush and all, but can we please take a moment to experience it here? Don't get me wrong, I loved it in Ethiopia with the Amanirenians, but I didn't get to see anything but the Amanirenians. Besides training outside a few pyramids here and there, we missed a lot." Aniah's eyes held the King's truth in them.

Hadiat was reminded of her love for her family and purpose. Then she remembered Nefertiti's words and accepted the Heir's as confirmation, they need time to be both innocent and heir. "Yes, shall we rent some vehicles. There are eleven of us in total, how do we do this?"

"How about a guided tour bus?" Hasan entered the room. "While we're there, I'd love to see where Mandela was born. Everyone from my tribe makes it a point to personally pay homage."

Everyone looked to Hadiat for a response and she shrugged with a cute chuckle as she realized their dependence and her need to let go. "This hajj doesn't belong to me."

"Did anyone bring my khopesh and katanas?" Aniah asked while she searching for fresh clothing to wear.

"Yeah, they were right by your side the entire time. Check on the bed." Khailia shouted as she strapped her sword onto her back.

"So, you just gon' walk out into broad daylight with a sword on your back? Like that's normal or something.... no time for blending in and being lowkey at all, huh? Why don't you just call the military and police and let them know you're here as well, just cut right to the chase. I'm sure there's some demons in the crowd."

Khailia laughed at her own absurdity. She was raised to move in a fashion of urgency and responsibility to the throne. "You're right. Where are you putting your khopesh and katanas?"

"I was just gonna carry them in a duffle bag. You want me to see what I can do to conceal yours?"

"Yes, thank you."

Aniah looked around the room at all the things they'd packed and knew it was all too much. Her family had packed so much stuff, but nothing more than what she was carrying could come with her. It only reminded her of how she worked her whole life for all the things she had back home and had to leave it in the blink of an eye. Material things meant nothing to her anymore. She grabbed her blanket and placed it carefully amongst her weapons then rested her hands for a moment as she remembered the families in the club. She felt a rush come over her as she realized she had no idea about their safety. Aniah figured she'd be able to help them more and for the long run by continuing her hajj, but even that felt like a cop out. Her mind was hung up on what to do until Nefertiti walked by and pat her on the back. Aniah snapped out of her worried heart and finished packing.

They had no timeframe or route in particular. None of the Heirs had ever been to South Africa and none were ever bold enough to ask specifics about the dreaded day. But all three wanted to know. They desired to share the load that Hadiat carried all these years.

The bus coasted on a cloud of ambition and propitious winds. They all knew nothing of what to expect, separate in thought but equal in position. The driver ushered them through miles and miles of plush green canyons, rolling hills and wild flowers. They spoke about what ideas went through God's head as He created it all. They inquired about the true purpose of such things and wondered if they themselves were being utilized as God intended. The Amanirenians joined them as sisters in laughter of the wildest imaginations and expressed curiosity about things as simple as the placement of trees while Hasan tried showing them the geometries behind their distance. The purest indigo waters, clearer than media or any book could ever distort, splashed on the shores. They recognized the beauty and worth of every tear spilled to reclaim Believer's birthrights. The trails of stories never told cried out to them and the louder they cried the more God's love made sense. Protecting the purpose of every tear drop and returning it to its correct being was of the most importance.

Along the way, they stopped at Nelson Mandela's grave site in his home village of Qunu. Hasan lit incense and said a prayer of gratitude. During the tour, Ebelle touched the blades of grass to get a sense of Mandela's spirit. She shared it with Hasan which struck a great chord between the two. Ebelle gifted him with being able to feel the passion left stained within the prison walls and he couldn't wait to use the energy in His ordained way. Still high from the continuation of love and shared duty between them, the rest of the drive Ebelle and Hasan sat close to each other affectionately.

Meanwhile, Aniah and Khailia looked out the windows at all the grandeur in the landscape, and most importantly, the people. Such beautiful people with cheek bones only God could create, with hair that gave the adored waters purpose.

Hadiat smiled favorably on all as she never really felt as though she had the time to stop and smell the roses. Sure, she'd sneak time here and there in between battles and assignments, but she couldn't remember fully enjoying the nothingness in everything. Then it hit her, she loved being herself even more. She loved being a mother and great great grandmother and so on and so forth. She loved simply watching them breathe. When her three girls were alive, most of their time was spent training and learning who they had to be, rarely celebrating who they were at that moment. A chapter that should have been written long ago was righting itself in front of her. She laughed to herself in thinking, God her Father was right after all. It made her believe in herself and her purpose once again, no longer a mere routine. It made her proud that her blood was strong and written for greatness. So she sat up in her seat a little higher and watched over them caringly.

The air began to grow stiffer the closer they got to Hadiat's burial site. The heirs grew cold upon seeing the reservations for the San and Khoi Khoi people. There was a sign outside the preserve stating it was now illegal to hunt them. 'What demon had the authority to make it legal in the first place?' was the expression of disdain and disgust written across everyone's face.

"It's right up this road." The tour guide announced.

"Stop, please. I'd like to continue on foot." Khailia got out the vehicle even before it fully stopped.

They unloaded while the guide continued on by pointing out the rich history. Aniah pulled out the duffle bag and began securing her Khopesh and swords to her back and she willed her clothing to turn into battle wear. She looked over her shoulder to see Amanirenians, Khailia, Ebelle and Hasan did the same. While they walked, the sullen quietness over her sisters and Hadiat hurt Aniah so much that all she wanted to do was fight. She could care less about her armored appearance through city streets anymore. As they continued, people stopped in streets and watch the sovereignty of it all. Aniah locked eyes with an elder which caused him to cry out. Her presence made him begin to profess the realness of the prophesied Heirs. All those who Believe joined in and storm clouds began gathering in the distance. A little girl with gold beads and string in her hair ran up and grabbed Aniah's hand, not letting go as they continued on.

The group traveled up a long hill and Hadiat's spirit could no longer hide, she wept. The thoughts of her torture returned. A few people brought various flowers up the hill and laid them around Sarah's remains.

Ebelle was vulnerable in the moment as tears flowed and she crouched into a kneel. She thought of all the torment Hadiat suffered simply so she could be. After wrapping her arms around the monument, she kissed the stone then pressed her forehead against it in silence. The outward display of emotion shocked Khailia and Seshet because they'd never witnessed any sorrow in her. She was hard to crack but malleable at the cries of Hadiat.

"Today, right now in this very moment," The elder began, "We give thanks to our Creator. And we show gratitude for Hadiat's endurance. To know the end and still possess the power to continue on is no sheer feat for any being. The Hendricks', Dunlop's and Cuvier's of the world seek to destroy our truth, honor and legacy…. But not one could undo His promise. We've said thank you in the ways of man's tribe, but right now we celebrate in the rites of the only true crown. We uplift our Queen! We celebrate her winning sacrifice as the price for God's victory." He held a staff in the air, "and in my time I'm grateful to witness and lay eyes on the Throne of God! Do you hear me? My people, do you see? God is merciful. Lay eyes on the prophesied promise!" He sang out in happiness and rejoice. "In His divine trinitarian wisdom, He gifted us with unsurpassed protection...Hadiat's triplets. Long live the Queen!" He turned to Hadiat, "The truth was never lost. We know who you are. The gift that never ceases to give." He kissed her hand, "thank you."

Hadiat eyes filled with tears. Little by little the scars from arkhh chains lifted off her and her spirit brightened. She looked up over the hills and mountains and took a long pause, "I'm ready to go back."

Everyone looked in the direction where Hadiat was staring, toward the Gamtoos river where she was bathing on that frightful day. While the people stayed and danced throughout the streets in celebration, the traveling caravan and Heirs followed Hadiat as she headed toward the river. She didn't know if she was ready to face the birth of her pain.

"We came here to fight off demons who had been attacking the villagers. Back then, hunting God's children was legal. Can you believe that? It was written on parchment stolen from their land that their genocide was legal! And trust me, demons were sure to carry out the verdict of guilty at birth to all Believers. The Guardians were out helping to rebuild the village and I asked the Amanirenians to go home and check on their families...told them we'd be okay. Jasir said he wanted family time. We came up to this private part of the river and had ourselves a day." In tears Hadiat recalled it all as she fought hard to get past her shaky voice. "The sun was high up in the sky and Jasir flew my babies around on his wings for the breeze. Mid-air, Aida, Liya and Zoya jumped challenging their father to catch them all before they hit the ground. He did just that too! He loved those girls with every bit of him. I had just finished spreading out a snack of fruits and nuts and decided to take a quiet moment to myself to bathe. He said 'Ah, my Sarai, you deserve this moment and many more.' Kissed me like he knew it was his last. We knew. Then he took them on the other side of that there tree and those bushes to give me privacy."

The air turned dark and storm clouds rolled in at tremendous speed and the wind picked up quickly on the bright and sunny day. The ominous look of the skies put everyone on guard.

"Ilum." Ebelle was ready for anything or so she thought.

Thunder struck repeatedly in between them all as everyone moved to dodge the blows. In a loud roar, the wind screamed at them. "Get off these sacred lands!" It was the King. "You will not deface my territory. GET OUT!" The storm clouds circled like a tornado until his image began to form among them. First his feet, then legs and torso. His majesty appeared as the storm. He viciously manifested out of the wind right before them.

"My King." Hadiat gasped out and held her arms out to receive him.

Nefertiti ran and tackled Hadiat before his fist could land. His spirit had grown angry over time and it overshadowed his memory of self. Clouds towered in rage as his fury continued. While no one could understand the reason for his attack, they defended themselves, nonetheless.

"Do you not recognize me, it is me, your wife, your Queen...." Hadiat cried out.

It was as if he didn't hear her at all while he continued fighting them all, screaming for them to get off his land.

"Father, it's me, Aida." Khailia tried to provoke memories but it didn't work.

"That is enough. Little Liya says enough!" Ebelle tried a different angle to no avail.

They were all growing faint and tired from taking hits and dodging lightning bolts. Aniah pulled her katanas and saw them swiftly leave her hands and landing into a tree due to a strong breath of wind by Jasir. When he saw his sacred tree being pierced, he howled so loud it shook the ground. A large gust carried Aniah into the air then slammed her to the ground. She trembled as he appeared before her and she turned to dodge the next blow. Jasir caught a glimpse of her backside and his khopesh. He knelt down below her face like a panther on the prowl then proceeded past any personal space. In a scooping motion Jasir lifted Aniah without even touching her. She winced. Jasir opened his mouth and blew so hard it pushed Aniah's backside into the ground. She finally opened her eyes and dared to stare into his. A soft rain began.

Aniah slowly lifted to her knees and loosened her khopesh while he was stuck staring into her eyes.

"I know you. WHY DO I KNOW YOU?!"

Using the soaked mud on the ground, she pushed off the King and spun around while pulling out the khopesh. She held it out in offering and bowed before him. While waiting to see what he'd do next Aniah finally looked up again, her eyes begged for mercy.

His body began to jerk as if a million arrows of remembrance were hitting him all at once. King Jasir's tears ran into his mouth and provided nourishment for the words that fighting for release. "Z...z...," he tried to spit it out through the overwhelming hurt.

"Zoya." Hadiat placed her hand on his shoulder.

He grabbed Hadiat by her face. "Sarai." He lowered his head in shame while trying to catch any bit of air into his lungs he whispered, "Please forgive me," and faded away.

Hadiat looked as if she had all she could take. When he faded her body felt as light as a feather as she easily she fell over. Her spirit cringed at the thought of having to go numb when her life was just with her. She stared into the sky trying to see if she could find him, but her head dropped when she finally accepted he was gone...again.

Khailia ran to Aniah's side as she lay bruised and bloodied while Ebelle and Nefertiti tended to the Queen.

"Now is not the time for crying. Give him time to feel the pain. He will find you. He always has and always will find his way back to you." Nefertiti reminded her.

Melaine and ZaQuaysia assisted Aniah up and held her on each side as they made their way back to the tour guide. Everyone in the group was consumed by a mixing bowl of emotions. The King hadn't been seen since his earthly death; no one was prepared.

Chapter 13: Anointing Tresses

They fazed into Mandela Bay and found a place along the beach for the night. Aniah decided to bandage herself on the balcony for a moment alone. Hadiat determined that Aniah had had enough loneliness in her lifetime and joined her.

"How are you, dear?"

"The better question is, how are you?" Aniah's heart was still aching from it all. She forced a smile because she didn't want to place any more burden on Hadiat.

"I've definitely had better days, but the best is yet to come." She smiled and grabbed Aniah by the face and began to see how much she truly cared for her. "You were so brave today. I'm proud of you."

"It takes a lot to return to the place where it hurts the most, huh?" Aniah tried to rush past the unfamiliar affection from Hadiat unsure of how to accept her love.

"Your sight is growing, no mere perception could've revealed that. With all I've been through and all I've seen, nothing horrifies me more than the sight of losing my King." Typically Hadiat would try to be strong, but she understood that Aniah's gift of sight was not one she ever really successfully hid from. With nowhere to hide, she found comfort in sharing her truth with the young heiress.

"It hurts." Aniah's involuntary tears gave in to their fight. The transparency Aniah was getting from Hadiat allowed her empathy to take over as her chest swelled in and out releasing a world of questions. Each tear Aniah shed made paths for the next one to trace; one drop asking why and the next inquiring how much more.

Hadiat grabbed a pillow cushion from a seat nearby and motioned for Aniah to stand. She placed the pillow on the ground then sat on the chair right above it. Then she lifted her hand and fashioned a comb from her own being, opened her legs and twice tapped on her chair. Hadiat watched her Aniah struggle to smile for her. She held her arms out wide toward the sniffling Heiress and Aniah took slow steps to her seat between Hadiat's legs as she pulled out some oil.

"King Jasir and I went to Honduras to meet with a tribe there once. The chieftain's wife gave me this oil, it's called Batana oil. You ever heard of it?" Hadiat started undoing the long braid in Aniah's hair. "Well the Moskito tribe, that's the name of the tribe you know, use this oil right from the Earth and it strengthens and lengthens their hair. They've used it for centuries, take it right out the trees."

Nefertiti, Hasan, Hathor, Seshet and the other two Heirs joined them on the balcony while the Amanirenians stayed on their watch right below the balcony still within listening distance.

"You've seen some of the stories on palace walls and ceremonial fires, heard it some and even read a little. But I guess I've never really taken the time to explain it all to you, and I apologize for that. In my rush I often forget His timing is never our own. I keep repeating that lesson." Hadiat parted Aniah's beautiful tresses straight down the middle then massaged the Batana oil onto the roots of her hair. "You see, God created all things in all the universe. He saw good in all He created but He favored what He created in His own image; for man has the capacity to love. It caused confusion for some beings causing them to hate Humans because of God's favor. But what He favors He gifts. And we, my dear, are His gifts. You see, The King and I were created to protect man from things they couldn't understand because love is blind until it isn't. As you are aware, protecting the blind is hard. Back in our reigning days Jasir and I would sometimes grow tired, he more than I. You see, he too, just like you, had the gift of sight. No matter how many people we saved or how many of the p'irveli shekmna he killed, there was always more pain behind the pain. It's as if the blindness was in layers and demon works spread quicker than black mamba venom in human veins." She took a deep breath and recalled stories from inside her story, "Jasir could only see people by locking eyes with them. Their stories unraveled and weighed on him so bad he didn't really ever rest. Sometimes peace seemed impossible. To share in relief of his pain, I would grab this here Batana oil and massage his scalp. I loved nourishing his long locs. And as I would rub his scalp, I'd sing to him. I made up random songs but his favorite one was, 'And then there's The Light in you.' It reminded him that in the darkest of corners is where he was meant to exist because the light in him reflected His truth. But God heard Jasir's pain and then came the prophecy. We were dirt old and not human but god and goddess, how could we possibly reproduce? God, Himself spoke life into both me and Jasir. He made it so and we birthed reminders to the world that no matter what, He is with us always, until the end. And that Jasir, ohhhh...he was head over heels about his girls. His love for those triplets made every swing of His khopesh stronger and truer than any other reason before because...."

The tears from Hadiat's face flowed onto Aniah's head anointing her with answers and her eyes lit up in indigo flames. Meanwhile, the moon and sun shined bright, the elements rang out and the angels played their horns. An alignment of epic proportions radiated onto them both. Without force nor traditional announcement, an organic embrace was happening before everyone's eyes. No one was mad but the demons hiding in shadows. Aniah embraced Hadiat and began learning and truly accepting her worth.

"....he'd be damned before he let any demon or being in this world lay an undignified disgustingly dilapidated finger on his baby girls or his Queen." Hadiat's voice regaled a truth so strong that she was overcome with pride, gratification, and reciprocal worth. "He made that message loud and clear. Problem was the demons heard it all too well and they knew the only way to get to him was through me. Prophecy or not, I was never ready to lose my King."

As the Heavens rejoiced so did all who Believe. The line of Zoya was forever free. The Earth shook and loud shrieks from demons and dark creatures repulsed and skewed for they knew it was only but a matter of time before their end.

Aniah let out a sigh full of joy and understanding as a million stars danced in the flames of her eyes. She took deep breaths accepting all that Hadiat just bestowed upon her life. She wiped the tears from her face and grew full of eagerness; ready to win. "Why is it that no one ever gave him a proper burial?" Aniah asked.

"Well, Jasir was not only the reigning god King, he was king and commander and chief of the Guardians. A Guardian's purpose is to protect that which they love. They accused him of not protecting his family and found him unfit for a King's burial."

"Who is they?" Aniah turned sharply to Hadiat.

"The Mansa-ibn," Hasan interrupted. "They won't honor him because they deliberated and found his work unfinished."

"Why is it up to them? What right do they have to judge the King?" Aniah sat back in her seat to allow Hadiat to finish rebraiding her hair.

"My tribe is the lineage of earthly kings and justices. As such, they control the scales of right and wrong for matters concerning this realm and have for centuries. The Guardians and Mansa-Ibn tended to argue with one another all the time which often led to the Guardians completely ignoring my tribe and doing as they felt necessary instead. As you can imagine, the Mansa-Ibn took much offense but with all their wealth could do nothing to stop the Guardians and the god King. So when King Jasir fell, they took advantage of an opportunity to bury his name and refused to honor him just as he refused to honor them."

"Was King Jasir not their King as well?"

"Yes, he was. However, unlike his Guardians, they feared his reign but mocked his death."

"The King believed they were compromised by demon infiltration and refused to make decisions based on what he viewed as financial gain." Hathor quickly added, "to this day the Mansa-Ibn's decisions are questioned by many Believers."

"It is my goal to right this. I've made it my promise to my paternal ancestral lineage, Mansa Musa, and maternal ancestral lineage through Septimius Severus. I will clean up house."

"In the words of your wife, what are we waiting for?" Aniah waited for a response but Hasan had none to offer. "I say the next stop on our hajj is that we go to your tribe and demand respect for the King. You will have my support, katanas and these hands." She laughed.

"And my bow." Khailia stood.

"I'll pull the trigger for you any day baby!" Ebelle smiled while hugging him from behind.

"Then it is settled. To Rome we go." Hasan smiled as though he'd just earned the sweetest reward while kissing his wife's hand.

"First, we need to sleep." Nefertiti reentered the room. "Today has been a day of reflection. We should take a moment to understand God's delivery of these occurrences. Meditation, my dear, provides a chance to align, center yourselves, and build confidence. Now that you have embraced, Aniah, you should be able to see a great deal more, do you remember his eyes? You, you heard the King, Khailia. In between his words, what did he really say? Ebelle, in anger you fought him, what did you feel?"

"I felt his wrath and fury. I felt frustration and elusive contradictions. He doesn't know how to feel, he's hurting. And he does he want to feel it but it's the only feeling he knows anymore. The brain blisters puss and it's comforting to his heart. Poison blinded him and took other facilities of his consciousness, an inner demon." Ebelle gasped at how powerful her touch was becoming.

"Indeed, I heard his pain." Khailia couldn't hold back, "His voice is ill-fitted to the numbness of it all, therefore he yells and screams, unbefitting of his throne. I heard a struggle in his breaths. He isn't struggling to breathe, he's struggling to die. He wishes the bullet justified the end."

Aniah closed her eyes and tried to relive it. Her powers weren't as strong in the moment with the King but her gift of sight was rapidly growing to reveal the past, present, and future. "I see his eyes. He is afraid and ashamed. He kept searching and relied on the stars to show him the path but every time he made it back to this place, he grew sore. The stars confused him. Their design couldn't have been true otherwise he would've found you many years ago. That's what I see in his confusion. His eyes jaded with malice for the heavens because he kept losing his way recidivally. What should he do next? Where should he go now? Each time he became heavier. In a world that is his, what does he call home without his family? Too much, too big, too unnecessary without his Queen. The fable of young, daunted, darkening hues of fear spewed out in rabid rage for over a century. Yet in the darkness he reacquainted with light, within his own eyes he remembered the truth. He knows the prophecy to be real yet again. It is time for the Rise of the King." Aniah gasped as she opened her eyes surprised at how she spoke. It was as if she was self-possessed, revealing a truth she didn't know was buried within.

"You saw my Jasir on his throne?"

"No. I cannot see any of his future at all. Maybe I'm not strong enough yet. But I know we can never be us without making the world call out his name. And if that means I have to go through my brother in law's tribe to do it, I will. May God have mercy on them."

Melaine ran into the room holding her phone out, "Look! Someone caught you walking through the city streets fully armed and went live on social media. Ya'll went viral in seconds." She waved her phone around, "They're all speculating as to who we are. It's happening. It's being televised. They want to know who we are! Look at the comments! Look how many times its being shared! The lie is up!"

"The two worlds are starting to converge. All of this excitement is a lot. I need some tea if I'm ever going to sleep tonight." Khailia smiled, "I'm going across the street to the corner café. Aniah, Ebelle, will you join me?"

....

It was dark outside, but the sky is lit up with stars. No one was out in the streets understandably with all the rioting over land, background noise. No one was safe at night. The Heirs walked into the café escorted by the Amanirenians. "I wanted some space to speak to the two of you alone." Khailia ordered her tea and pulled out a chair at a table next to the café's front window. "Now that Aniah has embraced Hadiat there is only one more step needed to unite us. You two need to form fik-iri. What can I do to help?"

"Find another Heir!" Ebelle scoffed out while taking her seat.

"Oh, look! I found her!" Aniah faked enthusiasm as she revealed her middle finger to Ebelle. "You're welcome. Go ahead, embrace it, please!"

"The twerker is no sister of mine?"

"Why do you insist on calling me the twerker?"

"That's all you Afro-American women can do."

"Black American women are responsible for changing the landscape of the entire world. But I've never forgotten that it's in our blood. It's in our origin. Shore to shore we are powerful, beautiful, and majestic."

"You removed the word Afro and replaced it with Black. Still don't know your worth or where you came from? Not proud to be African descent?"

"Nah, that'd be you who doesn't understand my worth. Of African descent and damn proud of it. And it's you who doesn't want to claim me as belonging. Childlike score keeper using your fingers to keep count. Petty one, don't forget when you point at me, there are three more pointing right back at you, therefore you're three times as much as whatever you claim me to be. And most importantly, don't forget to carry the one!" Aniah flicked her off yet again and walked up to the counter to get Khailia's order.

As she walked away a man entered the café singing beautifully. His song was so sweet that Khailia's heart skipped a beat. She decided to join in and adlib for him as she didn't know the words. She smiled at him brightly and he returned her favor.

"Do you feel that?" He asked her, "what is that? What's happening to me?"

The adrenaline rush swept Khailia off her feet as she labeled him her King, "I think we're forming iji mesit 'eti. I feel it too. Quick, sing to me some more…" She was so caught up in the excitement of everything that she hadn't realized the surge of energy she felt was her discernment's warning.

He continued by making up his own lyrics which included his name, James. He sang about his search for a Queen coming to an end in that very moment, perfectly laying out everything Khailia needed to hear. He was careful not to let Ebelle touch him and even more careful not to let Aniah see his eyes. But as for his voice, he knew Khailia wouldn't detect the deception because she was too hooked on the lies. James was no king. James wasn't even James, he was Trigon. Trigon wasn't just any demon, he was one of the first fallen angels, a p'irveli shekmna. Since his heavenly role was once singing in God's choir, his voice was his easy way in as it held enormous power. He got away with uniting with Khailia undetected as long as the other heirs couldn't get next to him which fed into his plan to divide and conquer. Since a p'irveli shekmna can only be killed by a

Guardian, he knew he couldn't be harmed. He gently pulled Khailia away to another table while the Heirs and Amanirenians watched from their original seating.

Hadiat entered with Nefertiti and introduced themselves to him while asking a few questions. After a very small inquisition, Ebelle stood and welcomed him to the family content at Aniah being the fifth wheel. Before she could hug him, he quickly placed his arms around Khailia to show his hands as occupied. When she went in to hug them both, he made sure to adjust it so that the only person she touched was Khailia.

"What tribe are you from?" Aniah asked.

"I am Bulawayo-Nandi tribe, relocated to Angola."

"I've never heard of this tribe." Ebelle interceded, "Why is that?"

"Well," Seshet walked closer, "his tribe was disgraced a long time ago and the Believers amongst them scattered throughout the world to wash the shame. But it's okay, we will not judge him for the errors of his forefathers."

"I'm assuming you mean we were disgraced due to Shaka's violent acts while grieving the death of his beloved mother, my Queen, Queen Nandi?"

"That and much more." Nefertiti spoke calmly, "He's hoisted up high in history books, but one must read in between every line as to why that is. So we'll give James a break for now."

"Thank you." Trigon smiled as innocently as he could.

"Well, I guess it's time to plan the wedding!" Hadiat announced. "We can begin tomorrow. It's been a long day, I need rest."

"I would think the demons would be attacking us from left to right at every angle now. Shouldn't we leave right away?" Aniah had a terrible feeling take over her eyes and a headache began.

"I think demons fear those eyes of yours too much to try anything right away. We'll be fine for the night." Hadiat softly exited the café.

They all walked back together while Aniah followed from behind. Everyone was caught up in the excitement of another Heir finding her king except Aniah. She couldn't quite read him but she knew something was off and kept a close eye on him.

Ebelle smirked mistaking Aniah's watchful eye as jealousy. "Always the bridesmaid, never the bride. I guess I'm not the only one unable to find your worth." She continued pressing since it seemed she was being ignored. "Hope your king isn't American. Afro American men tend not to see worth in any of you, prefer to crown non-*Black* women, as you put it. Oh, maybe he likes the mixed-breed ones. That's how they excuse it, right?"

"We're all mixed with something. Are you done yet?" Aniah remained focused.

When they returned, Aniah got her blanket and went to the balcony where she watched over all while they sleep, especially her soon-to-be brother-in-law. But Trigon wasn't really asleep and could feel her eyes attempting to pierce through and didn't want to risk her seeing his. He thought about Tiago's warning of how strong she was when they faced off, wondering how strong she was now that she'd embraced her ancestor.

Chapter 14: Mansa-ibn

The sunrise in South Africa was one of the most beautiful views in the world. Birds with lilac breasts, others with red crests and rare falcons, spread their wings and flew out to perform their part in the world. Aniah watched the birds in awe of the freedom they experienced in simply knowing where they belonged. Contrarily, she also pondered about their freedom to choose anywhere to be versus their purpose in creation. Or was it one in the same? Aniah's sight was growing in so many ways. On one hand she was visiting a land filled with colors defined prior to her existence but summed up as non-existent in all her public school books. On the other hand, the respect she was gaining from her new reality gave her pride about the legendary tales of her ancestral lineage. Where she is was always meant for her but wasn't quite home. The disenfranchisement was heart breaking.

For now, trying to understand her sight would have to wait. Aniah had to ignore tourist attractions to watch everyone wake up and begin packing to prepare for their faze.

"Where are we going?" Trigon asked.

"To Rome." Hasan walked over and introduced himself. "I guess we're to be brothers-in-law soon. Glad to have you along this hajj."

"Why are we going to Rome?" Trigon's heart began to race. "Someone visiting some Etruscan family or something?"

"We're going to see my tribe, the Mansa-Ibn."

"Oh really, wonderful. I happen to know a few good people in that tribe." He tried to hide his mind calculating the best next steps.

"Oh yeah? Well, we're going to discuss the honor of King Jasir."

"He's never had a proper burial, talk about disgraced. Why are we going to discuss him?"

"Good morning, darling," Khailia leaned in for a kiss, "we're not going for a discussion. We're going to demand they honor him. It's imperative to our destinies that his name be written in history."

"He's been gone for so long. Do they even remember him?" Trigon was amused at their pridefulness.

"He's not gone. He emerged yesterday. We saw him with our own eyes." Khailia smiled on unaware of the intel she was delivering.

"Thee King? King of the Guardians....that King? King Jasir-Amare?" Trigon rubbed his palms together to soothe his anger, then folded his arms.

"My husband. I can't wait for him to meet you." Hadiat smiled and handed Trigon a duffle bag full of Khailia's gear.

His face dropped immediately. He did not plan for the dead King. He needed to think of ways around meeting him as he was the only one who could identify him. Trigon knew he needed to get Khailia away from her sisters and hand her over to Draisien for sacrifice but he'd have to move quick. "Are we getting married there?"

"We can talk about that once we get there. It's time to faze." Khailia grabbed him by the hand and kissed him gently on the cheek. "Aniah, we will faze to one of the seven hills of Rome, the earliest one, the Palatine Hill to be exact. Are you familiar?"

"Yes." She held her hands out and ZaQuaysia and Melaine grabbed her hands to prepare for fazing. She left immediately so that she could see how Trigon reacted to the faze when he appeared. Watching him faze in with Khailia, her thought was right. He wasn't shook one bit. No disorientation whatsoever. She remembered how she felt the first few times and knew there was no way he should just walk away from it. When Hasan and Ebelle arrived, Hasan struggled to find balance. Aniah also knew Khailia was smitten under Trigon's spell. She feared being misunderstood so she kept her suspicions about Trigon to herself.

"Hadiat, are the Mansa-ibn enemies of the throne?" Aniah inquired trying to scratch up reactions for Trigon.

"No. They are supposed to be the balance to the kingdom. Jasir and I ruled, but that didn't mean we were deaf to the concerns of Believers. In those days, there were many. There was no way we would have time to hear them all. So the Mansa-ibns took on the task of being great leaders for all Believers."

"Why do you say 'supposed'?"

"The Mansa-Ibn were infiltrated by demons long ago, in particular, a p'irveli shekmna by the name of Draisien."

"Draisien...Draisien, why does his name sound so familiar?"

"I'm not sure, to my recollection, you've never seen him. If you did, you would remember."

"How did he infiltrate them?"

"By plaguing the minds of Believers with greed. Their greed led them to become decadent demon pawns. As such, they could move about freely and deliver intel to real demons almost without notice. The pawns are necessary because they can enter places demons cannot."

"Such as..."

"Neither P'irveli shekmna nor demons can enter The Hall of Kings, Aganjú – Olókun Passage, Queen's Cove, nor The Vatican. But for many years their spies or pawns have relayed messages to them. The Hall of Kings has never been supplanted. And though many have tried, neither has the Aganjú – Olókun Passage."

"Hadiat, what is a p'irveli shekmna?"

"A p'irveli shekmna is rare. They are the army of original fallen angels. Never forget that they were His first creations. They may have lost grace, but they possess great power, nonetheless. They chose to leave Heaven and place themselves as gods of men. They are highly skilled, extremely dangerous, very powerful, and hard to track. Currently, they pose the biggest threat to you as they can only be killed by a Guardian and we have no idea where the Guardians are or if they even exist anymore. Years ago, intel reported there are only three p'irveli shekmna left: Draisien, Trigon and Tien."

"That's not true." Aniah stopped mid-step.

"What?" Ebelle turned and headed toward Aniah, confused by her challenge to Hadiat's words. "How would you know? You're only just now learning what a p'irveli shekmna is."

"I saw it. Tiago is no regular demon. He is the most powerful p'irveli shekmna amongst the remaining. And I wouldn't be so sure about there only being four left. And Draisien, he's..."

"What are you talking about Aniah?" Hadiat approached with aggression placing her hands on her hips and squinting her eyes, "We've chased after them and hunted p'irveli shekmna for centuries. I think I'd know a p'irveli shekmna when I saw him."

"Only King Jasir and the Guardians could sense them, correct?"

"That is true." Hadiat backed away. "He led, we followed."

"Did the King ever meet Tiago or Draisien? Did he ever see any of the remaining?"

"No." Hadiat leaned to one side and crossed her arms. "Can you sense them?"

"I don't know. Maybe. I read it in Tiago's eyes. His story is different."

"We have intel? What else has intel told us?" Trigon's perpetration was at risk. He needed to know for how much longer. "Who is our intel?" He was careful to choose the power of inclusive words as mesmerizing spells.

"Just as they have their pawns, we too have our own ways. Some of God's bravest soldiers have penetrated their system. It has many weak points, the foundation is so fragmented." Hadiat smiled arrogantly.

"Well, where are these p'irveli shekmna? Can't we trap them until the Guardians return?" Trigon paced slowly, careful to dodge their gifts.

"We don't know where they are nor what they look like." Hadiat turned to Trigon and gave him her full attention.

"What about their pawns, have you identified them?"

"No. It's not easy. The one's we know of, we only know about after they've made mistakes, when they were caught in the act of espionage."

Walking the ruins of the Palatine Hill, Hasan watched Aniah's concern for how comfortable 'James' was getting with the throne. He too noticed how careful he was at dodging the Heirs' gifts and how easily he included himself as a part of the family. After kissing Ebelle's hand gently as she continued listening to the pretender, Hasan slowly drifted toward the back where Aniah watched over everyone.

"What do you see?" Hasan cut straight to the chase, "I'm not as won over either."

Aniah didn't trust Hasan much either as he was the husband of the sister who hated her. For all she knew, he was gathering information against her for pillow talks and conspiracy. She stared at him thinking, what man would proudly stand up against his own tribe to declare their 'enemy' as honorable.

"Read my eyes if you must..." Hasan didn't want to draw attention to their conversation so he relaxed his shoulders and took a step back. After he noticed he didn't have her trust either, he returned to the front of the line. "This way. My home is just through here."

"Do they know we're here?" Ebelle grew flirtatiously curious and added a playful skip to her walk, "I can't wait to meet your people."

"They've been following us throughout streets." Aniah mentioned without looking around. "We've all been so entertained by James, I didn't want to interrupt his and Hadiat's stories. All so interesting." She stared directly at the back of Trigon's head as she began to understand more and more why he refused to look her way.

"What's eating her?" Ebelle smiled and walked over to Khailia as she tried to figure out what was happening. "See, you and I weren't raised to be jealous. The reason her jealousy shocks you is because you think she's your beloved sister spewing envy, something we never did to each other. So this time, the jealousy is more of a betrayal. The treachery is real, watch your back."

Seshet and Hathor noted the conversation between the two and decided to stay close by them. Nefertiti also noticed the discord but wasn't ready to count Aniah out.

"Ladies and gentleman, we are here. Welcome to my home, Domus Severiana." He held his hands high in the air in excitement while everyone else only looked upon the ruins. "Oh, in my excitement I forgot, you cannot see what I do not reveal." He stepped ahead of everyone and due to his distrust for James he whispered 'truth in justice' in the ancient Mansa-ibn tongue. An entire scene fell twinkling before them, a modern-day version of ancient Etruscan Rome. The city streets were filled with his tribe people carrying on in everyday life until they noticed the Heirs. Footsteps slowed down and mouths hung open at the sight of the royal family. Hasan ushered everyone up the stairs and through the garden straight into the dynastic home of the line of Severus. High arching pillars stood at least four stories firmly arching over the entrance way into Hasan's home.

"Won't the tourists see us?" Aniah was shocked at the beauty and history of it all. She walked among the pillars taking in the bronze and marble engravings in the stones.

"Not unless they are Believers. These tourists believe in the Ancient Rome Hollywood sells them. Only a Believer can see what I reveal." Servants ran out to greet them with fresh flowers and water. They heard all the noise regarding the arrival of the Heirs and couldn't wait to see for themselves.

They greeted and hugged Ebelle welcoming their new Queen home. Ebelle nourished herself in their outpour of admiration and looked over her shoulder at every chance to see if Aniah was watching.

Aniah was more interested in the people. She walked around in close surrounding of Khailia, looking people in the eyes to learn their stories while trying to catch a reflection of Trigon's through theirs.

The interrogation of her eyes burned the back of Trigon's neck so much that he was having troubles keeping his hyena face hidden. However, he kept himself together for the charade.

"Pardon my maids, they still can't believe I married an Heir. No one saw this coming." Hasan approached Aniah when he spotted her away from everyone else, as she watched everyone from a corner in the room.

"No pardon necessary. So this is where you live?"

"Something like that." He smiled, "more like, this is where I keep up a public image. My family is one full of plots and twists. Please, come with me, let me show you."

Aniah stopped watching the room and focused her attention on Hasan's eyes. She looked into them and saw pure genuine truth. She saw how Hasan had immersed himself in his family's business with the goal of restoring the realm of Believers to their once beloved glory.

As she walked by, Seshet noticed their departure and drew Ebelle's attention closer to them. She'd always warned Ebelle of the succubus habits of American women and to always protect her king even when he was being misguided. However, Ebelle didn't believe neither were so bold at that time, so she didn't follow but simply took note.

Hasan guided Aniah to the center of the grounds where there was a garden with a fountain in the middle. Around the garden were several bronze statues. The columns surrounded old paintings describing his family's story. "That statue there, that is my super great grandfather, Septimius Severus. The real statue, not that marble crap demons concocted after his death. This one shows his real features. His real lips, nose and wild hair that looked like wool. Have you ever heard of him?"

"Yes, one of Rome's more famous emperors. Known for the power he invested in his military. His expansion of Rome came at a bloody cost."

"Why, yes. That was him. Ambitious in many ways, including the expansion of his throne, but even more ambitious in proving the worth of his skin. Having been Libyan, he gained the love of so many Africans and his soldiers. However, he lacked the noble acceptance of his European peers, due to the color of his skin. The weight of it all drove him to deny his own and led to the fall of the Roman empire."

"What do you mean?"

"Prior to marrying Julia who was the wife he's more known for having, he was married to a beautiful Libyan woman, named Paccia Marciana, her skin reminds me of Ebelle's. She and Septimius were very much in love. Known far and wide for her intellect, grace, and unmatched beauty, Paccia was a jewel fit only for his crown...and she honored that. All the Africans honored it as well, but the Roman politicians did not. In those days, Rome was a melting pot of people from many nations, but the firsts here were Africans. Unfortunately, chocolate popularity was dwindling due to decadent behavior and residents nor immigrants wanted to recognize Africans as royal in Roman society. While it is written that

Paccia died of natural causes, she did but in old age. History books tell one story, but the truth is she understood that Severus would never be completely happy unless he took his rightful place on the throne. Paccia felt like she was holding him back and loved him too much for that. So she packed up their daughters and left her home. But their one year old son, Lucius Septimius Bassianu, Septimius promised would one day rule as Emperor by his side for her sacrifice. So then he married Julia of Syrian descent and she adopted Lucius and aided in changing his name to Antoninus, which was done to align Septimius to his real father, Marcus Aurelius. Julia's aesthetics were more accepted in the ever-changing Roman climate and helped him climb social ranks all the way to the throne. However, she favored her's and Septimius' son Geta over Antonius and a bitterness grew. She treated Antonius less favorably. To put it lightly, she pitted the two brothers against each other. Imagine Antoninus' anger when he later grew up and after years of taking her abuse, he found out that Julia was not his mother at all. Arkhh matter wasn't necessary in this case for enslaving one's mind. Septimius died mysteriously and Geta was murdered by Antonius who later changed his name to Caracalla. While Caracalla was a great military leader, he was plagued by his father's curse, the need to prove his skin's worth. If only he knew, the world already knew."

"You come from a disjointed family as well."

"Yes. In this moment, allow me to tell why this story is so important."

"I'm listening."

"Septimius' closest friend was King Jasir in the days when Mansa Ibn and Guardians were one. The Guardian King encouraged that Septimius' blood was already royal and he had nothing to prove. You see, although Septimius was raised by an equestrian, his real father was Emperor Marcus Aurelius, no pardon was ever necessary. Seeking to validate his skin which was already legitimate would only bring corruption to his legacy. That was Jasir's warning. Septimius mistook this as everything but the truth and began to poison the Mansa-ibn against the Guardians, thus came the demise of the relationship between both sides. Divide and conquer, huh?"

Aniah understood where he was going and trusted her vision of his purity. "I guess when old folks back home used to fashion God as a comedian, they had you and Ebelle in mind. Ancient Etruscan marriages are more about uniting families than anything else. Your marriage realigns King Jasir and Septimius' friendship. Good thing ya'll were meant to be, otherwise it'd be a loveless union."

"History is repeating itself and we must not fail a test we already know the answer to. We simply need to show our work. I know you see something just like King Jasir saw Septimius' fall. Unlike my ancestor, I believe your sight is true. James' movements are very similar to corrupted peoples within the tribe. I know their motives all too well. I am not betraying my wife by protecting the Kingdom of God, however, she is jaded against you...something else I'm looking into. I will right Septimius' wrong with your help. You have my word, anything you need me to do to prove what you have seen, I will do."

"I can't see anything, he won't allow me to look into his eyes. He dodges my eyes however possible he can. He also dodges Ebelle's touch. That is all I have seen thus far."

"You have King Jasir's eyes, use them. We will not allow God's Kingdom to fall ever again." Hasan could hear Ebelle's voice approaching, "please, follow my lead for now. We have to play into this madness until it's time to show the truth." He looked Aniah directly in the eyes to keep her trust and yelled, "you will honor your throne and get your shit together! The fate of the crown depends on it. Humble yourself and take heed to my wife's words. Now ready yourself for The Vatican. Surely you don't intend to represent the throne looking like that." He pretended to be startled by Ebelle's presence, "oh, hello you. Well, do you like what you have seen?" He was careful not to touch Ebelle otherwise she'd pick up on the farse act.

"Everything is beautiful! I am so honored to have such a strong righteous man as my King." She relished in what she perceived to be Aniah's disgrace.

"Excuse me." Aniah ran out the room dramatically, throwing secret shade at Ebelle's ignorance.

On her way out, she ran past Khailia who was entering the room with Seshet and Hathor. Khailia sensed the insincerity of Aniah's cry immediately and began to wonder what the true commotion was all about. While Hasan continued speaking to Ebelle about the garden, she heard a lie in him. At first she thought, 'Could Aniah be attempting to seduce Hasan to spite Ebelle?'

Demonic confusion continued to cloud the minds of two heirs. Trigon didn't need a gift to understand the separation occurring. He took it as his queue. "So, the two couples, no fifth wheel, eh?" He joined Ebelle and Hasan in a short laughter. "Maybe this will allow us some time to discuss how to deal with the elephant in the room?"

"I'm glad you brought it up. I knew it wasn't just me seeing her jealous nature." Ebelle's conspiracy against herself pierced her husband in the heart, but she was too broken to notice. "Khailia, don't let that charlatan steal your joy."

Khailia felt uneasy with the conversation, "My joy was gifted by God, therefore no one can take it away. It is part of my birthright."

"So, we're going to The Vatican, huh?" Trigon knew he could not pass the city's walls. There was a strong hold over it. He got closer to Khailia and embraced her hips as he whispered in her ear, "I was thinking maybe we could stay behind and plan for our wedding. What do you think?"

"I'm sure my sisters won't need me." Her smile placed warmly across her face as she stepped closer into his arms.

"What was that?" Hasan quickly interrupted, "I hate to be the bearer of bad news, the Mansa-ibn will only receive all three at the same time. Khailia, you must be there. James, you're coming into the family at a wonderous time. The Heirs at The Vatican, there's a stirring in the air already. Sis, can't you hear them? Can't you hear my tribe making way for you? What are they saying?" Hasan wanted her to wake up from his spell and use her gift.

Khailia tried to meditate but it was as if she forgot how to 'ride her own bike.' Trigon was still in her ear laying out a happily ever after story.

"Heirs, please follow my house maids to your rooms. They will help you get dressed. I need to get to my room, my barber is waiting. James, feel free to join me." Hasan understood the need to be overly insistent and so he continued to push against the unseen danger of Trigon.

"Actually, I have a few things I need to get in order. I'm going to have to pass up your offer." His cunning grin didn't escape Hasan one bit. Trigon kissed Khailia on the cheek and walked away toward the front entrance. He took a seat on a set of stairs to the side of the grande entrance and began plotting how to kidnap Khailia.

Chapter 15: Growing Pains

Khailia and Ebelle followed the women to their rooms. Once there, they were overcome with hospitality. The best foods were lined out on a buffet table in the middle of the room with grapes and olives stacked high in the middle. The finest of clothes were on racks neatly hung for their choosing. Hair dressers and makeup teams were assembled to help them get ready.

Meanwhile, Aniah searched for a place to meditate. Hasan's words about having the King's eyes resonated with her and she desperately needed to know what that meant. His confirmation of Queen Hadiat's words couldn't scream any louder. Yet everywhere she looked for a quiet space, there was someone there, watching her, taking photos or offering something. Nefertiti walked by and winked at her in passing and that was when it hit her. Nefertiti spoke about having to operate while all eyes were on her, the mission was always to be present no matter the environment. She knew there could be no plan. She'd have to move under the veil of God to separate Holy from unholy. Aniah paced the hallways staring at the paintings. She focused on the painting that told the story of King Jasir and Septimius' falling out.

"Your majesty, please follow me. Your sisters are waiting for you." The servant lowered her head while she spoke to Aniah.

"Well hello to you too." Aniah smiled and lowered her head too, trying to find the girl's eyes. "You know, you can look at me. I won't be offended."

"I wouldn't dare. I am a servant of this house, unworthy of your presence. I'm shaking just speaking to you."

"What is your name?"

"My name is Abiya."

"Abiya, I'm told my very existence is to solidify your safety in order for you to carry out God's purpose for you. Therefore, it is I who serve you. I'd be honored if you let me read your eyes."

Abiya smiled. In her mind, she wasn't anyone special. Coming from a line of maids and butlers, she was raised to respect nobility, never thought things would be the other way around. She lifted her head and giggled nervously as she offered Aniah her eyes.

Aniah read her and smiled. "Don't worry about naysayers. Now is the time for realities in dreams. You've prayed and remained faithful. I see it in you, your mother and grandmother. All of your stories are so beautiful. You really want to be a teacher and you should do it. You can't be afraid to break every boundary and tell truths the world buried under dust. I wish I had a teacher like the one you're meant to be."

"You see my mother and grandmother?"

"Yes, I see all the prayers they poured into you. All their wildest dreams, with their very last breaths they whispered fulfillment into the air that surrounded you. I see your dad too. He's stern and very traditional and prideful. But mostly, he's proud about you."

"My dad? He barely notices my existence. Since my mother passed, he's rarely spoken to me."

"He sees so much of her in you and it hurts him because he really misses her. He pushes you away to atone for smothering your mother into accepting his plans for her and not God's. He realizes his mistake and doesn't want you to suffer the same, but he wants you to stay at the same time. He's not pushing you away, he's bracing himself for the day you leave the nest. It's a type of love he's never expressed and doesn't quite know how to."

Abiya smiled so hard her face reversed in time as her own tears cleansed her heart. She turned to hug Aniah but hesitated because of who she was.

"Hey now, wait a minute. I need all the hugs I can get." She laughed to drown out the truth, "bring it in!"

Abiya hugged Aniah tightly. All her years of begging God to give her a sign and He showed up in the most magnificent way. "Thank you." Abiya released Aniah but her smile stayed as she gently stepped back while holding her hand out and trying to wipe away her tears. She ushered Aniah into the room where her sisters were being pampered.

Aniah didn't engage them in conversation for fear of a worsening divide. Instead, she invited Abiya in as her guest and she listened to her talk about her love of education and children. As she listened, an epiphany occurred, her sight didn't exist solely in the eyes she sees, but as mirrors into every person's network. Her eyes not only bend light, they bend time as well; Aniah could see reflection's of other people's eyes through the eyes in front of her. She could see stories from centuries ago as if she were there. It was all happening so fast that Aniah's heart began so race into a panic.

"Aniah...Aniah...what is it?" Hadiat noticed Aniah's panic and raced to her side. She turned to Abiya, "please, bring water." She rubbed Aniah's arm vigorously trying to pull her back from. "Speak to me, what do you see?"

"I can't see. It's all a blur. I can't see anything. I don't know what I see? My head! It hurts!" Aniah's head turned from side to side hoping to see anything.

"Hear me, calm yourself and breathe. You are one with your gift. It doesn't control you and you don't control it, understand? Steady your heart and come back to my voice."

Nefertiti ran over and placed her hand on Aniah's shoulder, "It's alright young Heir. It's alright."

Aniah's panic slowly reduced and her breathing returned to normal. Her vision came back as she looked around and became embarrassed.

"It's your gift. It's growing and maturing in you. It's supposed to happen dear. Don't be afraid." Nefertiti nodded at her, "One step at a time. You can do it. Although they were much younger when it happened to them, your sisters went through this too."

"True, but we never got this type of gentleness with our gifts. You need the attention, huh? Had to grasp on any moment you could get selfish." Ebelle rolled her eyes and continued talking to Khailia about her wedding plans.

"Oh, no you don't." Nefertiti put her hands up to stop Aniah who was heading toward the balcony. "No more retreats. Face it with grace and dignity."

Aniah sat back down and motioned for Abiya to continue speaking while she finished getting her hair done. She wanted to leave to stop herself from fighting Ebelle yet again but she remained and endured her criticism and mockery.

When they finished dressing, they were escorted downstairs to the front entrance where Hasan and Trigon waited for them. As they doted over their women's beauty, Ebelle continued her glaring harassment of Aniah.

Hasan had already assembled a convoy to escort them to the Vatican and as they rode, the Heirs looked outside at the gathering crowd of people trying to catch a glimpse of them. Ebelle, Khailia and Aniah took in the sights of ancient Rome much differently than in South Africa. This time they were separated by singles and couples. Aniah sat in her back seat refusing to look in Ebelle's direction due to the endless nitpicking and catty words. Khailia rested on Trigon's arm with her guard completely down. What should have been a five minute drive, took twenty. And the closer they got to The Vatican the harder it was for Trigon to keep his composure as the blessed grounds would eventually force him to reveal himself.

"Wait, this isn't The Vatican. Where are we?" Aniah didn't understand.

"This is the inspiration behind the Vatican therefore we Believers call it the real Vatican. There are some that would argue the Lateran palace is, but only if you fall for the misconceptions of history. While others refer to this place as The Archbasilica, it is the highest-ranking basilica, originally founded by Septimius. Septimius laid foundation to the land before the Archbasilica was ever thought of. Underneath the surface is where you will find the truth. Blindness will lead you to believe this was a mere post for his calvary. However, Septimius built it to honor Calvary, true soldiers of our world. Believers were here long before Constantine who tried to wipe out the truth long before Napoleon. Centuries and centuries worth of pawns have always tried to distance Believers from themselves."

Trigon began coughing and panting for air, "Pull over, I think I'm going to be sick." Just as the Vatican City walls are impenetrable for him, so were the Archbasilica's gates, Castra Nova. In fact, Castra Nova's protection against evil was so strong that the nearness nearly drove him mad. The SUV pulled over and Trigon ran out. Khailia followed him trying to comfort him by attempting to rub his back. Passersby stopped to see what the commotion was all about then screamed out when they saw it. Trigon's charade was up, his Hyena face revealed.

"A p'irveli shekmna? Kishi demon?!" Hadiat screamed in disbelief. "How did he get so close?"

Aniah noticed some of the witnesses seeming to sneak away and caught their eyes. Her sight jumped from reflection to reflection until she found him. "Trigon!" She didn't have enough time to pull out her katanas so she grabbed Ebelle's dagger from her waist, rushed out the SUV and ran to help her sister. Aniah made it to Trigon right as he opened his mouth to clamp down on Khailia's head. She reached in his mouth and held it open. In her hurry, his long and powerful canine pierced her left hand all the way through. Her right hand held the dagger piercing his serpent like tongue.

Hasan ran over to snatch Khailia out the way. She was still in a trance while Ebelle pulled out her pistols and began firing on Trigon as the Amanirenians closed in.

Trigon tried to clamp down on Aniah who screamed out so loud it woke Khailia from her trance as she fell to her knees fearing the worse was her fault.

Trigon had no time left as Melaine and Grace reached him. He let go and flew away but not before Aniah yanked his tooth out.

"Quick, get her inside!" Hasan motioned the guards to assist Aniah while he and Ebelle helped Khailia to her feet to run inside. Next, in Ge'ez language, he spoke "Verily, verily, I say unto you, He that believeth on me, the works that I do shall he do also." Right before their eyes, the original House of the Lord in Rome appeared as they ran through the gates.

Aniah wanted to cry out in pain but she wouldn't dare guilt Khailia any further. Instead, she forced a smile. "I have a gift for you." She held out Trigon's tooth, "I am my sister's keeper."

"Oh Aniah, I'm so sorry! How could I let this happen to you?" Khailia knelt down with her sister in pain. "Why did this happen to you?"

Aniah saw Khailia's heart breaking not only for her pain but for love lost. She knew Khailia honestly believed she was in love, a distrust of self-tried to plant itself within her sister's heart. Aniah would have none of that. "This is not your fault." Aniah searched for Khailia's eyes, "You did not do this to me. You would never intentionally hurt me and I know this, remember?"

Khailia thought back to their discussion in Queen Nefertiti's home. Aniah never doubted Khailia's heart. She ripped the sleeves off her dress and wrapped Aniah's hand while praying for forgiveness and healing.

"I know it hurts." Aniah grabbed Khailia's face with her other hand. "We'll get through this together, I promise. But right now, my patience is wearing thin and we got shit to do." She winked at Khailia, "remember why we're here."

Neither Hadiat, the T'Malaks, nor the Amanirenians had ever imagined a bond so great. Both sisters were trying to comfort each other's pain as if their own didn't exist. Khailia and Aniah stood to their feet straightening each other's hair and clothes. Aniah nodded toward Hadiat after Melaine handed her her katanas and everyone slowly walked inside, staring back at the eyes staring at them. People lined the hallways and held out their cell phone cameras recording the group's procession to The Scales of Mercy Tribunal Courtroom. Whisperings of "its them," "they're real", "it's Queen Hadiat," "Queen Nefertiti and the Amanirenians," and "where have they been?" could be heard. Priceless artifacts of Mansa Musa's surrounded them as were stories of the Mansa-ibn tribe painted all over the walls.

Hasan stepped toward the front of the line and held everyone up for a moment. "No one from the Throne of God has entered these doors in over a century. While all knew this day would come, none ever expected it to actually happen. Not one King or Queen that holds a seat is missing today. They all came as soon as they heard word of your arrival to my home. When they realize, if they haven't already, that you've come to restore King Jasir's honor, much will be revealed to you. Stay focused and remember that you are the means to an end." He opened the doors and slowly escorted the Heirs down a long set of stairs surrounded by royalty, nobles and generals.

The presence of the Heirs rang so true that a handful of demon pawns excused themselves immediately and left the city. The Heirs made it front and center and waited for the loud whispers and seat shuffling to settle.

"Queen Hadiat. We heard of your death. Our condolences." A man at the front of the room sitting on what mimicked a throne spoke up. He stood from his seat and his necklaces wrestled against his sashes.

"Kwasi." She replied showing him no honor as a King.

"The much-anticipated Heirs to The Throne of God." He smiled at them while glancing them over. "Please, introduce yourselves to the court."

"I am Khailia, Heiress to the line of Aida."

"Khailia, is it? Welcome. You're as beautiful as your mother once was." He turned his nose up to Hadiat, "keeping company with demons too, huh? What's the saying about an apple...?"

Khailia dropped her head in shame which visibly angered Aniah as she lowered her chin ready to charge forward like an angry bull. Khailia held her hand out in front of Aniah to stop her from defending an honor she no longer felt worthy of.

The underhanded comment didn't shake Ebelle one bit, she chose to remain focused. "I am Ebelle, Heiress to the line of Liya, your honor."

"I see. And also the wife of one of ours, Hasan here. Congrats to you both. Hasan was engaged to marry my daughter. I guess he chose otherwise. She'll be happy to know why."

"King Kwasi, I am not here to discuss matters of marital status." Ebelle continued, "I am here to ask you and your tribe to honor King Jasir Amare in death."

An uproar swept the room as people stood to their feet outraged that his name was spoken in their midst.

"Quiet!" He slammed his gavel on his desk, "We don't say that name here and neither will you. Now, stand to the side, I want to see the final Heiress. The one no one could find."

"How did you know no one could find me?" Aniah read his eyes before she took her first step.

"What do you mean? Whispers everywhere about your absence swept over all believers."

"Whispers or intel?"

"Are you accusing me of treason?" King Kwasi's head turned as he slowly stood to his feet in a manner meant to threaten Aniah.

Aniah drew a katana with her good hand. "My hand hurts too bad to play with you right now. I'm not about to entertain you nor your bs.... your soul has the sold sign of Tiago written all over it. So, I'm going to say this one time and I mean... one time only. This is every single demon pawn, friend, sympathizers last chance to leave my presence. I will not count down and this is as pleasant I'm going to be about it. Amanirenians, ilum."

The Amanirenians drew their weapons, as did Khailia and Ebelle. Aniah wasted no further time approaching the so called King Kwasi while other demon pawns evacuated immediately. The conviction and determination in her eyes let everyone know of her sincerity.

Angered at his ousting, Kwasi dared not approach the Heir as he was no match for her. "I'll see you soon. We'll have our day, this isn't over at all."

Before another word could be uttered from his mouth, a loud burst of lightning shook the grounds and caused all the stained glass windows to break. Aniah smiled because she knew the world was getting ready to witness the worth of a daddy's girl. A strong wind swirled around the room that only the pure-hearted believers understood. King Kwesi tried to escape but was blocked off by a forming wind. It walked toward him like the world was on fire. The legs took shape, then the torso, chest, arms and face. King Jasir returned!

"You dare threaten my child!?" Lightning and fire flared out King Jasir's eyes.

"You have no power here!" Kwesi shouted in his face.

The King wasted no time in picking Kwesi up by his throat with one hand and crushing his neck until the bones cracked and eventually snapped. He opened his fingers and released Kwesi's lifeless body. He made sure to give that moment all he could so that all watching understood his power still held true.

However, Aniah saw that it drained the King to take that course of action but didn't want to reveal his weakness to everyone else. She sped things up a bit so that they could get back and rest, "I believe the reason for not properly burying your King was due to not protecting his family, right?" Aniah addressed the remaining of the tribunal.

"I speak for everyone when I say that ruling is overturned." Hasan stood tall as others from his tribe gathered behind him in support. He extended his hand to receive the King in the same custom as his family once did in a more loving time.

"You belong to Septimius." The King read Hasan while walking closer, "Septimius and Mansa Musa, eh. Your great uncle Mansa Abu Bakr II was a great friend of mine. Septimius, however, was once more of a brother to me. Your blood, blessed twice by royalty. How extraordinary."

"Please, allow my tribe the honor of providing you a proper burial."

"How can you bury me if my body never remained?" King Jasir smiled and tilted his head waiting for Hasan's reply.

"Good question. Well then, please allow me the honor of preparing a celebration in honor of your name, as it shall forever remain."

King Jasir turned to his Heiresses for their vote. They smiled with tears of joy. He then looked to his beloved wife and she too nodded in agreement. "I'd be elated. You and I have much to talk about. You married an Heir without my permission."

Chapter 16: Tested Love

Hasan sweated bullets the entire walk back to Palatine Hill while having a deep discussion with King Jasir regarding legacy, politics and Ebelle. Meanwhile, Ebelle rested comfortably under Queen Hadiat and Seshet's embrace. Aniah continued pouring love out onto Khailia, trying to convince her that everything would be alright as the Amanirenians, Hathor and Nefertiti kept watch.

The procession reminded Queen Hadiat of the old days when people came from far and wide to see her and the King. She remembered the flowers and gifts bestowed upon them from people showing their appreciation of the throne. However, that day people lined the streets with cell phones, recording them and speaking to audiences near and far. When they finally returned to the house of Septimius, they received a warm welcome. This was the first time in centuries anyone had witnessed the entire family unit together.

King Jasir walked around reliving days long past in shared memories with his wife. Everyone noticed their need for a moment and left the two alone. The King was grateful for their understanding. He slowed his steps and pulled Hadiat into him so they could be face to face.

"I'm so sorry Jasir. All this time and I…" Hadiat lowered her shoulders, opened her chest and revealed her bleeding heart in remorse.

"Sorry for what?" He lifted her chin and lovingly read her eyes for the first time in centuries.

"You died protecting me and I could've just killed those men. I wasted time and squandered my gift and it cost you your life. It cost us our lives."

"My sweet Sarai, you owe me no apologies. I came from out of the bushes like a mad man. I lacked discipline and rationale…just fear. I knew better than that. I am sorry for not protecting you better."

"It's not your fault."

"You know, for so long I blamed myself. Then I blamed God…then back to myself. The anger in me caused so much confusion. I was so lost and I just wanted to start over. For over a century, I thought out what a second chance would look like. I begged for anything but the present. Either take me back or push me to the good part." Laughter pushed its way through King Jasir's pain, "seeing you again, knowing all you've endured and how you've held it all together, sometimes hoping for hope…you're so beautiful. I thank God it's always been you and it will always be you. Everything is you. The most precious gift I could have ever received, my Hadiat."

She rested her head on his chest and wept as they exchanged what energy they had left. It was more than plenty to sustain them for what still remained.

King Jasir held her face against his beating heart while lightly massaging the side of his thumb against her temple. He kissed her forehead and continued, "And the girls, we just knew that we knew what we knew. God has His ways and I see it now. I spoke with the Kurati tribe before I came here. It's been hard for all who believe, but the restoration is near. We shall receive everything we lost and so much more."

"You went to The Kurati? How are they? What news do they have? Has Simeon seen Him? Spoken to Him?" Hadiat tilted her head and stared into her king's eyes lovingly.

"Hadiat, some things never change." He kissed her hand and guided her to the dining hall where everyone was waiting for them, "Soon, my dear, very soon. I'll tell you everything." King Jasir nodded at the servants holding the doors wide open for them, then he nodded again at a nervous Hasan who was standing at attention awaiting the King.

"Please, King Jasir, please have my seat at the head of the table." Hasan opened his arms out wide.

"Thank you, son. But please, take your own seat as it is your time now. Besides, I want to sit as close to Hadiat as possible." He looked around the table at everyone and whispered for God to be his voice. "The day I lost my babies I was planning a large birthday event in my head for my triplets' sixteenth and I was saving their gifts in my thoughts as though I was promised those years. They weren't even close to sixteen." He walked around the table to an open seat and pulled out a chair for Hadiat. "The other day when I saw you and the Heirs near the river, I couldn't make out whether I needed space for pain or joy. I came to the conclusion that it's okay to feel both at the same time. All the years I spent sowing and protecting have come to this. A lifetime spent thinking of ways to celebrate my girls only to realize He rewarded me the blessings of His gifts, and I'm grateful."

Hasan motioned for dinner to be served as he kissed his wife's hand. One heart from that table was enough to rekindle a million lights.

Although Khailia's own heart was heavy, there would be no deterring of their purpose and Aniah made sure to remind her.

"Do you hear the vibes in the streets? You remember the little girl who brought us flowers when we first arrived? Look, over there. She's wearing her hair like yours now, even dressing like you. I see she's found her superhero and favorite path to follow." Aniah leaned her shoulder into Khailia's arm.

"I loved a first demon. A damn P'irveli shekmna! I can hear the men whispering and social media slanderings about how I soiled my virtue and essence. I'll probably be an old woman by the time love finds me now. Maybe some man with a load as heavy as mine is all I'm fit for now....If I'm even worth that."

Aniah turned to face Khailia eye to eye, "You know sis, the one thing God keeps showing me over and over, Hadiat's lifetime and ours, is that His ways are not man's. For all you know, your King is much closer than you think. And I'm willing to bet my life that the miserable barking of the bitch-ass walking dead semi-believers aren't enough to keep Him from hearing you and blessing you beyond what you could ever conceive. As great as your purpose is, He means for you to prosper. He desires for you to win. And I'm here to make sure nothing stops you from all your destined to have and become."

"Ah, He desires that *we* win!" Nefertiti whispered her joy into their conversation. "Give me your hand Aniah, let me see it. And stop cursing or I'll shove soap down your mouth, hear me?" Nefertiti took a bite of her food then held her hand out waiting for Aniah's.

"People are eating, can't we wait." Aniah tried to keep her hand from Nefertiti who ignored her and grabbed her hand from underneath the table.

"ZaQuaysia found some powerful seeds. We prayed over them and Melaine made them into a gel. I'll plant them right here and they'll help reconnect your roots. This hand will bear fruit in no time." Nefertiti gripped Aniah's hand as she twitched a few times from the pain. Without looking up she could sense Khailia, "and you, no one lesson sums up your existence. How could someone created from love, in order to protect love, not be meant to love? You are to be loved. It's in His will. Chin up! Make it easier for your King to find you."

Hadiat noticed the entire exchange but never made any strong movements about her awareness. She leaned toward her husband, "Nefertiti always had a soft spot for Zoya. Even though all were commanded not to have a favorite, Zoya was Nefertiti's. Since she's been reunited with her lineage, she hasn't let her out of her sight." Queen Hadiat softly spoke to the King.

"I'm sensing some sort of guilt." King Jasir's whisper was overheard by Hasan, Ebelle and Seshet.

"Come," Seshet stood and smiled at Hasan and Ebelle. "The two of you have great works ahead. You need to rest." If the King's sight could sense the guilt of an innocent, Seshet didn't want her eyes read by him, at least not until she was ready.

Later that night while his family slept peacefully, the Guardian King stood watch. His spirit fed on their trust as they rested. He knew he was worthy of it again. However, his mind couldn't stop wandering through the century he spent apart from his family. While his bond with Hadiat seemed stronger than ever before, he struggled with feeling disconnected from his daughters, and was having trouble remembering himself and them. He spread his wings and flew to the rooftop and perched himself there daring anyone to enter.

Chapter 17: Fear Love, not Evil

If Trigon could scream out he would curse believers worlds over. Aniah left him unable to use his operatic illusory voice ever again. That part of his power was gone and he must now rely on other methods of narcissism. The dead bodies of demon pawns created a trail leading to his door. He left the path as a reminder to all demons, pawns, and foul beings that there was no honor amongst thieves, yet their allegiance was purchased for his exploits. Abandoning him would not be tolerated.

Tien, Draisien and Tiago laughed as they stepped over the bodies and entered the gated room.

"I count at least ten Mansa-Ibns," Tien chuckled toward Draisien and Tiago as they stepped over the bodies. He entered Trigon's room and addressed him jokingly, "I heard the American one forked your tongue." Tien slapped Trigon on the back of his head, "Now you can lick twice as many..."

"Gentlemen, is that all you can think of?" Draisien laughed. "What did you find out?"

Trigon ignored Draisien and turned to Tiago and opened his thoughts for him to read.

"The Heirs are still divided. There is feuding among them, specifically Ebelle and Aniah. Khailia, from the eldest line, you were able to expose and attack her lack of discernment. That allowed you to push the agenda and divide them further. Ahhhhh...Aniah is injured. You have her blood on what remains of your tongue? The blood of an heir on your tongue? Give me your tongue." Tiago never raised his voice while holding out his hand. He looked Trigon sternly in the eyes and impatiently warned, "You know the truth of my power now, no need for demonstration, right?"

Trigon demonstrated Tiago's power for him anyhow and cut off his tongue and handed it to Tiago. He placed it into the handkerchief Tiago pulled from his jacket pocket.

"What do you mean, the truth of your power?" Tien sat down next to Trigon and handed him a towel. "It'll grow back, give it a few weeks."

"Aniah, she has the King's eyes but much more. Her lineage's pain transfigured her sight. She's extremely strong. When she read me on the battlefield, she found a fleshy skeleton, only she still doesn't know that she knows. Yet and still, she has accepted her worth now. How interesting."

"Before Trigon's fun," Draisien looked down at a few bodies, "One of the pawns informed that King Jasir has returned. I'm sure he'll teach her how to use her eyes very soon. If he hasn't begun already."

"What skeletons?" Tien refused to let up from Tiago's tracks. He was beginning to understand the centuries he'd been distracted by over indulgence as memories of their fall from grace slowly returned to him.

Tiago noticed the curtain lifting and acknowledged it as his time. The time he'd been waiting for since his fall. Without any further care for discreet movements, he let it all spill out. "Draisien was never the strongest, I allowed him to believe it. And the two of you rode that wave. Now you know." Tiago stepped over the bodies and opened the balcony doors where his wings spread wide. "Trigon, I called for a priestess. She's on her way to fix your mouth. She'll be here in no time."

"Can't wait for your wedding." Draisien scorned. "Your bride awaits."

"You dare?" Tiago did not flinch nor look back as he felt his strength growing and the fear of his power fed him even more. "But she may be of use to me yet. Tien, I think it's time for you to reveal your true self. My Inkanyamba brother, teach them their place yet again. Trigon, revenge, you know it best. This time, let's make sure to keep the cameras rolling, you're still a star. And Draisien, you're not a leader anymore, never really were... but you have a following, a strong following. Let's empower them. Also, I need your flesh. Hold your arm out." Tiago didn't blink one time. His silent prowess spoke volumes of his peaking power. Draisien did as he was commanded and pulled out his own blade to cut away some flesh and handed it to Tiago.

Tiago opened the stained glass doors on Trigon's balcony and flew out to the other side of the estate landing before Victoria. She straightened her appearance and bowed down before Tiago. He walked by her and she got in line and followed him. His footsteps were urgent as he couldn't stand the smell of her. Tiago nearly sprinted down a hidden hall and opened a secret passage. Victoria hurried to catch the door before it slammed in her face. They entered a cold and somber laboratory. There were vials and medical equipment all around. A doctor stood at attention and buttoned his white lab coat as Tiago got closer to him.

"Use a very small drop of blood from the surface of this tongue. Transform her into something presentable." Tiago leaned closer and whispered into the demonic doctor's ear, "the rest of the blood, divide into two vials using this same casing and give to me. If you waste one drop I will personally see to your torment. Here is Draisien's flesh. Use it to turn her demon. I don't want her possessed." Tiago's sharp turn back down the hall left a frigid chill over anything in his presence.

Tiago was ready to stop hiding his power as well. It was time to show believers who they should believe. His arrogance grew with every step for he knew what God created him for as well and just how to use it in his own favor. Finally a fight worth preparing for had come upon him and he was sure to make it one that conveyed his own message. His intentions of reestablishing The Throne of God and branding it under his empire was mapping out better than he ever perceived.

The next day Tien found Tiago meditating on the roof of the estate. Tiago had never seen him excited.

"Why did you hide your strength? You kept secrets from me, your brother?" Tien spoke up as he continued walking toward Tiago.

"Yes, I did. These walls have eyes and ears not connected to the greater good for us. So what if Draisien had their fear. It also brought him attention and made him a target. Meanwhile, I've been able to fly under the radar for centuries. Building, plotting, devising, and now Tien, it's time for our real reign to begin."

"I'm listening." Tien sat down on the ledge next to Tiago. He looked over his shoulder as Trigon appeared and sat down beside him

"Trigon, for your troubles, we will burn your name into every city under His watchful eye. They will pay." Tiago joined them on the ledge. "We must be skillful about this and move quickly. The last thing we need is for the return of The Guardians. We'll draw the Heirs out of training or hiding, whatever they're calling it. And when we do, the only thing I ask is that you leave Aniah to me. As for any and everyone else, enjoy the spoils of war." He pulled out his hand and cut his palm to allow the hate to spill. Trigon and Tien did the same to complete the pact.

They went back inside and marched through the halls of the estate to the throne room where a crowd awaited their arrival. All bowed as Tiago took his seat on the throne.

"We've had our fun with limits. Now we will show Him, their God, His mistake in ever turning us away. Tien, the Cyrusians are still loyal to you, begin with them. Trigon, your line of embittered seedlings, summon them to you. Add gas to their fires and bury the extinguishers with their mothers just like we did with Shaka. Draisien, call forth your top disciples and execs. We need access to their privilege. Bring her in." He commanded a guard at the closest door.

Victoria walked in with a new stride. After participating in her demonic rebirth she drank a potion containing the drop of Aniah's blood; the vixen emerged. "Do I please you now, my king?"

"You'll do. It's a shame. Your roots grew from soil stained and nurtured by the blood of Aniah's ancestral line and still…" His lack of thrill didn't pause to halfway look once. Her soulless walking corpse held a putrid stench no matter how she looked. "I will place you on a pedestal for the world to see. Trigon, your seedlings, make them respect and adore her. Make them praise her high above the blinding truth. Women need to look at her and want to be her while shunning the woman she's molded from. Draisien, leave no stone unturned in giving her all she desires and keep the cameras on her at all times. Floor seats, backstage passes, designer everything, access to every coveted pedestal you can find. Victoria, the world will celebrate your stolen essence and you will culture it as your own. No more hiding."

A demon walked in and handed Tiago the remaining blood in two small vials. Tiago spread his wings and left to hide them in places only he would know. Then he went to his retreat, a place fabled as one he fears, its existence unknown. He paced circles around the location where he fell. Unable to let go of the day for over thousands of years, he revisited every angle of the moment he was dragged out of Heaven. The confusion banged relentlessly on his still beating heart so that even he trembled at the thought of his next move.

"I still carry the engraved features from your very ink. You wrote me into time and forgot your reason. To call me perfect but love them more, preposterous. Once, I had no issue with you, but you forced my hand when you poured out these so-called champions to protect your favorites. Protect them from what? Your perfections? You gift humans with god and goddess to your throne, well then, what was I for? You don't lack omnipresence so I know you hear me, traitor! I will reign supreme and not disgrace myself to even spit in your face for the rewrite I will complete will bury your memory forever more. If you think what I've accomplished thus far is something, then I can't wait to see your face now that the End begins. I hate you…the world's first absentee Father. You get no vote here." Tiago knew God could still hear his call. So he continued to curse and remind God of all the atrocities he'd encouraged and created thus far. Threatening God with every misunderstood breath his Creator permitted neither cooled nor heated him. It created a vibrating standstill. Tiago wanted very much for God to present himself and fight. Since He never showed, Tiago continued to provoke, using his hate to dare God unto him.

Chapter 18: One Hurts, All Hurt

The Etruscan city of Believers was alive again. People danced within the city streets with music blaring loudly, laughing and throwing flowers, streamers and confetti in the air. The realm carried on purifying the air with hummings of hymns new and old, all proclaiming "To God Be The Glory." Within a few days, Believers were remembering themselves with every genuine hug and selfless deed for one another. They put themselves to work visiting hospitals, reading books to young children, and simply giving their time and love where needed the most.

When in the shield of The House of Severus, the Heirs practiced honing their skills by continuing their fight training and growing stronger. Ebelle's powers multiplied rapidly. She shared all she knew and promised all she'd ever become to her husband Hasan. He reciprocated by working to ease her heart while promising he'd never allow anything nor anyone to ever hurt her. Hasan was voted into King Kwesi's old position and when he held court, Ebelle sat right by his side to be respected and felt through her presence. She learned the truth in her touch and how to respond in favor of God's will.

Seshet kept a close eye but from a distance. She often thought back over the years she'd spent protecting the line of Liya and the sacrifices she made to ensure the Kingdom's balance aligned with longevity.

Khailia stayed close to Hathor and spent the passing days in constant meditation. She no longer wanted the Spirit of discernment to evade her. Her appreciation for her gift made her realize that if she couldn't hear the most important voice of all, she'd lose everything she loved. She was showered in constant love and admiration by her little sister Aniah who reminded she'd always look up to her no matter what.

Although Aniah held Khailia high, she kept her there because it was the easiest point from which to protect her. As much as she could, Nefertiti stole every extra moment of Aniah's time to train her to channel not only Zoya but Sekhmet's strength as well. Aniah took hit after hit from Nefertiti and never complained one bit. She was growing into the understanding of what it meant to own a gift so rare. The more Aniah learned of Sekhmet, the more honor she felt to have her strength and valor.... But she also knew that too came with the price of holding herself accountable to how she's show appreciation for Sekhmet's sacrifice.

All three girls were careful to spend time embracing King Jasir and Queen Hadiat. However, Jasir grew worried for Aniah because her distance was obvious to him and he blamed himself. On a more quiet day, where he was able to train Aniah alone, he made sure to invest into her gift.

"Raising three girls meant being in a constant state of madness." He chuckled while cleaning his khopesh after training. He nudged at Aniah's shoulder when she sat down beside him and pulled out cloth and Holy oils to clean her katanas mimicking her father's every movement. "They all had different personalities which made it easy for me to realize who was who even if I couldn't see them." He paused to show Aniah how to properly anoint her blades then handed her the khopesh back. "While Aida was known for her level of maturity and peace, she was also a fireball that didn't mind snapping off at a moment's notice. Liya, my sweet baby girl Liya. The brains on that one and she had a heart that matched, beautiful through and through. But Zoya, people thought her mischievous and too bold. And she was those things but that was her peace, that was her level zero so to speak. We only saw Zoya get mad one time ever. She was only seven but she took on two demons standing over the bodies of two little Aboriginal boys. We burned the demons' bodies and left Australia and immediately headed straight to Ethiopia to Nefertiti's so that she could start training Zoya. She excelled in fighting but her gift, it was stronger than even mine. She couldn't stop seeing those boys' eyes. She used it to connect her to the world we kept hidden from her and she saw it all. Not one time did she tell her sisters for fear they'd be as heavy as she was. I was murdered when she was ten. Found out my baby spent her sweet sixteen birthing a nation at her death."

"I can't see her." Aniah slowed her hands a little, hoping for advice.

"It's the pain. You can't keep it to yourself. Zoya kept it from her sisters and now you're keeping it from yours. Look at the distance its creating."

"I'm close with Khailia."

"Yes, but even that is at a distance. She hears your pain even when you try to hide it. Makes it hard for her to know the right words to say."

"What do you suggest I do?"

"Let them experience you. Give them the truth."

"I have to figure out what that is first."

"No, the truth is not only in you, the truth is you. You must look inward first. Don't fear your own gift, open your own eye. You my dear are gifted beyond measure. You possess the strength of not only your lineage but one of the greatest warriors I've ever known, Sekhmet. Every large battle I fought, I rode in protected. The protector being protected and not just by my Guardians. Hadiat was always by my side, and Nefertiti by hers. But when Sekhmet would join in battles, we knew the victory would be overwhelmingly swift. Her presence could be felt by any manner of being, and she lives in you. I saw it with how swiftly you dealt with the pawns and Kwesi in the Vatican... that was Sekhmet through and through... definitely something she'd have done. It's one of the first things anyone inside the realm can sense about you. In addition to your natural born powers, you have her in you too. She gifted you for a reason, don't waste it."

"My natural born powers?"

"Ahhh, yes. You haven't quite learned how to silence yourself and hear your ancestors. Therefore, you're unaware of all the powers you possess. Zoya is your first and eldest ancestor of your line. Your direct lineage to your throne and the reason you're a goddess. However, she's only the beginning of what flows through your veins. American slavery tried to erase your genealogy and history. It's not uncommon. You see dear, eons before Christopher Columbus and other colonizers, demons taught invaders of the real ancient Africa to erase their history by burning books, scrolls, tapestries, artifacts and murdering elders who held verbal and written histories of Believers. Ancient civilizations of Babylonian and Persian empires get a lot of credit for first this or first that, but truthfully, they weren't. And you're the evidence of this. The moment I locked eyes with you, I read parts of your story. Whether you know it or not, you blocked me from the rest. Which, I must say, only exemplifies your incredible strength. What I can tell you is, you have royalty running all through you. Your biological father was a king, only he didn't know it." King Jasir stood up and started to walk away. "You also possess a Guardian amulet, may I see it please?"

"If you mean the blanket, sure. Yes sir." Aniah dug in her bag and pulled out the blanket. She stood and held it out for the King.

He touched it and silently mourned for all he'd missed. "May I borrow this?"

"Yes sir." She handed him the blanket but gripped it tighter to hold his attention, "You speak to me of truth and royalty, but I know you and Hadiat are hiding something. I see you creating a labyrinth within your pupil the closer I get, but the memories in your tear ducts give you away. I mean this in the most respectful way."

"I'll show you soon, but not today. I think it's time to get dressed young lady. There will be a Colosseum full of people waiting to see you shortly."

"Yes sir." Aniah was overcome with gratefulness. The honor of baring her father's name had been elusive prior to the hajj. The simple favor of being a daddy's girl brought her an elevated sense of worth and she wore it like the most sacred treasure she'd ever received. Prior to knowing him, she never let that blanket go to anyone and would fight tooth and nail to keep it. Now, the blanket was more a memento of her journey to him than a necessity for comfort.

The slow walk down the hallways of The House of Severus, Aniah paid close attention to the newer marble walls and all their engravings versus the bronze artifacts. Her eyes revealed the authenticity of the stories engraved in bronze as they began to emerge from the walls. She took note of Geta's name and face being etched out then within the mural a guide appeared luring her to a truth which she followed without fear nor hesitation. She was led to Caracalla's private quarter. It was a locked bronze door and blatantly inscribed in a dead language that no one should enter. Aniah continued to read until she found Caracalla's eyes engraved within the stones and his eyes begged her to read further. Then she heard footsteps drawing near which stopped her from going any deeper. Aniah noticed the guide's panic and in her peripheral, caught Seshet sneaking in to observer her. Curious to see how much Seshet would reveal of herself, the Heir took the guide's warning as more of a suggestion and desired to look further as her heart instructed. When she went to reconnect with Caracalla, his eyes were gone. So instead, she continued to her room to get dressed and pretended to be unbothered and unaware of Seshet's presence.

....

The Colosseum was filled with Believers from far and wide. Every tribe that was represented wore their insignia, patterns, tattoos and colors with a resilient pride they hadn't felt in ages. Shoulders were light and hearts were full as smiles, laugher and jubilation took over the night's air. All one could feel was heard, understood and pure happiness in knowing *it* was happening.

Shades of soft greens, ivory and gold flowed through draperies, table cloths and décor. Columns over one hundred and fifty feet high were wrapped in hanging candles to brighten every corner of the feast. The smell of fine foods tickled bellies that hungered for the savory deliciousness they'd soon partake. Accents and languages from various nations filled every space the venue would allow. Everyone stood at attention waiting to witness the god King and goddess

Queen together again. The mention of their existence was enough to draw out large crowds, but the addition of the made the event much sweeter. No more waiting, the time was past due.

   The procession of King Jasir and Queen Hadiat kept everyone's breath hostage with each step. The King proudly wore a black and gold dashiki tuxedo his girls gifted him with. The small tail of the Queen's purple gown drifted behind her as they flowed down the aisle. Nothing else mattered over the years to any Believer in that moment. It was all summed up at the sight what had come to be. As they walked, Jasir pulled Hadiat closer to his side, unable to withhold the lifetime of moments stolen. His love poured out with every step and glance into her beautiful being. He lifted her hand and placed it gently against his lips. His anger eased as his silence begged for forgiveness that was granted with each stroke of prophecy years ago. Hadiat allowed his energy to fill every crevice and void within her soul. Not one word spoken as they walked but they were communicating now more than ever before.

   Hasan and Ebelle entered next. The newness of wedded bliss shined over both faces. Placing their feet in the trailway of royalty was comforting to them. Not in their lives had they ever denied or refuted their ancestry which included that very moment's prominence. Seshet stayed tightly behind them securing her centuries old work.

   There was a large gap between them and Khailia as she fought the desire to run away. Her feet sludged in the heaviest doubts and fears and if they were to move too quickly, it'd only be to run the opposite direction. Aniah could see every heartbeat and hear the stutters. Breaking the traditional promenade of the occasion, Aniah caught up to Khailia and grabbed her hand and pulled her into an embrace, whispering and laughing at Ebelle's expense. She poked fun at Ebelle's arrogant walk calling her clumsy. Khailia giggled through her objections and gave into forgetfulness for Believers' sake. Hathor tried to get their attention to remind them of proper etiquette but Nefertiti begged their pardon to have just one more night of healing before more scarring came.

   After the astonishment wore off not one believing hand was idle as everyone applauded gratefully for God's remembrance of them. The royals were seated at an elevated head table overlooking the others and were served food as the night had just begun. Tribal leaderships were offered their opportunity to address the family in front of the multitudes. The revered Barcas known for their Moor ancestry gifted their renown elephantine daggers. The Chapu-Ambar sultanate tribe who were responsible for the rise of honored civilization in India gifted three dead sea scrolls and a few rare pages of Enoch. The gifts went on and on but one specifically stood out. A blind man from the Levantian tribe asked to be read by the King. The Levantians were a tribe that held the forgotten truths of origin and in the war to come, they had yet to announce allegiance to either side. The King obliged and the blind man gifted the King with the only map known of ancient Jezreel. The King stored the truth in his eyes and told no one. Others came forth with gifts specific to their tribes, and flowers from every secret corner of Earth were laid at their feet. Once they were done eating, the King, Queen and Heirs separated to greet and acquaint as many as they could.

Aniah hadn't been groomed for all the attention the throne was promised to bring and it weighed her to remember formalities when she sought purpose. The last thing she wanted was material things and small talk. Yet, she smiled through the evening event, trying to ration her gift as though there was a numerical supply. She could see truths more and more, and even amongst Believers, it wasn't pretty. Wanting to steer clear of judgment, she tried looking for the nearest exit until her attention was drawn to the entrance.

The whispers of the latest arrival were more of a scream to Khailia and avalanched her ears causing a sharp pain. Aniah immediately fazed to her side and prepared for what was making its way through the crowd. There was a man veering his head at onlookers and showing his teeth. He and his friends pushed their way through wearing the skinned furs of various animals. The one leading, wore lion across his shoulders with an all-white button up dress shirt and pants blended of denim and leather. His hair was loc'd in an updo with a strange pattern causing Khailia to wonder what tribe he belonged to. The onlookers backed away while attempting to remain brave and taunt back at the same time. Aniah placed her hands on her katanas. The man and his small following made their way to King Jasir who smiled at the ruckus. He embraced the man and laughed at the dramatic entrance.

"Your highness! My father sent me to escort you to our home safely. I insisted it'd be you that'd be the one keeping me safe but..." The man's words were cut off.

"Who is it?" Khailia grabbed Aniah's shoulder and leaned into her. She could barely stand the pain shredding through her ears. "I can't hear anything. I'm scared Aniah!"

Before Aniah could respond with her own curiosity, the man sharply turned in their direction. His eye began to spasm as he searched for her voice. He graced his way through until he stood face to face with Khailia, their hearts pounding to chaotic rhythms.

"It can't be." The man's disbelief quieted everyone. "How could I be worthy of…"

"Who are you?" Khailia fought through the roar of his heart and could only hear his voice. "What is happening? What is this?"

"Etienne Idris. My name is Etienne Idris. And you, you're an Heir. And us…we're…"

"I could hear you from miles away." She was still unsure if iji mesit 'eti was truly happening this time or if she was simply hoping too hard through it all.

"I… I'm… We Kurati are heard most by understandings beyond this world." He took a step forward and was stopped immediately.

Aniah drew her katana and placed it firmly between he and Khailia. She flicked the blade upward to catch a glance of his eyes in her blade's reflection. She couldn't see much but she saw enough to know he was no immediate threat. Before she could lower her weapon Khailia heard the blade's memory and could only see her sister's wounded hand.

Khailia's eyes swelled with tears at the sight of the pain her mistake in love cost the ones she loved haunted her still. "I've heard enough." She backed away and left the Colosseum with Aniah following her every footstep.

Chapter 19: Kurati Homecoming

The next day Khailia said not one word, just paced while others packed for Kurati, the next stop on their hajj. A storm brewed in her spirit and the winds called to her. She wished for foresight and the creativity to craft a plan, but the storm inside of her wouldn't cease long enough. She heard the discernment loud and clear amongst a few other things. Etienne Idris was her king but she couldn't push past the doubts that didn't matter...or did they?

Etienne Idris walked the sidewalks praying for her light to emerge. He was reluctant to grow weary for he knew how long she waited while he squandered away his inheritance. The chill of the world dare not find his feet because for once in his life he stood in the place of knowing. He wanted vengeance for Trigon's deception of her virtue but how could he seek it without crucifying himself for his own similar transgressions.

Khailia continued to pace in circles until she came to a point within herself where her storm called forth her inner warrior. "Aniah, Ebelle...with me." Her sisters strapped on their weapons and dressed for the occasion because Khailia never asked much from anyone at all.

King Jasir and Queen Hadiat felt the Heirs were up to something and ran to them immediately. "Are you forgetting you are to meet with the Kurati today? They are waiting for you. Khailia, Etienne is waiting for you." Queen Hadiat was in shock to be having the conversation with Khailia, typically the most obedient.

"I will not marry him. He does not fully understand. I hear him. I will not take my love for granted ever again and I won't allow him to either. I know he does not understand this." Khailia secured her glove and bo. Her sisters and Amanirenians followed them.

"What doesn't he understand, dear? What more does he need to know? Come. Sit down and let's talk things out." Queen Hadiat's surprise took breaths away before she had a chance to receive them.

Seshet tried to intervene, "You've been spending too much time with Aniah. Return to yourself right now!"

"Excuse me!" Nefertiti took offense. "What did you just say? What is your meaning?"

"Khailia was raised to be a Queen, not a rebellious drifter."

"You mistake rebellion for revolution." Nefertiti's eyes grew and she placed her hand on her sword, "where do you stand? Which side are you on?" They argued further as the small battalion continued past them down the hall.

"Ebelle! Ebelle!" Hasan ran to his wife. "What is going on? Where are you ladies going?"

Ebelle touched Hasan's hand to search for his comfort. There was none to provide in his worry of the unknown. "I know how this feels, but this is what it means to be married to an heiress. My job does not stop because of our love, the responsibility grows instead."

"And what about the accountability? Who are you accountable to?"

"God alone." She tried to kiss his cheek but he pulled away. Understanding his pain, she continued down her path with hopes to align on an understanding once she returned.

As the group entered the city streets all business and bypassing ceased. Etienne tried to catch Khailia's attention but she refused him the simple formality of unspoken discussions. King Jasir watched from the roof and without question granted his blessings by telling Etienne and the others to pack for the land of Kurati, ensuring the girls would meet them there later.

"Aniah...Ebelle...," Khailia gathered them close to her call. "I can't marry him without an understanding."

Her sisters nodded in allegiance.

"You'll need a coat, it may get a little nippy." Khailia held her hands out and her sisters obliged and their clothing changed into warmer battle gear. The Amanirenians grabbed onto available hands forming an unbreakable v-formation, changing their clothes as well.

The faze landed them outside Lake Arpi National Park, right on the borders of Turkey, Georgia and Armenia. Nippy was most certainly an understatement. It was unseasonably freezing. The howling blizzard's wind revealed an entire army ready and waiting to shed Heiress blood. The Scythians, a long forgotten and lost tribe, had the numbers of Xerces. Despite the numbers, Amanirenians were known for killing "greats."

"May we help you?" A pale woman with hints of melanin hued skin, icy blue eyes, and wild floor length blond hair stepped forward. Her sarcastic smile baited Ebelle into revealing her pistols. Another woman stood firm to meet Ebelle's threat without hesitance. "Why are you here?" The pale woman held her head high staring at Khailia.

Khailia walked in their direction and dropped her fur coat into the snow. She held her finger in the air asking her sisters and the Amanirenians to hold their position. With the Amanirenians stayed behind and the Scythian soldiers relaxed their muscles just a little. Their comfort changed to pure shock when Khailia pulled her arrow and gutted the pale long-haired woman. The Scythians froze in terror as their anguish mounted. The arrow dripped a greenish blood when she pulled it from the woman. Khailia then drew her bow and released the arrow in between the eyes of a soldier standing on a hill. On the soldier's head was a crown. The glare in Khailia's eyes dared anyone to say or do anything about it. Then she reached in to the pale dead woman's chest and removed a large ruby, turned her back on the army then slowly walked back to her sisters.

"You had me get dressed for this?" Aniah chuckled causing Khailia to finally smile. "I finally put thought into an outfit and I couldn't even throw one jab? Not even pinch a heffa?"

Once Khailia was shoulder to shoulder with them, they all turned and walked with her into a faze.

Chapter 20: Orisha Gatekeepers

An experience untold, their faze to the land of Kurati was interrupted. The Heirs and Amanirenians were unsure as to why. Aniah was the first to pull her weapons, katanas in ready stance with her khopesh on her back, the others joined unaware of if she'd seen something.

"Never knew the time or place, just that I'd see you and you see me as well... don't you Aniah? Don't you see me, too?" A male's voice whispered over the wind. "What do you fight against? What are you ready for?"

"Can't be!" Ebelle dropped her guns in astonishment. "They're just a tale, a myth."

"The most intelligent amongst you will learn the truth is not found in years of studying alone. Where are your works?" The voice whispered again.

"Show yourself!" Khailia demanded with her new-found strength.

"My voice is all you need or maybe it's the silence you deserve." A gust of wind took shape in front of them, "Soldiers to protect those created for protecting? Still not ready for your gifts? Then, give them to me? You started several wars, and one just moments ago. Didn't you hear the bells toll?" The voice chuckled.

Ebelle collapsed unable to feel anything around her. Khailia grew more confused as the hearing she'd learned to depend on went away. Aniah held her composure as the dark grew around her. The Amanirenians lost all sense of bravery and valor.

He appeared in front of them, someone they weren't prepared to meet. One of the Orisha gatekeepers, Esu. "You seek to cross over into the land of Kurati, but are you worthy of such balance? Have you been spoiled into only existing for what is defined as right? Tell me, how do your scales fare? In the lands where good and evil respectfully coexist, how will you place yourself amongst them?"

The heirs were more disconnected than ever in the face of lack of preparation.

"I see you." Aniah spoke up.

Esu turned toward her hurriedly and mocked her blindness by waving his hand in front of her as she stood still.

"You asked me if I could see you. My answer is yes. I see you and I see your message." She slowly lifted her katana while Khailia braced Ebelle on her backside and led the Amanirenians to find comfort behind them."

"Why do you fear me?"

"I thought you said you can see me? Clearly, it is you who cannot see."

The trickster smiled. He started to speak further but received a message from another Orisha gatekeeper that his inquisition is unnecessary.

Khailia intercepted the message, "You cannot take what you did not give." Her voice rose higher than before which moved Ebelle to stand upright and the Amanirenians to unsheathe their weapons once more. However, Aniah remained in the dark.

"Ah, and you, heiress. Don't you want to see again? Don't you believe in who you are? Come into the light."

"Your little prank became pointless when you made the mistake of believing I couldn't see in the dark."

"Or your real comfort exists there..." He smiled at her waiting for her to reveal yet another layer of herself. Instead he came to understand that her silence carried more weight than her words and revealed himself. "I am Esu, an Orisha. Gatekeeper to the land of Kurati. I will not hold you any longer. I know what it's like to anger Queen Hadiat. I don't want to feel her chastisement ever again. And since I prefer being on her good side, allow me to escort you to your destination. No more tricks. You have my word."

"I thought you Gatekeepers were fables." Ebelle continued to straighten her pose. "Where have you been?"

"Waiting to be summoned, brain child." He snickered, "I'd apologize if only I could mean it. Sarcasm and pettiness bring me great joy. Alas, I better stop before you tell mommy."

"And you, other Gatekeeper, will you be escorting us as well or will you remain hidden?" Ebelle felt the presence of another, "show yourself."

"I would love to escort you to your family." A strong gust of wind blew through and a beautiful slender woman wearing a long light gray gown appeared to them never missing her stride. "I am Oya, keeper of the winds." She bowed before them. When she lifted herself back up she made sure her amethyst eyes connected with Aniah's. "But please, allow me to take the load off your travel." She lifted a pearl jewel into the air and controlled the wind. The tree leaves shuffled as clouds came through, one for each rider. Oya peeked over to Khailia and Ebelle and smiled warmly at their astonishment. "Try not to be so surprised young heirs. Who do you think taught your beloved Hadiat?"

They all took steps onto their clouds, some remained standing while others choose to be seated. The clouds smoothed their way through the jungle's leaves and trees alongside the Zambezi River. The Heirs and Amanirenians gazed in amazement at the hidden beauties of nature. They took note at all the creatures and animals that peeked out to see them pass by asking the Orisha to name the ones they'd never seen in pictures. All except Aniah. The closer they got to the Kurati the more distant she felt in her heart. While the sights held her interest, so did the fact that she would soon be the only sister unwed, the only sister still catching up, the only one holding up fik-iri, and most importantly, the only one holding up the Kingdom of God. She stared into the distance until they came to a point where the river seemed to end.

"Great thing about all that He created, right where you think life's story ends, is the exact place where it begins again." Oya's eyes held the reflection of the dancing waters as she gently glanced over her shoulders then turned to face the river. "Yemoja used to say that to me all the time..." She lifted her jewel again and the waters began to rise, "Do you begin with balance or do you begin with alignment?" She peeked over her shoulders at the heirs yet again, "Asayenyi." She spoke through her jewel and Esu held up his gold bracelet.

The river grew before their eyes leading them straight into the land of Kurati. King Jasir, Queen Hadiat and Simeon, King of the Kurati, in his lion form straightened their posture as the girls got closer. A pathway through a crowd of all sorts of beings was made for their approach. To their left and right were the Aziza fairies, Kishi demons, Yomboe zombies, Eloko dwarfs, Believers, Tikoloshe sprites, Jengu spirits, lions, leopards, gorillas, and more. Circling the skies were phoenixes, griffins, sphinxes, kongamato pterodactyls, eagles, vultures, and majestic roc eagles. All manner of creation came from near and far to lay eyes on the heirs.

As they got closer Etienne Idris came out and stood by his great great grandfather, King Simeon. He smiled brightly as his fiancé approached, however she didn't return the same display of emotion.

King Simeon stood in a slightly bewildered stare. His hazel – amber eyes couldn't quite understand Khailia's intentions behind ignoring his own heir. He straightened his shoulders high with pride with his mane blowed delicately in the wind and watched as Khailia pulled the heavy ruby jewel from her backpack. King Simeon's heart melted as the entire crowd, including King Jasir and Queen

Hadiat gasped for air. King Simeon bowed down at the sight of the jewel. All other lions circled him as he lifted his head and roared at the jewel so loud it was heard in Heaven.

    The ruby shook and shattered into thousands of pieces suspended floating slowly in air. Queen Hadiat stepped in immediately moving her hands throughout the air, gathering the elements around her shifting the remnants of the ruby into a form. After shaping the fragments of the ruby, she uplifted Oba, her great friend, the lost Orisha. Nefertiti took off her long robe and wrapped it around Oba's shoulders, clothing her bare skin.

    Oba's beautiful dark deep flawless skin and magnificent long blonde hair captured every creatures' eyes. She stared at her free hands and held the sun's embrace as she finally was able to touch her own face. After thousands of years being trapped inside a gem, its real value shined brighter than her weight in gold. Rivers of tears rushed from her blue eyes and led her straight to her love, King Simeon. She hugged his shoulders and ran her fingers through his mane until he once again took human form. No one had seen King Simeon that way since Oba's disappearance. Their story was one for the ages. What was meant to be never passed them. Then Oba grabbed her great great grandson, Etienne Idris, by the hand and kissed his palms while resting her head in them. A grandmother's love transformed his heart completely, as he once again trusted love and understood his wife's meaning.

Chapter 21: A Prodigal King's Worth

Etienne Idris' heart was worth the war Khailia had just started. And she needed him to know that she would stand boldly against unknown risks and dangers if it means him returning to himself. She'd call on her sisters, a force greater than any on the Earth and ride into uncertainty if it helped him connect the pieces of himself. He had to know that she would not proceed until he understood his own value, for without it, how could he ever protect, lead or love his Queen. Her love was uncommon, the kind only God could create. And she needed him to know God still existed within himself no matter what he'd ever done, the mirror projection was for a reason. Khailia stepped away without a word and Ebelle followed. Etienne reached for Aniah's shoulder as she began to follow suit.

"Why won't she speak to me? How long will she be this way?" Etienne's eyes stayed on Khailia and longed for her to turn around and come back to him.

"There are endless words in her silence. Follow their meaning and that's where you'll find her. She's been waiting all along." Aniah tilted her head to catch a glimpse of his eyes then smiled and turned away, "Welcome home Etienne." She read his story in a matter of a few blinks. "And welcome to the family."

Hathor, Seshet and Nefertiti left with the Heirs and led them to their rooms. They were King Simeon's honored guests and as such stayed in a private villa looking out on the safari. Everything from the wood and stone architecture to the wild plants became subtle reminders of God's grace. Khailia wished to stay there forever with life's organic rhythms in hues of blues with whispers of greens and fragrant purples with fiery orange and red dirt. She inhaled wonder and exhaled appreciation so deeply that the winds awaited her command. Her gift was blossoming once more in the beauty of love and all its intimate fascinations, but most of all for the one created as Etienne Idris. Meanwhile, celebrations of Etienne and Oba's return filled every corner of Kurati lands and beyond.

Ebelle and Aniah helped their sister prepare for her marriage while Hathor and Hadiat helped Oba with the wedding plans. Etienne circled Khailia's bedroom window in hopes for just a glance, and she bathed herself in his longing which made her blush. Khailia's biological parents arrived with Ebelle's and Hasan's and the uncharted lands lit up with excitement by the Believers. Tribes from Anatolia to Oceania had come to honor the Heiress and her soon to be king.

Legendary mythical warriors from Kurati beginnings appeared for the homecoming as they stepped into their human forms to help ring in the occasion over that week.

ZaQuaysia and Melaine found Aniah sitting on the porch one afternoon and confirmed she'd read Etienne's eyes then asked her to share the story of Simeon, Oba and Etienne.

"Well, I'm sure you know Simeon, King of Kurati, holds a greater title than king in God's heart. He's his best friend. Simeon was there with God in Eden. He was with Daniel in the lion's den. He helped Jesus carry the cross. He laid beside the tomb until Christ was arisen. All of those wonderful stories and more I'm sure Simeon can give more passionate detail than I can. However, I'm sure what's more pressing is what just occurred with Khailia outside the Caucasus Mountains on the borders of Turkey, Armenia and Georgia. Let's take a few steps back to the story of Daniel in the lion's den. After Daniel was pulled from the lion's den, his accusers and the accusers' families were sentenced to death and fed to the lions, which just so happened to be King Simeon and his soldiers. Daniel's accusers were people who hated Believers also known as evil Babylonian, tainted Persians, Scythians, Caucasians, whatever you may call them. They were an evil sort. They even caused smears to their own state and gods, a careless and reckless bunch. Well, after their bodies were devoured by King Simeon's and his lions, the accuser's souls never left this earth. You see, prior to dying, they cursed themselves with unnatural life so that they could have revenge. Now, fast forward to around the time Jesus was born, King Simeon met and fell in love with Oba who had just been banished from her throne. The two would go on to marry and have a family. Well one day, God sent Simeon to meet Jesus on the road to Calvary and asked him to be with His son. While this was happening, Oba was kidnapped and cursed by being trapped in the ruby by a tribe of particular Scythians who were actually Daniel's accusers' souls. They basically took over someone else's body. Oba had been trapped in that ruby for thousands of years. They swore in order to find Oba, King Simeon would have to dig her out from where her heart was torn. Oba's family had searched for her all that time in all the wrong places, causing her sons to leave home and be referred to as prodigal...far from the truth. Oba and Simeon's lineage were kidnapped away into slavery as well and distributed all around the Caribbean islands. They forgot themselves and none of them had been quite able to mesh their lion form with their human form, that metamorphic training was a rite of passage that occurred here in the Kurati lands. That all ended when Oba returned to restore their memories: King

Simeon can now take on his human form and slave lineages descended from their blood can now take on lion form. The best part is Etienne Idris is the strongest Kurati alive and he's about to marry a goddess Heiress to the Throne of God. Yet again, proof that what evil means to destroy always works out for those who Believe in the end."

"So two great families are about to unite. And Khailia brought the whole kingdom back together again."

"She knew Etienne wouldn't understand her love for him if she didn't. He needed to be whole before they married so that nothing could stop their united alignment with God's purpose for their lives." Aniah looked up at the villa's terrace and saw Grace returning but couldn't see her eyes to read her. It's as if she was purposely hiding them. Grace went straight to Hasan and closed the door of his and Ebelle's room. Aniah continued on, "I'm still trying to figure out the rest of the story. You see, the woman who Khailia ripped the ruby from was once an honored warrior. There was some sort of power shift I'm unable to see that she participated in. Remember the other woman with the crown who Khailia killed as well? She's no royal, she's a decoy. In fact, their real queen wasn't even there. Whoever she is, I could see her face, but her actual identity is unknown, even to her own people. Something tells me she'll want revenge, and she ain't shit to be playing with."

"And we'll be ready when she decides to embark upon her suicide mission." Hathor joined them on the porch and poured herself a drink. "In other news, have you heard about King Simeon's decree this morning?"

"Yes." Aniah sighed a sullen reply.

"Well? Are you excited to know who the reigning Queen will be? And he agreed to reveal it even though you and Ebelle have not formed fik-iri yet, talk about a plot twist! We always thought there had to be a specific order to everything, He's always got surprises." Hathor sat down on the rail, "All these years of waiting and watching and protecting and its finally happening! I'm so excited. I'm just glad to be here! We made it!"

Seshet joined them on the porch as well. "Oh, I can't wait! Do you think God will grace us? You think He'll come?"

"What makes you think He ever left?" Hathor was confused at Seshet's question. "All these years of knowing His word and the prophecy, I have to say, I'm shocked at you."

Aniah and the Amanirenians remained silent as Seshet and Hathor went back and forth. No one else but Aniah knew that Nefertiti was on the side listening the entire time.

....

The day of the wedding arrived and Khailia held the envy of the biggest star in the sky. Her beauty was too majestic for words or tradition. She opted for a very nontraditional wedding as she couldn't find a predecessor for her specific story. She braved a forgotten road to get back to herself and him in one; it was a process of merging two powerful families together by striking the enemy simply so that one man could know love unparalleled.

The ceremony's attendees added unscripted splashes of vibrancy on each side of the aisle, all waiting for the wedding to begin. There was no defined boundaries just open field and an altar. Ebelle was the first to walk down as the next oldest in line and of course she was stern about her part in honoring tradition, but no one cared, so Khailia let her have her way. Ebelle's spirited footsteps accompanied by her smiling at Hasan and smirking at a loveless Aniah. Aniah followed Ebelle but paid her no mind. Instead, she prayed her tears of joy wouldn't cause her makeup to run.

The heartbeats of the pride stood still as Khailia's echo vibrated so high that no one could escape its trance. She wore a dress made of vibrant reds, purples and yellows. There were bloomed petals hand-stitched into the tiered skirt of her dress made only in the finest of linens in Asia. Her long wavy hair softly rippled around her delicate cheekbones. The shimmer of her eyes showed the transparency of her heart.

And when Etienne Idris finally saw her, his chest jerked and every chain he ever placed around his heart dissolved all at once. The lion-hearted man's tears resounded elations of untampered happiness. To understand that God's love for him transcended any and every careless mistake he could have ever made regarding his worth and prominence was everything. And although God's love was more than enough, He then gifted him with her. His her. His forever her. For the first time he heard her heart loud and clear. He heard the courage it took for her to face his enemies and own his losses as hers with no respect to time or diligence, only the urgency for him to know.

And she, her radiance filled the entire land worlds over. Khailia slowly proceeded down the aisle walking hand-in-hand with her birth father. She favored him but was the spitting image of her mother. Khailia found her discernment when she heard God's voice in Etienne, and she was glad that he finally knew. Every step was intentional. There was clarity of past moments understood between he and she alone because when they became them, nothing from their past mattered. She loved her wait and cared none about what happened before destiny.

King Simeon waited at the alter for her. Ecstatic to unite his own with such great royalty. Simeon found himself caught up in reaffirmations that He had been here all along through each trial and journey of Believers stemming from the beginning. Yet, in this moment he believed in its future. His bloodline ensured that hers would always have a friend and never have to face ill repute or love alone. When Khailia finally made it to meet her King eye to eye, Etienne Idris took her face into the palms of his renewed hands and worshipped her with their first kiss. While a few whispered at their lack of care for order of the church, others eased back as Aniah smiled, mirroring King Jasir's. Permission wouldn't be requested or needed.

"Ahem," King Simeon begged their attention, "I guess we better get this over with...quickly."

The crowd chuckled and took their seats.

"I won't tell you why we're gathered here today, rather I'll ask you to remember. Remember a time when the name of our Heavenly Father melted the hardest of hearts and cleansed them with abundance and overflow. All those years, I would walk with him and talk with him and listen to His greatest concerns. I remember He healed the paralyzed man simply because his friend believed. Being His best friend meant I had the privilege of trying to pour back into Him quicker than He poured into this world. Needless to say, He showed out a lot." King Simeon smiled and turned to Oba, "And I thought there was nothing new under the sun until I experienced His greatest ordinance through the sacrifice of another. And although I've seen a great deal," he returned his eyes to Etienne and Khailia, "I've never seen the righteous forsaken. I'm so glad He knew exactly who to create for each other. His best kept secret, never ruined by any force." He stepped forward and joined their hands together, "Etienne Idris, Judah, my tribesman, my heir. Love her, cherish her, remain her friend always. As her King, know there are no more ifs and execute loyalty to God always. And Khailia, Heiress of the eldest line. The voice that hears the opportunity to insert love. Always hear Etienne that way without needing to translate its meaning. Accept its truth."

Etienne's brother handed him a ring to place on Khailia's finger and Ebelle handed Khailia a ring for Etienne. Khailia's mother and Oba stood behind them and a high standing halo crown appear upon Khailia's head and the crown of Kurati appeared upon Etienne Idris'. Their hearts and their union was communicated throughout the airways as Heaven opened up and approved.

Chapter 22: Higher

The wilderness was filled with celebration for the next few days. Per usual, Ebelle rejoiced in Aniah's pretend exile, taunting her of rumors of forever loneliness and death for the line of the unloved. It made Aniah train harder and learn faster. However, she wouldn't lie to herself, she too wanted to love.

One morning after training, resting with her eyes closed, Aniah remembered how it all started. Thinking back to her alarm forcing her eyes open although she'd been awake the whole time. Was it duty that called to her? Or fear that made her wait? As the sun lifted up with the birds' songs, so too did Aniah's eyelids as she watched the scene trying to imagine herself escaping in it.

"How did this prophecy come to be? What caused its purpose?" She slowly opened her eyes when she felt Nefertiti come close.

"Why do you ask me?" Nefertiti sat beside her to catch her breath. "It's time to get dressed."

"Do I have to go?" Aniah smiled and sank into Nefertiti's shoulder.

"Actually, no. The choice is and still remains yours." She passed some water to the Heiress.

"Eh, I think I've kept everyone waiting long enough." She drank water while a breeze sifted through them. "More gatekeepers, huh?"

"Where?"

"One watched us train the entire time. I believe his name is Orunmila."

"Why didn't you tell me?"

"He was right there, not hiding. How did you miss him? Ori, just arrived. That was him walking by a moment ago in the breeze." Aniah stood up and wiped the dirt from her pants, "I guess we should get inside."

Nefertiti helped her prepare while Hathor and Seshet assisted the other heirs. They dress almost in complete silence until Aniah spoke up.

"So, how's it feel to be married?" She grabbed Khailia's hand gazing at her ring and smiled.

"Eh, you wouldn't understand." Ebelle laughed and sipped her wine. "Do you think you'll ever be ready for marriage? Or do Afro-American men have to wait as long as we did for you to show up? Do you prefer I call them Afro American, or Black or Negro. You all don't know what you want, nor who you are. No wonder why American men love all the others."

"You've seen your mother-in-law, right? You know she definitely checks the other box, right? Hasan is half 'other,' dumb ass! Meaning your kids are gonna have some other in them too, right?" Aniah softly chuckled, "keep speaking ill toward me if you want, looks like it just comes back to you in the end."

"I feel great! I honestly feel free from myself with him." Khailia smiled at Aniah and then looked to Ebelle sitting off her left shoulder. "Must you insist? Today more than any other, we need unity."

"You're right. Doesn't change any other truths, but you're right. Cease fire, Aniah?"

"I'd rather stop it all together. I'm too tired for it anymore." Aniah stood to her feet and walked toward the balcony. She looked out on the crowds walking to the mountains in the distance to find out which Heiress was to become the reigning Queen. "Ebelle, I don't understand your hate for me, but I'm happy to have your back for life. Even with all your misdirected anger, I wouldn't want to live in this world without you. Khailia, you have my blades and fists til the end. I'm proud to belong in anything the two of you are involved in."

"Same here! I'd follow either of you into the ends of this world no matter what! Just don't make it anytime soon...just got married...wanna do a couple thangs with him, uninterrupted if you catch my drift." Khailia swatted at Ebelle.

"You trying to give him some babies?" Ebelle laughed.

"I'm trying to give that man several babies!" Khailia swung her hands in the air pointing at the sky like she found the right spot.

"I've followed ya'll into battle. Followed ya'lls lead on several occasions...wouldn't mind spending life following either." Ebelle got closer to the mirror to check her lipstick. "Besides, who else going to save ya'll?"

"I seem to remember us saving you!" Khailia screeched. "And if you put on any more lipstick every circus clown near and far is going to demand purchase limits." She noticed the silence underneath it all and decided to turn on some music. She thumbed through the records trying to find the most befitting song. Then her favorite moment with her sisters nudged her hand to play Prince's "I would die for you." Without reluctance, her sisters joined in.

The moment came and they were escorted to the crowning ceremony. All Orisha gatekeepers were present in the same space for the first time ever. Every Amanirenian stood counted for. The living lineages of Aida, Liya and Zoya all present.

King Simeon took his human form and stood before King Jasir and Queen Hadiat with his back toward the crowd and kneeling heiresses. "To walk with

Him and talk to Him on a regular basis and still not know His every move, my Friend continues to amaze me. No speech I could give would ever resemble the greatness of this moment." He turned and stood before them, ready to crown the reigning Queen. "One to Free, One to Heal and One to Lead." He paused to ensure every Believer was in tune. "Once all His children are free, someone must heal every pain, until then, they will not be led. Not one heiress is more important than the other, equal in every aspect except one. Your gifts were never for you, from birth you were meant to love. Ebelle, rise."

Seshet's heart nearly jumped out of her chest. She couldn't and at the same time she fully believed Ebelle to be the reigning Queen.

"There is no touch in this universe as great as yours. You will heal many nations and reaffirm Believers far and wide." He touched her hands and placed them in Seshet's. "Khailia, the voice that moves mountains, soothes egos, and breaks chains, freedom flows from your very essence."

A silence covered all of nature as all eyes were on Aniah who fought hard to not look up. "Please choose one of them. I can't do this. I don't want this." She whispered to King Simeon.

"Your birthright was never your choice, however your acceptance always has been and always will be. You, the eyes that see simplicity, truth and love. You were created to lead. Will you rise and accept your crown?"

Aniah looked up and over at Nefertiti who nodded her head in agreement ushering her to stand. Then Aniah looked at Hadiat, tall in gratitude encouraging the heiress to choose the crown. Finally, she looked at Khailia, eyes full of relief and peace while Ebelle snared. Hathor scooted in front of Seshet and Ebelle to refocus her on what was rightfully hers. Aniah stood and looked King Simeon in the eyes. Piercing through their amber beauty she saw God sitting under a tree by still waters waiting for her. He looked back at her and smiled at how calm she was with their likeliness. No pupils for her to search, He held the Universe in His eyes and she smiled back at the stars twinkling at her. She walked in and sat down beside Him careful not to step or sit on His ocean robe or long locs that looked like tree roots. He stretched out his hands face down, their brown hue comforted her. He turned His hands palm side up and watched life begin in the center of his palm and end on His fingertips, then circle back to begin again. There were so many "why's" she had in mind but refused to bore Him with questions He already knew she'd ask. So she leaned into Him and rested her heaviness on His shoulders as His embrace renewed her spirit. One blink and she was back in front of King Simeon.

"Even you, Aniah, are worthy of His embrace. He who is in everything and is everything adores you. You are not finished. You've only barely begun. Queen Aniah, reigning goddess Queen to the Throne of God, we exalt the God within you, my friend. Now open your eyes and lead."

Overwhelmed with innumerable feelings, Aniah's body tried objecting but her eyes knew the truth. She stood there feeling like the new her was older than the old her. Khailia jumped to hug Aniah, sweeping Aniah off her feet. Etienne Idris joined in on the hug while others slowly piled in. Others except Ebelle, Seshet and Nefertiti.

"He would squander His wealth on her?" Seshet's words stabbed the entire crowd in the back. "She had no idea of what an inheritance even meant or that it even existed, and He would waste His essence on her? I don't believe it. Let Him come down and tell us this Himself." She turned and grabbed Ebelle's arm, "Until then, we're leaving! We don't need this type of bullshit. We can handle this on our own. No peasant will reign over us!"

Nefertiti drew her sword daring Seshet to take another step with the blade at her neck. Seshet slowly released Ebelle's arm and as soon as she started to speak, Nefertiti touched the tip of the blade to her skin.

"Ebelle, your sister's crown does not diminish your own." Hasan tried to speak life into his wife, but she heard none of it.

Ebelle stepped past her husband's words and confronted Aniah. "Why you?" Her tears fell out fast, "I hate this! I hate all of this! I have literally worked my ass off my entire life! Khailia and I both sacrificed any resemblance of normalcy with His purpose in mind. We were persecuted for His name's sake! Denied sleepovers with friends. Couldn't go to the mall for smoothies with non-believers or believers, isolated to remain pure to our gifts. Saturated in His word, we can quote the Truth verbatim! We've stood in cold rains and snows to pass out charities. And we trained. We trained in so many different styles of fighting until we bled streams. Left every time with new bumps, bruises and cuts, bloodied to the sole. We understand His people more than you, studied them even when our eyes closed for sleep. And then here you come. Out of the blue. Don't even care about worth, can barely spell it and He chose you. You rotten American, tribe of Quadroons and Octaroons unworthy of your own blood! Masquerading as queens and kings bring shame to this crown! You deserve to remain unnamed in death!" She could barely see Aniah. Her own tears blocked her sight. She pulled out her pistol and pointed it directly at Aniah's head. "...why not me? I would've even been alright with Khailia, but you? Why did He give it to you?"

"Enough! Aren't you two tired yet?" Queen Hadiat stepped forward to put an end to the bickering.

Khailia stepped in front of Queen Hadiat in peaceful resistance stopping her from breaking them a part. King Jasir placed his hand on Hadiat's shoulder to let her know it was alright.

"Ebelle, what you fail to grasp is that nothing has been given to me. It's always been mine. The very thing you despise in me is within you too. But you won't believe until you see." Aniah's eyes began pulsating an indigo glow as her powers surged within. "You want my gift?" She plainly asked but went from zero to a hundred without counting a second for a response, "DO YOU WANT MY GIFT?! HERE, SEE!!" She knocked Ebelle's pistol from her hand and touched her forehead.

Immediately, Ebelle's eyes rolled into the back of her head as a light inside her reached from beyond the dark begging to breathe. Ebelle started choking and tried to take Aniah's hand off her head but it was too late, Aniah was tapped in. Khailia heard Ebelle's and Aniah's pain and her chest began asthmatic rhythms. Aniah's powers were so great that the ground quaked beneath their feet and it felt as if the world was spinning out of control. Everyone that had grown to mean something to her was now caught up in her vision—Khailia, Ebelle, King Jasir, Queen Hadiat, Hathor, Seshet, Nefertiti, Melaine, ZaQuaysia, Grace, Hasan, Etienne Idris had no choice to but to succumb to His sight.

Fighting as hard as she could, Ebelle gritted her teeth as saliva purged her words and no negativity could escape. She tried using her powers to feel for Aniah but Aniah was too strong. Aniah's hair grew wild and free as her new powers rose to the forefront. Khailia's air escaped her lungs and small yelps jumped out into echoes until they all screamed.

"DO YOU WANT THIS GIFT? HERE, SEE WHAT COMES WITH IT!" Aniah fazed everyone to Goree Island.

The panic on everyone's face as Aniah was able to revisit the past and show everyone the sight of brutality suffered by millions hundreds of years prior. Etienne Idris vomited both from the faze and the colonizers whipping and torturing Believers. Children looking for any familiar face listening for any familiar tongue while being pushed into the bosom of strangers forced to believe any teat was better than none. Then they saw it. As clear as the day it happened. Seshet shackled then passed Zoya into rotation and then slipped away.

"FEEL IT! You felt the warmth of your line's protection. FEEL MINE!" Aniah still had her finger on Ebelle's forehead pressing into it as she slowly knelt down, bracing herself, her hands touched the ground and the stains of blood, vomit, tears, screams and pain filled every crevice of her being.

Ebelle's fingers grabbed into the soil tight as she searched hard for an end. Khailia screamed out in pain as she felt both sisters and heard the details of fallen Believers for herself. Everyone tried to stop Aniah because the glimpse hurt so much, but she had to make them experience it for themselves. Knowing was one thing, hearing another, feeling was close, but seeing it up close was something different and she refused to let go. She allowed her inner vision to take it from there.

Fazing everyone to the voyage, they watched as protesters jumped in unmeasured waters chasing their babes and dead friends. Still chained in arkhh matter, they screamed for rebellion but the fear of bullets, whips and rape cornered them into planked positions. Some charge forward, others tried to believe different. "See what I see!" Aniah kept on through the terror.

Meanwhile, ancestral Believers felt the truth from beneath the waters and the Tribesmen of the Aganju – Olokun passage peaked out to witness the final fik-iri. Sensing the demons closing in, they opened the passage's high blue watery gates around them and pulled the group into a safe space. But the Heirs and company weren't there for a visit. The faze rushed them through the Passage as they all stared at each other until resurfacing in Suriname.

Aniah kept her finger on Ebelle whose eyes were still rolled back while the light took over. They all watched as the Believers were forcefully stripped from their identities and spit on for their birth. Etienne tried fighting the colonizers but he wasn't permitted to release his own pain, simply rewarded the harshness of sharing the slaves' voices. Queen Hadiat's head shook back and forth absurdly because she had seen it all before and having to witness it again took something from her while giving her something much more. King Jasir tried to inch closer to his heiress but he too was consumed with the pain and anger.

The Saramakan tribe peeked from their homes to witness their own history, calling for the drums, they mimicked the heartbeats of all Believers. Nefertiti steadied herself to keep her blade at Seshet's neck without killing her, her focus in alignment with her new Queen's. Hasan knelt down and began to pray helplessly while the male buck breaking proceeded only two feet away. Meanwhile, the reenactments of slavery continued. The wind whipped hard guiding them into their next faze to South Carolina. Through the swamps and rivers of the worse colonizing terrorists, the slave owners. Slave babies being used to bait dark swamp water creatures while mothers helplessly watch during forced penetration. And then they understood and no longer tried to stop Aniah, they all saw her. Sweet Zoya birthing her uncrowned heiress then dying with her eyes wide open, praying her child caught her sight. They were standing on Zoya's burial site, unmarked with the dignity of her name. It was now personal to everyone. From nearby, a kindred woman watched and waited as the energy began to calm down.

A fik-iri of epic proportion between Aniah and Ebelle finished with an unexpected gift. Zoya's spirit appeared and placed her hand on Aniah's arm to quiet the pain. King Jasir and Queen Hadiat's souls begged to hold Zoya but they were stuck in the presence of her glow. Zoya spotted Nefertiti and smiled brightly then blew her a kiss. Ebelle crouched slowly and wept as she could now feel every bit of her sister's journey. Khailia finally stopped screaming as she had awakened Believers near and far. In need of reassurance, she began to hum and rock herself back and forth. Zoya kissed her heiress on the forehead and looked her in the eyes. She felt avenged with pride seeing all her heiress had summed up to be. In between their glance, she leaned in and whispered, "all of my dreams, passed down onto you. Now what will you do with it? May this love lead the way." Zoya stepped back, held her head high, shoulders erect, and smiled as she faded away.

Sniffles and whimpers filled the still air. Nefertiti finally lowered her sword and Seshet stepped back. Ebelle now knew the truth and was struggling to forgive her narrow-minded protector. The group bestowed a temporary grace to Seshet as they knew the next time they saw her would be her last, she turned her back and walked away.

Khailia couldn't speak to soothe anyone because Zoya's words to Aniah convicted her too. Yet in that moment, Khailia understood that she could be heard by all seeking alignment and rang out freedom. *"Lift every voice and sing..., til Earth and Heaven ring, ring with the harmonies of liberty..."*

The remarkable occurrence continued to lift as God's army of Believers, far and wide, stretching to every corner of earth, joined in with same song adding their own tribe's blood onto each verse. All at once, Believers united and chains fell to their sides while emotions sang out to touch Ebelle. She reciprocated a higher vibration that endowed each Believer's heart with an embrace of unique healing proportions. And the Believers could feel God's arms embracing each and every one of them in His own special way. The energy grew and reminded everyone of His favor.

A war cry true enough to be heard in nations amongst galaxies had begun and the Heirs were finally all embraced. Aniah glanced around for her part. She looked for where to lead while she watched their unions grow. There was a panic creeping in and stealing her breath and focus. She quieted her heart to commune and a sharp pain befell her eyes. Stricken and drained by the blow, she fazed everyone once more to the City of Brotherly love in the middle of noon day traffic. Before she could uncontrollably faze again, King Jasir grabbed her to quiet her storm.

"Let's find somewhere to rest."

Chapter 23: Beside the Still Waters

The night's sky was filled with a business that reminded Aniah of home. She stared quietly out the hotel suite's window watching the reflection of everyone else. While she didn't share her awareness, Aniah knew to immerse herself in that moment. Something was coming, and it would shake them all. Additionally, they were being followed by a woman seeking kinship but had yet to announce herself. Aniah let her be and her sisters didn't question.

"It's been awhile since I was last here in Philly." Aniah turned to face everyone. She felt refreshed and ready to let loose. "Let me show ya'll a lil spot I like to go to, a club, ducked off away from all the cameras, live feeds, and cell phones. I love to go there and dance from time to time."

"Yes, please and thank you!" Khailia jumped up ready to go.

"Girl, you're gonna have to show me how to twerk first!" Ebelle chuckled softly but her sarcasm escaped Hasan. She straightened up when she saw his face. "I mean, sure, we'd love to."

"I think us old heads will pass. I for one have had enough excitement for one day." King Jasir smiled.

Queen Hadiat stood in agreement. "I think our girls could use a lil free time, and those Amanirenians look like they could use some rest."

United under the cloak of His love, the Heirs, Hasan and Etienne walk the streets of Philadelphia enamored with today. There were fewer cameras being pointed their way as they were in a land where Believers were coming to realize themselves, hands were no longer as idle. They entered a club where the owners knew Aniah and treated her like the Queen she'd always been to them before her crowning. Once introductions were had and everyone shook hands, Ebelle could feel the relationship between Aniah and the owners who once worked together for prison reform. And Khailia heard just how personal it was for them as they had a brother awaiting his date with death as an innocent man. Their powers had grown and their alignment now irreversible. What one experienced through gift, the others did too. The club owners led Aniah and her family to her favorite table. A view of the entire club from one seat was always necessary for her, always on a throne, from day one.

That night there just so happened to be a large group of dancers with various styles. From Chicago style steppers to Detroit ballroom dancers, hand dancers, kizamba, they were all gathered in one venue to put the weight of the world into foot work and jazzy sways. Ebelle and Khailia were caught up in the beauty of it all. To experience Aniah's views within their gifts was intoxicating. The vibes were so different that it made them love the diversity of Believers all the more. Then Aniah was asked to dance by an acquaintance, and she obliged.

"Watch me twerk!" Aniah's light heartedness laid the roses at their feet for them to join her in laughter. But when she danced, they saw her. With each twirl spin and glide, they saw her. They watched her etch her story into the wood flooring and paralleled it to their first dance together. Without the glow and Sentinelese, she had been there all along. Aniah was never departed from grace or favor. God never left her side though she was an ocean away. The way she closed her eyes but knew every move and never missed her partner's queues, her sisters got her now. Aniah gave herself to the beauty of the lyrics and melodies and personified every adlib for all to see. When her dance ended, she returned to the table to sip a little more of her water and wine but right as she reached for it, the sharp pain returned. It felt like something was knocking at her and pounding harder and harder. She and her sisters went to the restroom to regain composure but when they returned, the party was cut short. The police broke the party up off a tip that there was narcotics being sold, only Aniah knew this was a ploy. Instead of starting a fight in a room full of Believers still trying to find themselves, she decided to leave as quickly as possible to keep the peace.

On the way out, they noticed the brutality of several men in particular. These Black men's faces were being smeared into cement with guns pointing at their temples while they pleaded their innocence and begged for the police to check them for proof...all but one. He offered no tear or scream. He wouldn't energize them with the fear they were searching for. It all seemed so routine to him that Aniah tried looking into his eyes to see how many times he'd been put into the predicament, but he closed them, patiently waiting for the policeman's knee to be removed from his spine.

Aniah's headache intensified until they reached the hotel but eventually is faded into a manageable annoyance. Ebelle made her a tonic so that she could rest peacefully then went to be like everyone else.

That night, while everyone rested comfortably, Aniah woke up and snuck onto the balcony. She sat out on the ledge staring out into the city's nightlife. Unexpectedly, Queen Nefertiti joined her. They greeted each other with a warm smile then Nefertiti sat next to her on the ledge.

"I've never allowed you to read my eyes. Yet, you never pushed or questioned. Why?" Nefertiti asked while handing Aniah some water and placing a blanket around her shoulders.

"You treat me differently than my sisters, why?" Aniah smiled and took a sip.

Nefertiti took a deep breath and gave herself permission to be free. "You saw Zoya's eyes. You know our bond. The triplets respected me as an aunt but that Zoya….it was as if she were my own. I loved all three but I favored her most." Nefertiti's mind escaped to a distant past, "I was there the day those girls were born. I cried as I remembered birthing my own girls. The Queen held Aida and the King was holding Liya so I got to hold Zoya. It'd been ages since I had been asked to hold a baby. I had become a creature of war. Zoya was the first baby I held since my own." She chuckled a bit, "I spent centuries existing as I pleased and no one really knew me, the true me, but then I looked that beautiful baby in the eyes and she…she smiled. I'm not sure what I did to deserve such love and trust, but I promised her that I'd protect her and place her life above my own."

Aniah placed her arms around Nefertiti's shoulders and kissed her cheek while resting her forehead on the side of Queen Nefertiti's temple.

"I never let you read me because I was ashamed. I failed her and everything that happened to her…her entire lineage…you, it's all my fault. I never should've let Zoya out of my sight. I'm so sorry Aniah!" Nefertiti wanted to cry but didn't feel she deserved to after everything Zoya's line had been through. "I was supposed to protect her."

"Zoya never blamed you and I do not blame you. It was not your fault. And the promise you made to her you continue to be fulfilled through me. She simply loved you just because and so do I. You don't owe us a thing, never did."

Nefertiti tucked Aniah into her embrace and pressed her chin to the top of her head. "When the day comes, I will kill Seshet for her betrayal and I will show no mercy, so please do not ask it of me."

"Now that she's free to roam without having to hide her true self, she'll lead us to everything we need to know. All I ask is that you wait until we know everything."

Chapter 24: Rise of the King

The next morning the sun ascended over the city beaming beautifully over people awakening. King Jasir stood in the middle of the suite's living room, his eyes full of memories relinquishing tears of joy. Hadiat, Nefertiti and Hathor entered the room concerned, wanting to ask him why, but Etienne Idris placed his hand on Hadiat's shoulder and nodded in the direction King Jasir was staring.

Khailia, Ebelle and Aniah were sitting out on the balcony tangled in each other's arms sharing a laugh. No one could hear what they were saying because the sliding glass door was shut. They saw Ebelle laying across Khailia's lap twisting one hand through the air while the other hand reached for the bowl of fruit Aniah was holding. Aniah's back was resting on Khailia's shoulder and arm. She reached up and behind her and her hand landed in Khailia's hair. She gently grabbed a handful of her hair and strung it down her own forehead and smiled. Khailia playfully took her hair back and wrapped it around Aniah's neck pretending to strangle her with it and they all laughed a little harder. Hasan, Melaine, Grace and ZaQuaysia entered the room and became as hypnotized as the others watching the Heirs fuel one another.

"Aida, Liya and Zoya were the exact same way." King Jasir finally wiped his eyes without changing his view. "I remember this one time at the Hall of Kings, we had all just come home from Eden. The girls were supposed to be in the bed sleeping but as I walked by I noticed a light shining from the door. If I would've went for the door they would've felt it, heard it or seen it a mile away. So I went outside around the backside of the palace and flew to the roof. I slowly crept toward the edge of the roof right above their window then gently hovered to the side and peeked inside. Those girls made a tent that opened toward the window and they were wrapped around each other laughing and enjoying the night skies. Liya had made a batch of bubbles and scented it using the gardenia and valeria flowers from the bazaars in what is now known as Kassala. She used to collect flowers from everywhere and anywhere we went. Well, she was blowing the bubbles out the window while Aida tossed grapes into their mouths and Zoya popped the bubbles that came her way. They were giggling about nothing at all until they fell asleep. I didn't even bother putting them in their beds. I left them in each other's embrace."

"Let's keep that energy and let them enjoy each other. Finally!" ZaQuaysia made her way into the kitchen and started to prepare breakfast for everyone. "So what's next for us?"

"That would be up to Aniah now." Hadiat joined ZaQuaysia in the kitchen and pulled out a knife to help cut some fruit.

"Well, I fazed here for a reason. Not too sure why just yet." Aniah entered the room and her sisters spilled in behind her.

"Well, are you feeling up to touring the city? We've never been here. The United States is so different than what we thought." Ebelle wanted to touch the landscapes in search of history's recorded errors. She wanted to know what cures lie beneath its surfaces.

"Can we go to Love Park?" Khailia tried to persuade in Ebelle's interest.

Aniah knew there was something in between it all, something they weren't even aware they were saying just yet. Aroused by curiosity, she obliged their requests.

After breakfast the group left the hotel and reached Love Park. Her sisters and brother-in-laws took photos of each other while others took pictures of them. The crowds were back and in full force following the Heirs around. All the meshed walks of life occurred in one space, Aniah waited and watched for a sign. The Amanirenians stood guard and King Jasir and Queen Hadiat stood protectively over Aniah trying to see what she was receiving. While the woman following them kept her distance, she was joined by someone new, a shape shifter. He too appeared to mean no immediate harm, so Aniah continued allowing them to follow unquestioned.

"Hey Aniah, how far is Independence Park from here?" Ebelle asked.

Aniah's eyes tremored at Ebelle's words and her mouth began to speak her sight. "Can you feel the blatant disregard for us? The sadistic irony spilling upward out from the cement. Can you feel that?" Aniah's head began to hurt again. She continued while her sisters came closer trying to piece it all together. "Can't you hear the rocks crying out?" The entire group gathered around Aniah as she continued. "The shot heard around the world, the real one, the one that killed a man born free before he was ever shackled, his wings were never clipped."

"You mean, Crispus Attucks? But that happened in Boston, we're in Philadelphia. What's this about?" Ebelle was struggling to piece together anything that could make sense.

"That man, John Adams, said Crispus Attucks scared his murderer. John Adams said fear justified the murder of a Black man. He admitted it right there.

He admitted his own cowardice in that spot there. He came here to speak about Crispus' murder and said fear justified the end. He walked these very streets when they were unpaved, right where you're standing. He paced them while Quakers stirred about over there and here exporting materials for akrhh matter while speaking of freedom. Fear is the direct lineage of hate, but we're here in Love Park. They named this love but it was built on hate stained foundations."

"Aniah, what's this about?" Khailia tried to hear her over the pain in her head. "Maybe we should keep going, let's see where we end up? What direction is Independence Park in?"

"John Adams lived that way." Aniah started walking in the direction.

The group got back in travel formation. However, when they reached the Philadelphia Criminal Courthouse, they stopped to debate how to continue. Aniah's headache pounded harder. It shook a tear from her eye. There was no more ignoring it. With fruition in sight, she followed the pain and ventured away from the group. Nefertiti, Melaine, Grace and Queen Hadiat caught Aniah's movement and hurried to catch up with her. Without a bit of fear, Aniah entered the courthouse with her stronghold of women beside her right as a forcefield surrounded the entire building.

The demons spotted them immediately but Aniah wouldn't be deterred. The closer she got to wherever the pain was leading her, the more intense the throbbing got. The first demon approached and was quickly put down with one jab as Aniah continued to where she could silence the pain. Queen Hadiat, Nefertiti and Melaine pulled out their weapons freely setting off every alarm fighting their way through as Aniah dismantled any objection to her being there almost without effort. Demons couldn't stop her from what she was created to do. She reached the 8th floor and tears flowed freely tracing an exit path for the pain. She pushed open the courtroom door that caused her the most hurt and found a judge in the middle of a hearing yelling and screaming obscenities at the defendant who happened to be the man familiar with pain from the night before with the police knee in his spine. Aniah looked at him and saw his silent frustrations. Mothers in the courtroom watching grasped their children and held them close to their bosoms whispering warnings, telling them not to be like that man. He had yet to be convicted or ruled guilty of anything. The judgement upon the innocent man from those under demonic spells angered Aniah.

The judge snared at Aniah and motioned for the man to be chained to the table while demons brought out more akrhh matter promising to chain her as well.

"Buck him!" The judge commanded at the demons who are struggling to hold the man still.

The demons smiled and salivated at the idea of a traditional bucking in front of all the young Black children in the room. Teaching them fear was one of the demon's greatest victories to date.

Aniah finally pulled her katanas out, "not today. Melaine, Grace...with me. Queen Hadiat and Nefertiti, protect the witnesses.

They all fought as though they needed to deplete their gifts in one battle. Aniah threw a katana directly in between the eyes of a demon standing behind the innocent man. The man struggled and fought hard with bound hands to protect himself from other demons. More demons poured in while the judge yelled for someone to call Tiago.

Meanwhile, outside, Ebelle and Khailia fought with all their might to break through the forcefield while passersby pulled out their cell phones to record. Etienne, Hasan, Hathor, ZaQuaysia and King Jasir searched for ways inside until conceding to strike the force field as well.

Aniah did whatever she could to keep the demons from penetrating and castrating the man. She screamed louder with each blow she delivered giving her entire being to her cause. She saw the man's pain with every step closer to him. The man fought to wiggle away from attempts at his manhood and by perfect chance, looked up at Aniah heading his way. It was then that she finally saw him clearly but the pain in her head intensified so much that Khailia and Ebelle felt it too. Afraid that their sister was dying, they fought harder and screamed as loud as Aniah. Tears ran waves of purge down Aniah's eyes the closer she got to the man. The more she read him the more she saw past his pain. The more she understood him and believed in him. Her love for God grew but the pain kept ringing out. If she could only open his eyes to see himself in her too. So she fought harder, laying down multiple demons at a time. Snapping necks and twisting heads off while using demon spine to kill other demons. The man continued to dodge advances but was both mesmerized and caught off guard by Aniah.

"Don't give up, keep fighting!" She yelled at him, "I'm almost there!"

The man's strength increased off her words but a headache began for him as well. He started to see the pain she endured up until that point and felt a sense of responsibility to protect the one that was laying her life on the line for little ol' him, or is he that simple after all? Aniah's belief fed his belief as he continued to emerge within himself. Through all the sneak attacks she fought viciously. Her own blood being shed too, she refused to give up and he refused not to honor her fight for his. She finally made it to him only to be stopped by the cursed ankrr chains that she learned were supposedly stronger than her. Her katana couldn't break through and every time her skin grazed the chains it drained her. She looked him in the eyes once more as his eyes confirmed she needed him. Gracefully wrapping her fingers around the links she pulled and screamed out, losing energy with each try. Demons fought tooth and nail to get to her but she wouldn't bite, while Melaine and Grace fought hard to block demonic attempts on their Queen. Aniah pulled at his chains with every ounce of strength she had left...and they began to break.

The first link broke and a pain swept over the man that hastened him still. Outside, his brothers heard the call. Hasan began to see algorithms he'd never seen before and Etienne grew wings. A convention of fraternities and sororities nearby heard all the commotion and lined themselves in war formation as though they knew the steps they never practiced their whole lives. In identified unison, they marched and began their first circle around the forcefield walls outside. King Jasir heard a sound he hadn't heard in a very long time and cried out his psalm. It was happening. The return of the Guardians was upon him.

Inside Aniah pulled harder even through her own pain. As much as it hurt her, she knew how much the system was meant to kill that man and she wouldn't lose him. The second break of the chains and the man's eyes looked toward Heaven as his pupils lit the way for a message to be received. He was remembering himself. Everything he knew about himself and everything that had ever occurred in his life was making sense. He didn't want Aniah to hurt any further but he knew why she had to do it. His pain had always been her pain too, before the beginning of time. So he looked her eye to eye in order for her to join in on the new strength he was receiving. He desperately invited her to be a part of His rise. Aniah screamed louder, barely able to see past the tears but she found a little more strength hidden in places she had yet discovered...and pulled once more, her king was free. A demon finally shot at her and right as the bullet got close to her, the man pulled her into him as his wings cover them both, not allowing the bullet to touch her skin.

The world, the turmoil, the current circumstance quieted for them as she buried herself into his chest to hide from it all. He covered them with his enormous indigo Guardian wings and enclosed them in a place no one could enter. Instead of allowing her to hide, he told her they'd get through the pain together by lifting her head and finishing the story in their eyes. This time when they looked at each other, an escape of conjoined minds occurred and they shared a space that no one else would ever see but them. It was their first time there and it tickled them, iji mesit'eti.

"Aniah, that's a beautiful name. It means God has answered. Did you know that?"

"God's sense of humor is unmatched," she chuckled, "yours means higher. Eli...He lifts you higher. Your calling has always been in a space that only a few others could ever faintly see. Eli-K'ali Gibeah. Your mom meant it, huh?"

"Yeah, she was a character."

"You've come a long way from where you started." She took pride in her man.

"Crazy, this is how we meet. In the middle of all this around us. Is this supposed to be our moment?"

"This is our right now today. Our right now will forever be wherever we are no matter the time or circumstance. It was always meant. Ancestors of those whose skin dared to rejoice in reflection with the sun. Those who danced trails leaving footprints across oceans leading us back to the path of Believers' first love. We unite a million right nows, You and I. I am always yours to find. It was us before He landscaped the first star." Aniah was free to be herself and feelings she's longed for poured out with ease.

Aniah's love for Eli erased generations of heaviness. He saw her as evidence of a forever truth that loneliness never had space to exist within. He held his self-evident truth as a tangible reality that his whole life had meaning beyond any supplanter's statistic. He forever mattered and always would. A strength grew and His purpose aligned. All he had to offer was now multiplied exponentially beyond defined electoral counts. She saw him and opened her heart wider to accept everything he was without doubt or fear. Eli wore Aniah's understanding of him as trimming around his newfound wings with a golden ferocity that protected him from past fears. She would never judge him for everything meant something. He was the same and brand new. His duality in sight before time. He found love. He didn't fight the tears that Baptized them both in the midst of battle. Unbreakable.

"Since we have always been written, we've never been alone. Even before today, it was forever us. I don't feel so broken even as a child. I understand I was always won, twice over." He hugged her tighter knowing he'd soon have to fight. "That means we still have a ways to go. We in this, together. Forever, right?"

"I mean if I have to be stuck with anyone in this world, I guess you're alright." Aniah's sarcasm gave them both a second wind as they prepared a for victory foretold.

"If I'm getting the hang of this, seeing what you see and all, I believe you just took us spiritually somewhere else. While this, to me, is Heaven, we need to return back to the physical world and finish this up. You got a lil more left in you?"

"I'm ready." Aniah grit her teeth and gently dug her forehead into his chest wanting to beg for just one more second to share the closeness between them. But instead, she released his eyes trusting it was now theirs. "I'm gonna make them beg for the days when reparations was an option on the table our ancestors built."

Her sight became his fuel. Her words pressed the gas as he spread his wings and rolled her around to his backside to protect her while grabbing her khopesh. "You don't mind if I borrow this, do you?"

She smiled while some demons tried to escape from their own trap running toward the doors of the courtroom. The Guardian King was reborn and they knew that meant hell for them.

Outside loud drums and horns rang out and the rhythm was being set. The steppers reached their 7th time around the walls and the force fields of evil fell down from around the courthouse. Everywhere on the Earth, Guardian wings were being reborn. Men purposed for the role remembered themselves and were coming to their call. King Jasir saw his own strength returning like an invisible algorithm and stretched his arms while cracking his neck. The energy of self-realization took over and he let loose as though days long past were repeating themselves and he never was lost to any of it. Demons spilled out into the streets and the war was televised. The Amanirenians redirected their attention to protecting the witnesses as others pulled up and joined in. Guardians started landing in to join the fight. King Simeon had sent his flight army of griffins and sphinxes into battle.

In the courthouse, Aniah and her King fought side by side in sync avenging the years lost to demonic plagues. Stunned by their fight, Queen Hadiat watched mesmerized at the fulfilment of God's word releasing from beating and spirited hearts. Every step the new couple took was perfectly choreographed dance steps they never learned but enjoyed learning together. Their bond was happening for all to see. They killed demon after demon creating footstools as exits.

Tiago arrived in enough time to catch a seat atop the building next door and studied their moves. Tien and Draisien joined him but Trigon wanted revenge and joined the fight.

Eli wielded the khopesh with every swing bringing him closer to it always belonging to him. Aniah fought beside him weaving in and out of his footsteps, a balance with rippling effect. King Jasir stood firm and proud with every loving emotion he'd needed to pour out over the past century. He worshiped his Creator in heart for he was permitted to witness a promise fulfilled. The evidence of Aniah and Eli's match being destined continued as demon after demon fell beside them every step of the way until they reached outside to complete their battle.

Eli swung blood off his khopesh as the battle was coming to an end. He slowly stepped toward a guardian who had captured Trigon and was waiting for Eli's judgement. "Trigon, one of the last of the first. Your first last breath has come." Eli held his khopesh high.

"I don't mind at all. I took a few good ones with me." He nodded his head in the direction of his bloody massacre. There were bodies of Believers scattered all across the ground that led to him. "Dozens of eyes for an eye. Today was a good day to die." He snarled at Aniah as if to make her feel at fault for the bloodshed. "Get it over with!"

Chapter 25: Higher Still

Aniah couldn't help but weep when she saw the spilled blood running through the streets. The cost of war and love was great. And she saw it. Still, it hurt more than any growing pain she'd experienced. She tried to see and not see hoping for a different picture every time she blinked, but picture remained in focus. She saw how Ebelle and Khailia gently stepped over bodies to get to her made the reality feel worse. The path they had to take to comfort her was something she hoped to never see again. The fallen couldn't understand the stories Aniah could see fading in their eyes. They couldn't see how much they were needed and would be missed...a gift Aniah could not share. Each life held value, unweighted mounds of gold couldn't amount to their price.

Suddenly, Aniah heard someone gasping for air and cries for help from a child. She tried not to step on anyone until she found the source. A Guardian lie in the rubble, his wings wanting so badly to soar as they strained to flex. He saw her and although he was struggling for air as his lungs filled with blood, he mustered strength to point in the direction of a small pile of debris two steps away where the screams were coming from. Etienne and Hasan raced over to lift the heavy rocks and street signs and found a child sitting there balled up screaming and afraid. Khailia lifted the child and began rubbing her back while Ebelle searched her body for any broken bones, bumps or cuts.

Aniah couldn't hold back the pain in her eyes so she held the Guardian's hand and shed tears with him. She had a hard time looking him in the eyes and seeing his story, but she knew he deserved his truth being known. So she fought her own will to look away and shared whatever memories she could and he willingly showed Aniah just how blessed he'd been. The little girl escaped Khailia and ran to, her father, the Guardian dying in Aniah's arm, and screamed for him to get up. He kissed his little girl's hand then the light left his eyes. A woman ran over and collapsed onto him rocking herself and her child.

All the Heirs' powers couldn't make the moment right. One life lost felt like losing themselves.

The need for justice swole up inside Eli. He felt an enormous energy surge through his legs and into his chest. It then moved to his arms and he turned while swinging his khopesh, beheading Trigon then looking to Tien, Draisien and Tiago as if to dare them. Only Tiago paid no mind. His sight was set on Aniah which nearly drove Eli into an immediate fight. Nefertiti placed her hand on his shoulder to calm Eli knowing he wasn't fully ready and the firsts spread their wings and departed.

Eli found Aniah standing with silent streams running down her face, each drop held reflections of the stories of the fallen. There were no words, he simply shared in her vision so she wouldn't have to carry the weight alone.

A heavy hearted feeling swept over all Believers after watching how much Aniah loved, cared for and desired to protect them. A sense of not only belonging but being needed melted onto every believing soul. It was this feeling that also allowed them to understand how important they were to each other, a true kindredness. The sight of bloodied martyrs became more personal with every heart beat and breath they were still alive to appreciate. The sacrifice of their loved ones gently placed itself on every heart. Ebelle helped the woman with her child. Khailia began to hum a song while a few Guardians came and picked up their fallen brother. The multitudes began to do the same, gathering their fallen and draping them in whatever shrouds they could find.

Aniah and Eli led everyone on a long and much-needed journey to the Atlantic shore. In their hearts, it was the least they could do to honor those who awakened to their bravery and gave their lives all in the same day. Every Believer needed that walk for a moment to mourn because in the battle to come that vengeful energy would have its place. So, they walked to the ocean to release the life force back to the God who created and designed it all. Small rafts built for each body lined with fresh flowers drifted into the waters holding the fallen's bodies. The heirs walked into the water after each raft deployed and meditated for a way to inspire a nation of Believers hurting for love's sake.

From a small distance the water began to glisten and a small area turned golden. A strikingly beautiful being slowly emerged from the waters. Walking toward them with long locs that nourished the ocean, she looked directly into Aniah's eyes and acknowledged each other's greatness. The woman introduced herself as the gatekeeper, Oshun. She was there to assure safe passage. Without warning, Aniah and her sisters majestically ascended into the air while Amanirenians and Guardians let loose burning arrows and set flames to the new spiritual guides. The fallen's souls were free. Oshun lifted her elbows like a flamingo lifts its wings. She raised her arms and sprinkles of water rose upward from the ocean leading the new ancestors to rest. Khailia's mouth glowed blue and Ebelle's hands glowed blue and Aniah's eyes lit up blue. The souls released from their Earthly temples and praised joyously the whole way to Heaven as God lit the skies in jubilation and acceptance. Souls lifted from every corner of Earth informing the Heirs of how far and wide Believers stood in agreement.

While the spirits ascended, a weight was beginning to lift from the Believers as they watched happy souls rejoice their way into the sky. For although no one wanted to pay the price of kindred blood, the martyrdom each life gained was worth more than any return on investment that could have ever been projected. Aniah euphorically smiled and twirled the souls of four little girls who were bombed in a church in a circle then placed their hands into the hands of others on the same path. The comfort of His spirit filled all who heard Khailia's voice from shore to shore. Ebelle smiled while nudging a young man wearing his hoodie as a crown then placed an elder man wearing a bomber jacket's hand in his and they communed along the way. The blood drying in the Heirs' hair and tattered clothing didn't matter as they understood everything they'd gained.

The Heirs began their descent to the ground to return to their love-filled duties. Suddenly, in a flash, Tiago swept in and stole Aniah away before anyone could react. He spread his wings and disappeared. Khailia gasped as she felt the air snatched from her lungs and Ebelle felt chills down her spine. Eli stood stuck in disbelief.

"We just got her....We just got her..." Ebelle, of all people began to panic as though her life left with her little sister. "Where'd he go?!"

"Calm down, dear. You're the smartest person here. Think!" Hasan stepped in. "Where would he have taken her?"

"You're Ebelle.... and you.... you're Hasan, right?" Eli was never formally introduced to the sisters or their kings. "Khailia," he pointed to her, "and Etienne Idris. Your majesties, Queen Hadiat and King Jasir." He made his way around using the visions from Aniah calling everyone by name. "The Heirs are all connected now, right? All aligned?"

"Yes." King Jasir stepped forward intrigued at how rapidly Eli and Aniah's bond was growing.

"Well, your gifts should lead us right to her. How do you commune and use them?" Eli tried to sort his way out of the confusion.

"We haven't had the chance to learn..." Khailia slowly spoke. "Hathor, teach us..."

"I...I don't know this part." Hathor felt defeated, "we never made it this far."

"Nefertiti?" Khailia sought wisdom.

"I'm not sure dear...," she slowly stepped back. "This part was always up to you three." She nearly collapsed. Her mind was racing in circles at how it's all happening again for her and she finally walked away to cry.

"Does anyone know? No one knows what was supposed to be next?" Khailia's voice started to trail, "I need her." She barely got out the words before as Etienne Idris caught her before she could fall.

"The torch is now yours to carry," King Jasir stepped up barely able to keep his shoulders erect. "Eli, some bonds were built stronger than time. And what's tradition to time, right? As unorthodox as this question may sound, seeing how you two aren't married, can you use her eyes at all? Can you see her anywhere? Do you feel anything? Focus, son."

"I just got here, I'm still trying to grasp it all myself. This is a lot all at once. I see her, but nothing makes sense. I'm not sure what all this is. I don't know how to describe it all." Eli put his hands behind his neck then closed his elbows covering his face and sat down trying to catch his footing. Ebelle and Khailia began to meditate in order to commune with God in hopes to find their sister.

King Jasir stood firmly in front of Eli and waited for him to reopen his eyes. Once Eli did, the king wasted no time reading him. "Can't be!"

Everyone stopped in their tracks and waited for the king to speak what he saw. Instead, he cried.

Chapter 26: Fallen Love

Tiago returned to the place of his constant shame and abuse. He'd been there so many times to curse God until he figured to curse God. He built his own private kingdom on the exact place he had fallen. On that mountain, he placed a mansion to which he only started to build once Aniah read his eyes. They stood there, she with her katanas drawn and he, plain and simple.

"You read me." He took a step back slowly, "You're the only one who knows."

Aniah twirled her katanas ready to fight.

"You can't kill me. Only your little boyfriend or one of his winged peons can do that. But of course you already know this. Let's not do this. I don't care to hurt you so don't tempt me."

Aniah started to put her katanas away.

"No...no, please keep them out. I trust you more with them than without." He chuckled, "your reputation with fists is well known."

"Hmmm, man sack still bruised from our last encounter?" Aniah finally spoke up.

"Actually, it's an 'angel' sack, and yes. Specifically left one roughly around 250th hair from the right, if you must know. No matter what they tell you, no matter how many labels your tribes give me, at the end of the day, I'm an angel and you know this, don't you?"

"Why are you being nice? You do know you cannot seduce me." She read his game but knew she didn't have much time until he'd become irate.

"I wouldn't insult you that way. You're not like the rest." He sat down on a chair and slowly took a deep breath. "No one knows the truth about me except for you, and yet you haven't used it as a weapon against me."

"One who bears truth is the weapon, no need for gimmicks."

"You sound just like him. You sound like God." He sighed, "If He cares so much, why won't He do it Himself? Why you?" Tiago aimed but found no weakness. "I can remember my days in Heaven. The others can't but I can. I roamed all over creation, not just this world but all His creation and I was revered. You think this world is something, wait until I show you the rest. You wouldn't believe it. This puny world is nothing compared to the rest. Ahhhh!!

These damn memories. It's like one more kick, right to the tip, you know. Well, of course you don't, being female and all. I can remember everything and have always had the ability...everything except the actual fall. That was, until you read my story. Now I remember everything."

"You never wanted to leave Heaven."

"I wasn't a part of the initial traitors. I just knew them and loved them as my family. I fought for my family to stay together. I wouldn't forsake them, even if He had."

"When they were cast out, you just happened to be in the vicinity and you allowed them to pull you down with them."

"I didn't allow it. It just happened. I was pulled by another who was fallen."

"Accountability, you should try it. Wrong crowd, much?"

"It wasn't my cross to bear."

"Who were you loyal to? Your confusion and lack of steadfast loyalty led you here."

"How dare you! You of all people know what it's like to love those who run from Him? You know what it means to see the need to protect them from themselves. I AM NOT TO BLAME FOR THIS! I DIDN'T CAUSE ANY OF THIS! I TRIED TO TELL THEM TO STOP! I TRIED TO TELL HIM..."

"You cried out to Him to let you back in. As soon as you fell, you wanted back in. YOU SCREAMED IT WAS A MISTAKE! YOU TOLD HIM YOU WEREN'T READY TO MAKE A DECISION! But, Tiago, indecisiveness is a decision. In the face of hate, to make no choice is a choice."

"Why are you the only one who knows? Your own father couldn't see that! Hell, his Father, couldn't see that. So why you? Why did you care to try?"

"What do you mean?"

"This love you have. How does it surpass even me...? or him...? or Him?"

"If you sought out His truth and His love more than you lust for me, you would have heard Him loud and clear. You chose."

"You're right. I desire you in every way. First time for everything."

"Yikes, it's not mutual at all."

"Yet, my dear, not yet. With your sight and my power, we can rule the worlds." Tiago stood and approached Aniah, "Actually, the universe and the uncontested. You wouldn't have to deal with the hate from your own sisters and the betrayer like Seshet. They all would bow down to you."

"I don't share your cause for greed nor reprisal."

"No. But you share my cause to win and my cause to live."

"I have a King."

"You and I would need no permission or cause at all, in fact. I can show you better than I can tell you." He speedily made his way to Aniah who shoved a blade in his kidney when he tried to kiss her.

She held the blade there and twisted it, "I do not share your means."

Tiago grunted then slowly removed the katana from his body, "Do not insult me. You cannot kill me, however, I can kill you." He threw the one sword across the room and slapped her to the other end of the room then sped to meet her as her body connected with the wall and bounced off. "Now, it is your turn to choose. I seem to remember a similar circumstance with Hadiat. I didn't want her as a wife or partner but she was useful. She chose death and pain for her little brats causing your line a century of avoidable drama. So what say you? Life with me or the demise of all those you love?"

"Same difference big dummy. Besides, I already have a king." She wiped the blood from her mouth and stood herself up.

Tiago threw a punch but she dodged and fought him back. They exchanged blows as she eloquently managed to cut him to and fro only for him to heal almost as soon as she sliced him. For Tiago, Aniah's betrayal cut him more than any blade ever could.

"YOU'RE ALREADY MINE! WE CONNECTED AND I KNOW YOU FEEL IT TOO!" He roundhouse kicked her in her back and sent her flying to the ground yet again. "You can't even connect with that little winged weakling yet. It requires some sort of marriage or something, right? But you and I forego ritual and His rules. We don't need that."

While Tiago walked slowly to her, Aniah felt another force in the room. With only a few seconds to spare she engaged His spirit and saw a message coming through to her, "Hurry...," she whispered aloud. She looked over her shoulder panting for air and saw Tiago was approaching. "I was always His. Therefore, I belonged to the winged weakling you fear before you ever fell or existed." She stumbled to her feet and raised her fists. "If you want, we can keep fighting, but this battle is already won."

"Now why did you go and do that? We were just having a conversation, gaining an understanding, and you went and called Him? I see you're as stubborn as your mother and you like it rough." Tiago unleashed his wrath upon her as she tried to dodge every blow.

Aniah managed to withstand his attack but her strength was fleeting. He punched her hard enough for her body to fly across the room once more. She grimaced in pain as she slowly stood again and wiped blood from her nose. She had yet to recoup from the battle in Philadelphia and a faint feeling was creeping onto her spine. With the strength she had left, she stood to her feet once more. She ran to grab her katanas and sheathed them. While racing, she saw a spell, and drew it out with her hands, then casted it into the air. The energy from the spell caused her to sweep up into her own forcefield, impenetrable by Tiago. Within the forcefield, her eyelids closed and she shifted horizontally in a comatose rest while she waited on Him.

    Tiago circled her levitating body gently grazing the forcefield even though it hurt him to touch it. He stared at her and his desire for her grew more and more. His toxicity wanted to hold and cherish her. He never took his eyes off her even when Victoria snuck into his lair and peeked around a corner at them. Tiago could care less about who knew his need for Aniah. He stretched his arm out and a heavy chair glided into the room and stopped behind him. He sat down, leaned back and waited.

    Shielded from everything and everyone, the fate of the world rested with Aniah...and the hope that her King would find her once more.

Jess L. Jackson is a fiction writer whose first novel, *Amidst Dreams*, debuted September 2020. Her second novel, *The Heirs of Sarah: The Hajj*, is the first in a series and is set for release late summer/early fall 2022.

Jackson was born Jessica L. Jackson on May 8, 1984, in Columbus, OH. She was a scholar-athlete in high school and graduated with honors. Jess has a Bachelor of Arts in political science and history from Ohio Dominican University and also possess a MBA with a concentration in project management.

With her two children, Jess finds crazy adventure in discovering infinite paths to one simple truth: that they are evidence of God's unconditional love.

Her style of writing boldly seeks no definition and respectfully, yet unapologetically, sidesteps passive permission. She has a voice that urgently seeks to bridge gaps by relating people through stories pushing readers to be unafraid to heal, laugh, cry.... or do whatever else one's soul has been restricted from.

Ms. Jackson grew up in the rougher parts of the north side of Columbus, OH and at many points in life has lacked in almost everything and every area but never in belief.... and that's awarded her degrees, prominent career paths, and a host of other things, but most importantly, the courage to see and the purpose to love.

For more about Jessica, you can find her on Instagram @jess.l.jackson, Facebook: Jess L. Jackson

Made in the USA
Middletown, DE
19 October 2022